A COLLECTION
OF SCARS

A COLLECTION OF SCARS

Cover & Interior Design by Stone Ridge Books

ISBN 978-1-7777973-0-0 (paperback)
ISBN 978-1-7777973-1-7 (ebook)

10 9 8 7 6 5 4 3 2 1

HEATHER HATALEY

A COLLECTION OF SCARS

To my family and friends for your continued support.

Slavery Act of Harasa

By order of President Althu and his ministers, the Slavery Act of Harasa will come into effect immediately as follows:

Criminals, the unemployed, the maimed, orphaned children, enemies of the state, and any persons deemed a threat to the economical wellbeing of Harasa shall be sold into slavery to provide labour for whomever purchases them. Slave purchases may occur at local markets where a member of the Guard is present.

The Guard shall gather slaves by any means necessary. Any working citizen who wishes to join the Guard in this honourable task shall receive monetary compensation for each slave gathered.

1. Terms of capture and release

a) Criminals:

Any citizen found to have broken a law of Harasa shall face trial and, where convicted, may be determined a slave by a judge of the Court of Harasa. Upon a criminal fulfilling their assigned years of slave labour, they shall be released back into society. Criminals who are convicted three times shall no longer be eligible for release.

b) Unemployed citizens:

Unemployed citizens shall provide two years of slave labour, at which point they shall be released back into society. Any citizen who fails to acquire employment within two seasons following release shall complete an additional two years of slave labour.

c) Maimed citizens:

Maimed citizens, having disabilities that prevent them from providing optimal work in society, are not eligible for release.

d) Orphaned children:

Orphaned children, having no adult supervision, shall be sold to a master. Orphaned children shall provide slave labour to their master until they attain the age of twenty years, upon which they shall be immediately released into society. Orphaned children with unknown birthdays shall be assigned a birth date.

e) Enemies of the state:

Any person found taking part in any form of protest may be captured at the Guard's discretion and, where convicted, may be determined a slave by a judge of the Court of Harasa. Any person found to be a rebel against the president or any of his ministers shall not be eligible for release into society.

Any slave found to have attempted escape from their servitude shall be penalized with an additional term of servitude of up to two years.

2. The rights of a slave

Slaves have a right to:

-be fed and sheltered; and

-be released from their servitude at an agreed upon date (where applicable).

3. Expectations of a slave

Slaves are expected to:

-provide honest labour for the duration of their term; and

-refrain from any criminal or rebellious activity.

4. The rights of a master

Masters have a right to:

-receive honest labour from their slaves;

-execute punishment as they see fit; and

-sell and trade slaves as they see fit.

5. Expectations of a master

Masters are expected to:

-report any slaves taking part in criminal or rebellious activity;

-report any slaves found to have attempted escape;

-feed, shelter, and clothe their slaves;

-protect their slaves from abuse or harm caused by other citizens of Harasa;

-maintain the health of their slaves until their release; and

-release their slaves at an agreed upon date (where applicable).

Prologue

The local children often played in the gully, including Yonah and her siblings. It was there that they were ambushed by the Guard.

That morning, their mother had sent Yonah and Sayzia out for the day with their little brother Obi. She had given them money to buy meat at lunch and told them in her sing-song voice, "I love you, my little mice. I'll see you tonight."

The three siblings walked straight to the gully, a strange oasis in the middle of the hot city. The rock walls of the gully were a pale brown and were coated in gravel. A stream ran along the centre of it, shaded by a handful of trees. There were several clumps of boulders on which the children loved to climb and sit. It was towards one of these boulder clumps that Yonah veered, wanting to sit with the other twelve-year-olds. Sayzia ran towards a group of boys climbing a different set of boulders. She nimbly clambered past them to the top and stood proudly with her fists to the sky. Obi chose to join the other younger children at the stream where he immediately got his clothes soaked in the cool water.

"Your brother's not going to another protest, is he?" Yonah heard one of the girls ask as she joined the conversation.

The boy to whom the girl had been speaking replied, "Of course, he is. And I might go, too. We're not scared of the Guard."

"You should be," Yonah said, memories of her own father's altercation with the Guard filling her mind.

The boy looked unabashedly at Yonah. "If we're all afraid of them then nothing will change."

Another girl spoke up. "Nothing has changed for years." Yonah knew the girl was an orphan and thus a target for the Guard to capture and sell into slavery. There was a mix of orphaned and parented children here in the gully, living wildly different lives from each other.

"That's why people need to keep protesting."

A glint of light flashed from the top of the gully. Yonah squinted her eyes and looked up at it. It came from a black metal object that was attached to a bigger form behind it. The form was a person, Yonah realized, and the metal object was the barrel of a gun. It was the Guard.

The back of her head tingled in fear and her stomach dropped. She didn't know how many there were. She glanced around the top of the gully, trying to find other figures. If there were more, they were hiding.

Nobody else seemed to have noticed the arrival of the Guard. Yonah, trying to look as though everything was alright, slid away from her conversation and made her way to the bottom of the gully towards Obi. She tried making eye contact with Sayzia, willing her to stay hidden among the boulders.

A gunshot went off.

Without looking to see if the bullet had hit anyone, Yonah raced to Obi. She scooped him up in her arms and briefly paused to search for a hiding spot. There was nowhere to hide but the boulders, but all the children were racing towards them. Her eyes followed the path of the stream. It came from a crevice along the side of the gully with room enough for her and Obi to squeeze into.

Yonah ran in the opposite direction from the other children. It was just a few metres to the crevice. She crammed herself and Obi inside. Once nestled in between the rocks, she looked out at the chaos.

The children were still racing for the boulders, and now a few members of the Guard were climbing down into the gully. From her position, Yonah could see about a half dozen of the guards perched at the top.

Among all the action, Yonah saw something that made her stomach leap up into her throat. Sayzia was making a mad dash towards Yonah and Obi's hiding spot. Based on her trajectory, Yonah guessed that Sayzia had managed to sneak some part of the way before having to put herself out into the open.

Yonah thought her sister had gone without the Guards noticing until the sand and stones around Sayzia's feet started to spit as the odd bullet kicked them up. Sayzia started climbing the side of the gully, climbing right past Yonah and Obi's hiding spot.

Within a few moments, the shots near Sayzia stopped. No body fell. Just loose stones tumbling past Yonah and Obi and into their crevice.

There was still a commotion at the bottom of the gully as some of the guards began grabbing some children and shooting to maim others. Yonah could feel her body begin to petrify into stone-still fear.

She had to believe Sayzia was safe. She and Obi needed to get out of here while the guards were still distracted and find Sayzia.

"Obi, we have to climb up out of here, okay?"

Her little brother had been silently crying. She grabbed his trembling hand. "Obi, look at me." Her voice was hard, masking her fear. He looked at her with wide eyes. "All you need to do is hold onto me. Can you do that? It's just a piggy-back ride."

Obi didn't respond.

She shook him. "Come on, Little Bear. I need you to be a big bear today. Can you hold on tight?" She fought hard against the panic rising in her chest, against her own trembling limbs, and her wish to crawl deeper into the crevice and never come out.

"I can be a big bear," he said meekly.

"Roar," Yonah whispered with a smile that felt like a lie.

He giggled.

"Grab on."

As Obi wrapped his little arms around her neck, Yonah emerged from the crevice and scrambled up the gully wall, scraping her hands along the way.

As she and Obi clambered over the top, Yonah gasped with relief. Then she felt a searing pain in her arm. She fell to her knees, mostly out of surprise.

"Yonah, run!"

It was Sayzia. Yonah looked up and saw her sister was hiding in a cluster of trees. With Obi still hanging off her back, Yonah stood and raced for her sister, ignoring the blood oozing from her arm.

Together, the sisters and their little brother raced through the cream and brown streets of Kelab back to their home. Yonah's arm ached, although she didn't think she had been hit very badly.

They burst through the open door of their small home. Their mother was singing in the kitchen and jumped when her children burst into the house.

"Ma, Yonah's hurt!" Sayzia said. "The Guard came to the gully. They've never come there before."

Their mother knelt next to Yonah, looking at her bleeding arm. Then she sadly stroked Obi's head and kissed him. She grabbed a cloth from the table, dunked it in a bucket of water, and pressed it to Yonah's arm.

"Were you followed?"

"I don't know," Yonah answered. She looked at Sayzia.

"Maybe," Sayzia said.

Their mother pursed her lips and tied the cloth to Yonah's arm so tightly it pinched. "Go to the bedroom."

The children went to their shared bedroom and sat down, huddled together. Their mother continued sweeping, removing any loose clumps of dirt from the packed floor. It was silent in the house, which made the children nervous. Normally, it was filled with music.

A man wearing black with a red sash—the uniform of the Guard— entered the house. He strutted with his pistol held casually at his side.

Unseen from the main room, Yonah peered from inside the bedroom.

"I need to search this residence for illegal persons." The man said.

"Only my children and I live here."

"Then you won't mind my searching your home." He brushed past their mother and strode straight to the bedroom. Yonah scrambled away from the doorway with Obi still clinging to her. When he entered the room, the man stood and looked down at the children with a sneer on his face.

"These children were with the group of urchins we just came across.

They'll have to be sold." He grinned at the thought.

"These are my children." Their mother stepped between the man and the three siblings. Her voice was strong. Yonah couldn't fathom how her mother could possibly be so brave.

"The president will see about that." The man made to move around their mother, but she stepped in his path.

"You are not taking my children away," she said with a fierceness that would rival a lion.

The Guard member lifted his gun to their mother's chin. "You don't tell me what to do. Now get out of my way."

"No."

The man grabbed their mother and shoved her to the floor. Yonah pressed herself towards the wall, hiding Obi from view and trying to stand in front of Sayzia.

Their mother threw herself on the man, trying to wrench his gun away from him. He turned angrily, threw her to the ground, aimed his gun, and shot.

Yonah flinched at the sound. She stared at their mother's trembling figure as a pool of blood spread beneath her, her eyes looking tearfully on her children.

Their mother gasped, "Run." She closed her eyes and she was still.

The man turned to the children, his teeth gritted. "Guess you're coming with me."

A flame erupted in Yonah's chest, one that would burn inside her for years to come, and she screamed, "You killed our ma!" This man wasn't supposed to be here. They had been safe.

"Don't make me kill you, too," he said, coming closer.

Suddenly, Yonah saw her sister throw one of their heavy clay toys, which hit the man squarely in the face. He brought a hand to his nose as he shouted in pain.

"Let's go!" Sayzia yelled. She grabbed Yonah's arm, leading her brother and sister to the window. Yonah jumped out first with Obi, then Sayzia. Just as Sayzia landed on the other side of the ground-floor window, the Guard grabbed her dress and began pulling her back in.

"No!" she shrieked. Yonah grabbed the Guard's hand and wrist and bit down on his thumb as hard as she could. The man cried out and pulled his hand away.

"Go!" Sayzia pushed Yonah and the three siblings ran. The man clumsily climbed out the window after them, but their head start was enough that they lost him in the city's alleys.

They ran. The only sound Yonah could hear was her breath pounding through her ears. Sayzia was only a few steps ahead of her, looking back every few minutes to make sure they were never too far apart. Her face was hard, furrowed in determination. Obi was silent on Yonah's back, a round ball of fear pressed tightly against her.

All Yonah could think of was to get as far away as possible. She and Sayzia just ran *away*.

Eventually they stopped, gasping for breath. The longer they stood there, the more quickly the reality of what they had seen washed over the older sisters. The worst had happened. Their mother was dead. They were orphans, and now they would never be safe from the Guard.

"What happened to Ma?" Obi asked. His first words since their escape from the gully. "Did she… Is she gone?"

Yonah blinked away the tears forming in her eyes. The awfulness of it overtook her and she sobbed loudly. She howled, "She's gone."

The children were quiet for a few minutes, unable to do anything but mourn the loss of their mother, their safehouse, the woman who sang to them and kept them warm and healthy and happy.

"What do we do now?" Sayzia finally asked. All her strength had withered away into emptiness.

Yonah didn't know. She didn't know how to look after her siblings. She didn't know where was safe anymore. She looked between Sayzia in front of her and Obi over her shoulder. There was only one thing she knew with certainty.

"We stay together."

Chapter One

"I thought I told Zabira to tell you to wash up."

Yonah was standing in front of the most beautiful woman she had ever seen at the slave entrance of Master Puru's palace. She could tell the woman was a slave like her because of the copper collar around her neck. "I did," Yonah said. "In the river."

The woman pursed her lips and wrinkled her nose. "And what is that?" She pointed at Yonah's right arm where a pink line was etched into her skin.

"It's a scar," Yonah answered. "I can work fine." Ever since her mother's murder seven years ago, she had been plagued by people staring at her scar.

A short puff of air came out of the woman's nose in a silent scoff. "I know you can work. But you might draw the wrong kind of attention." The woman seemed to be thinking about loud. Yonah wondered if she was going to be sent away.

With a sigh, the woman finally said, "Follow me," and set off at a brisk pace down the hallway. "Close the door behind you."

Yonah followed and underwent her transformation – a shower sourced by the same pools she regularly cleaned as an outdoor slave, getting dressed in a cropped, long-sleeved shirt that jingled with decorative coins, having her face done up in makeup for the first time.

It was disconcerting having a stranger wield a pointed object near her eye to line them in black. The girl doing Yonah's makeup also applied blush to Yonah's cheeks and colour to her lips. Then she brushed and dried out Yonah's hair as best as she could. When she finished, she pulled a hand mirror out and held it up so Yonah could see her reflection for the first time since she had been orphaned.

Yonah was surprised to find that she looked so much like her father, like an adult. At nineteen years old, she was nearly deemed an adult in the eyes of the law and nearing the day of her release from slavery. Her skin was slightly darker from years in the sun. Her face was gaunt with a square chin. Her lips were thin. There were deep purple bags beneath her eyes and the makings of wrinkles on her forehead. She barely recognized herself. It was difficult for Yonah to imagine her old twelve-year-old face in the one she saw right now.

Then her eyes drifted down to the copper slave collar around her neck. She and her siblings had been outfitted with them the day they were captured by the Guard three years ago.

She didn't even notice the makeup on her face.

Then she was whisked away to the kitchen and then to the dining hall.

Armed with a pitcher of wine so large that her arms quickly started to ache with its weight, Yonah wound around the guests who milled about the hall during the first evening feast. The interior of the palace was just as splendid as its exterior hinted. There was an entire wall made of intricately panelled tin that glistened beneath the flickering candles that were perched in silver chandeliers and sconces. The wall across housed several massive paintings of the master himself – in one he was seated next to a lion carcass, and in another he was aiming a rifle.

The guests did not remain in their seats throughout the feast. Instead, they picked at the food that lined the long tables as they travelled, jovially greeting one friend and then another. Although Master Puru remained on the dais at the front of the hall on which his table and most esteemed guests sat, even he meandered from one end to the other.

Yonah's mouth watered at the food selection: pork, hare, poultry, fish, platters piled with fruit, smaller dishes filled with candied fruit, wines and ports imported from across the country.

Throughout the night, the hands that held their empty cups shook more and more and Yonah tried to her best not to spill any wine. She was constantly dodging the guests as they plundered around the hall, changing directions suddenly and rocking back and forth with laughter. For the most part, she was invisible to the slave owners, for which she was grateful, as she felt uncomfortable dressed in only loose pants and a cropped shirt that left most of her torso exposed.

Every so often, a man or woman would look Yonah up and down, but they would usually leave it at that. One woman said to a man next to her, "I don't understand what Puru has to celebrate besides his own health. He appears to have lost all of his decent-looking serving girls."

The girls to which the woman referred had succumbed, along with nearly half of the household, to a terrible sickness that had recently passed through. Yonah had been brought inside that evening as their replacement during the feast. The feast was in celebration of Puru's survival of the same sickness.

While Yonah was refilling her pitcher in the kitchen, another one of the slaves said aloud for the others to hear, "I heard the cities faced the fever, too. It's awful. There were bodies lining the streets and bandits raiding everyone's homes."

"There'll be more orphans and criminals for the Guard to sell into slavery," the beautiful woman who had brought Yonah into the house said with a hint of bitterness in her voice. Bitterness also coursed through Yonah as she recalled the day the guards had picked her and her siblings off the streets, forcing their separation.

Throughout the night, Yonah continued to gather bits of information from the rowdy guests.

"Did you hear what happened to Otto? The moment the sickness took him, all of his slaves ran away, not before stealing all his weaponry and jewels, of course."

"Rya's household attempted a rebellion against her. The savages figured they were better than her just because of the sickness. 'An equalizer,' they said. Ha!"

"Well, now you really can't trust them. They all whisper to each other, scheming, spreading rumours, putting false hope in their hearts."

"There is a group building in Kelab trying to protest the slave trade."

Protesters. Like Yonah's father. But that was a long time ago.

"Be careful, Aveen, you might put ideas into their heads." The man who had spoken was one of the few static people in the great room. He sat casually, his hand caressing his cup.

The woman named Aveen looked from the man to Yonah. "Then perhaps I should tell the slave what happened to Master Rya's household when their rebellion failed." She took a step towards Yonah, so they were only a foot apart. "Every last man, woman, and child was executed that day. And now their remains lay buried in the desert."

Yonah's mouth opened, but she quickly closed it. Instead, she glared back at the woman with a hateful stare.

"Ah, the girl wishes to speak!" the man in the chair said, leaning forward with interest.

"How wise of her to hold her tongue," Aveen snarled. She drew away from Yonah and disappeared into the crowd.

Yonah went to continue her work, but the man wrapped his hand around her wrist, firmly, but not in a rough manner. She looked down at him in shock.

He looked to be only a few years older than Yonah. His short black hair lay in curls on top of his head and his closely cropped beard and moustache were shaved in sharp and neat angles. Brown and gold eyes looked intensely up at Yonah, paired with a perpetual smirk on his face. She found him quite handsome.

"What is it you wanted to say?" he asked.

Yonah tried to draw herself away from him, but he wouldn't let go. "I shouldn't." While she had been told that she should always answer a master when asked a direct question, she didn't think the advice pertained to political discussions.

"I want to hear it."

"I shouldn't," she repeated.

"I promise I won't tell," he teased.

Yonah glanced around the room. Master Puru was busily conversing on the dais. The other wine pourer was occupied with dodging a group of men who were reaching for her skirt. She could not see any other servers.

The embers of her angry flame burned in Yonah's chest. She poured wine into the man's cup and said, "Masters aren't allowed to kill their slaves. Master Rya will be punished."

"Is that what you think?"

Yonah stared at the man. His smirk lingered on his face.

"There will be a trial," he said. "But I imagine the context of their deaths – a household revolt – will weigh in Rya's favour."

But that was wrong. Even if the slavery act needed to be abolished, at least it protected slaves from murder.

Yonah said stubbornly, "Then both the executions and an unjust trial will fuel the protesters."

"Will they? Are you more passionate than ever about the rebellion, then?" The man looked up at Yonah with a soft smile on his face. He was charming, in a boyish way, although he continued to hold on tightly to Yonah's wrist.

"I am only pouring wine and listening to the conversations around me."

"You must be hearing many interesting things, then. From low-stakes gossip to political unrest."

Yonah kept silent as she looked at the man, wishing he would leave her be. She could feel his gaze burrowing its way through her chest, searching desperately for her soul and all its secrets. "I have to get back to my work," she said.

"Of course." As the man finally released her wrist, a wave of relief swept over Yonah. "Come back in a few minutes to refill my cup."

As she turned to leave, Yonah felt her senses heighten and she became acutely aware of the man's gaze on her, even as she walked further and further away.

IT WAS VERY LATE WHEN the last of the guests decided to stop drinking. Yonah had never stayed up so late in her work as an outdoor slave, but it appeared to be a regular occurrence inside.

The woman who brought Yonah into the palace – her name was Lari – brought Yonah back to a small room where she would sleep for the night. It was sparsely furnished with only a bed and a small table. Yonah would apparently be needed inside the palace for the duration of the celebration, which could last for days, if not weeks.

Yonah hadn't slept in a room by herself since she had lived in the big house with her family in Kelab. She had shared a room with her siblings in the small house. While they lived on the streets, the three siblings had always slept close enough that Yonah could easily brush her hand over theirs if either one of them had a bad dream, and as an outdoor slave she had remained squashed between the others in the huts that served as their shelters. Now Yonah felt cold without another body next to her, and lonely without the sound of another person breathing. It was absolutely still in her private room.

A loud knock startled Yonah upright. The door opened and Lari peeked inside.

"A Master Naris wants you to visit his room," she said softly.

"What?" Although sleep hadn't yet come to Yonah, she was still groggy from being on her feet for so long and so late.

"Get up." Lari stepped inside, bringing a candle with her. "Are you still dressed? Let me look at your face." She held the candle up to Yonah's made-up face. "Hmm, I think it will do."

"Who's Master Naris?"

"One of the guests. He must have liked you."

Yonah's stomach twisted as she remembered the man who had pestered her.

"Yonah," Lari said suddenly. "Have you ever…," she trailed off. She looked sadly at Yonah. "Have you ever been with a man?"

Yonah felt her skin prickle, shrinking away from the air that touched it, searching for safety. She understood what Lari was referring to. She had nearly found herself caught up in the business when she was living on the streets, looking after Sayzia and Obi, but Sayzia had talked her out of it.

"No," Yonah told Lari. "Never."

"Do you know how it works?"

"I think so?" Her voice wavered.

"Come, I'll give you my advice along the way."

Lari led Yonah away from the slave quarters, up the stairs to the palace, up more stairs, and down several hallways.

"Try to relax as best as you can. He knows what he wants, so let him make the decisions. I find it helps to think about," she paused, "happy things."

They stopped at a large metal door that was painted in bright colours and patterns. It must have looked magnificent in the daylight. Yonah had been so distracted on the walk up that she hadn't thought to look at the rest of the palace. She began to tremble.

"He's already seen one of the girls," Lari muttered. She put her hand on Yonah's shoulder. "Come see me when he sends you back. We'll fix you up. Now, go ahead and knock."

Yonah turned to face the door. She knew she was one of the lucky ones to have come this far in life and avoided this. She was lucky enough to have had parents looking after her for as long as they did, and then to have her sister looking out for her when their parents were gone. It really was only a matter of time.

She lifted her fist and struck the door with her knuckles slowly, three times.

"Enter," a voice called. The man from the feast.

"You'll do fine," Lari whispered before leaving. Yonah listened to her footsteps fade into silence, leaving her alone in the dark, expansive palace.

She pushed the door open and stepped inside.

The room was large, dimly lit with a few scattered candles. In the little light there was, Yonah could see there was a large bed to her right with posts on the four corners that hung with airy white curtains. The bedsheet was wrinkled and unkempt, and a single blanket lay on the floor next to the bed. The walls were lined with jewels near the top and painted with shades of blue. Chaises and wooden chairs were huddled at the other end of the room, to Yonah's left. They were gathered around a short games table. The man from dinner – Master Naris – lounged on one of the chaises.

He looked up at Yonah and flashed a charming smile.

"Good! You've found me. Come, sit."

She did as she was told, sitting at the opposite side of the square table on the edge of a chaise. He sat up on the edge of his own, facing her. He had changed from his dinner attire into a plain white linen shirt.

"The other wine pourer told me your name is Yonah. Is that true?"

She had to force the word out, but she said, "Yes." She was distinctly aware that her cropped shirt did not cover very much of her torso.

"And have they told you my name is Naris?"

"Yes."

"I had a pleasant time talking to you during dinner."

Yonah was unsure what response was expected of her. Slaves were not expected to converse with their masters.

"I was just doing my job," she finally murmured.

Naris smirked and stood up. "Would you like something to drink?"

The question startled Yonah. She stared up at the man with round eyes. She must have looked incredibly perplexed because he laughed.

"Please, Yonah, relax." Her name on his tongue made her ears prick. He walked over to a short cabinet on the far wall that was lined with bottles and glasses. He poured two drinks from a tall, thin bottle and handed one to Yonah. "What do you think of this?"

She peered into the glass. The liquid inside was a light colour. When she looked back up at Naris, she saw that he was waiting for her. She took a sip. It was wine. She had tasted it once as a child with her parents.

"It's good," she said, politely.

"Is it?" He sat on the chaise with her, leaning towards her.

His eagerness alarmed Yonah. The hairs on her arms were standing on end as if on high alert for any unwanted touch. "Yes?"

"It's from my vineyard."

"Oh."

He furrowed his eyebrows. "What do you like about it?"

Yonah looked at the wine in her glass. "I like..." She didn't know anything about wine. "It's just very refreshing. I haven't had anything other than water for a long time."

That caused Naris to pause. "Would you prefer water?"

She was worried she had insulted him. "No, this is fine." She took another gulp to illustrate her sincerity.

He smiled again and raised his own glass to her before taking a drink.

"So, Yonah." He shuffled closer to her, leaving only an inch of space between them. "You seem new to serving."

"What makes you say that?"

"Seasoned servers know better than to try to challenge a master like you did."

A combination of fear and resentment welled up in Yonah's chest. "I didn't. I didn't say anything to that master. And you made me tell you what I thought."

Naris chuckled as he said, "It's alright, Yonah. But you *are* new to serving?"

She looked at him. "I am new to serving, yes. I am not new to slavery."

"What's that story?"

As she spoke, Yonah inched away from Naris. "The sickness took many of the slaves here. They needed more help for the celebration." She wished that she was outside sitting around the fire with her friends like normal.

"What do you normally do here?"

She drank from her glass again, trying not to shake as she did. It was empty now. "I normally work outside. Today was my first time inside the palace."

"And what do you think of it?" Naris took her glass and walked back to the cabinet to refill it. Yonah recalled how only a few hours ago their roles were reversed and it was her job to make sure his cup was always full.

"Even the slaves who work inside live more luxuriously than those of us who work outside."

"Does it make you jealous?"

She shrugged. "They're also expected to stay up until all hours, so I suppose there are trade-offs."

Naris was grinning as he walked back to the sitting area with a fresh glass of wine. He sat down close to her again.

"You are not like the other girls I've come across."

Yonah didn't answer. Naris pressed the glass into her hand.

"Why are you different?" he asked. "Why are you more interesting than the others?"

"Maybe because you've given me the chance to be interesting." *Instead of merely taking me to your bed.*

He laughed again. "Believe me, I've given plenty of girls the chance to be interesting and they've all failed." He downed the rest of his wine. "It's the way you talk. You have a mind of your own. And there's intelligence in what you say."

Yonah's little voice was telling her to be silent, but she said, "Not generally a trait masters like in their slaves."

"No, not generally," Naris replied with a nod.

Yonah sipped her wine. Even if this master was fond of her, she was anxious to return to the safety of the slaves' quarters.

Naris said, "Where are you from?"

"Kelab."

"Ah, the big city. It's been a while since I visited there. It's where all the interesting people live." He nudged Yonah's shoulder, causing it to burn at his touch. "Including those pesky protesters. Are you a protester? Is that why you're a slave?"

Yonah looked defiantly at Naris. "No, I'm not a protester. But my father was." She was surprised the words had come out of her mouth. She didn't normally talk about her parents.

"And what is he now?"

"Dead." She said it so coldly that Naris was momentarily dumbfounded.

He broke the silence by quietly asking, "From the sickness?"

Yonah frowned at Naris. "He was murdered nine years ago. At a peaceful protest." A dull fire burned in her chest. She had been ten at the time.

Instead of responding, Naris went back to the cabinet and poured himself a second drink.

The room was quiet and still but for the flickering candles until he finally said, "Sometimes family isn't all that it's made out to be."

Yonah wanted to reprimand him for being so tactless, but the steely calmness he emanated made her stay silent.

"Do you like games?" he suddenly asked, turning and choosing to sit on the chaise across from Yonah.

"Yes, but I haven't played anything in a long time."

"What games do you like?"

She thought back to her childhood. "I remember enjoying playing cards with my—" she stopped herself, gauging Naris' mood. He looked fairly pleasant again. "My father."

His lips twitched, like he was trying to hide a grimace. "And your father thought that was a good use of his time? Playing cards with his daughter?"

"I imagine he thought I would gain various skills from cards. My father was a university professor and he was very concerned with our education." She was still watching for any change in Naris' demeanor. "Especially after the new president took over."

His face gave nothing away as he said, "Then you would enjoy playing a game with me."

Yonah, too, tried to hide her emotions from Naris. "If that is what you wish."

They looked at each other for what seemed like an hour, waiting for a tick, for someone to break. Yonah had had no intention of challenging the man – she wanted to get out of this room as soon as possible – but she did not appreciate the assumptions he seemed to be making about her father, assuming that he was wasting his time with his children, considering him a 'pesky' protestor because he stood up against slavery. Yonah's father had paid the ultimate price for standing up for what was right and Naris, who could command whomever to do whatever he wanted, believed him to be inferior.

"I am tired, for now," Naris suddenly announced. "You may go."

Relieved, Yonah silently set her cup on the games table and stood up, the coins on her shirt jingling softly. She was just opening the door when Naris called, "Have a good rest, Yonah."

She rushed out the door, eager to remove herself from his piercing gaze.

Chapter Two

Yonah was nine years old the day everything changed.

She and her family were living in the big house. She had woken, as usual, in her bedroom, the sunlight pouring through the glass-paned window onto her bed. She dressed herself in a blue dress that reached her knees, wrapped a white linen shawl around her shoulders, slipped into her sandals and raced down the stairs to the common area.

Her mother was singing while spreading jam on flatbread. Her father stood next to her, washing a dish in the kitchen basin, his lips curled into a pleasant smile.

"Morning!" Yonah cried from the stairs. She dragged a wooden chair out from the table and climbed into the seat.

Her parents chorused, "Good morning, Yonah."

"Are your brother and sister awake?" her father asked.

Yonah answered with a shrug, "I don't know."

Her father kissed the top of her head before saying, "I'll go check on them," and walked up the stairs. Meanwhile, Yonah's mother set a plate in front of her with two pieces of flatbread covered in jam.

"How come you're always down for breakfast so early, Yonah?" her mother asked.

Without a moment's hesitation, Yonah said, "So I'm not late for school." She took a large bite out of her breakfast.

At that moment, Yonah's sister Sayzia came down the stairs. She was one year Yonah's junior, but still much smaller. There was a frown on her face.

"Good morning, Grumpy," their mother said. "Where's your brother?"

Sayzia's voice was growly and low. "Obi is hiding from Pa."

With a chuckle and a sigh, Yonah heard her mother say, "That child."

Once Sayzia had plopped herself onto the chair next to Yonah, Yonah turned her head and stared obviously at her younger sister. "You shouldn't be so grumpy. Today will be good."

With a steadiness that seemed out of place for an eight-year-old, Sayzia turned to return Yonah's stare with her furrowed brow and deep eyes. "You don't know that."

Yonah raised her eyebrows at her sister with nonchalance.

"And you, my grump, don't know if it will be a bad day either," their mother said, setting breakfast in front of Sayzia.

Whether Sayzia had no argument for her mother, or was simply done with the conversation, Yonah wasn't sure, but Sayzia merely took up her breakfast and ate in silence.

A short, shrill scream burst through the house, following by raucous giggling, the volume of which rose until Yonah's father appeared at the top of the stairs with her little brother Obi over his shoulder.

"Where do you want him?" their father asked with a grin on his face.

"At the table," their mother answered. "Preferably in one piece."

As their father set Obi into a chair, their mother set a plate with breakfast in front of him. Obi's chubby fingers clumsily grabbed at the flatbread and he immediately had jam all over his hands.

Looking at the clock on the wall, their father said, "My girls, we should go. We don't want to be late."

"I think that would be fine," Sayzia said, but Yonah zipped out of her chair to the door where her school bag was waiting for her.

"Can't I come?" Obi whined.

"No, Obi," Yonah said, "you're too little for school."

"Next year, Little Bear," their father said.

Their mother wrapped her arms around her youngest child. "You get to help me!"

Every day Yonah walked with Sayzia and her father to school. From there, she knew her father continued to the university, which was the largest school in Kelab, the city they called home. He was a professor there.

"What are you teaching today, Pa?" Yonah asked as they walked down the brown and cream streets.

"We'll be talking about the old civilizations."

"You do that every day!"

"There's a lot to learn."

Yonah entwined her fingers with her father's. "Pa, will I get to go to your school one day?"

"If you'd like. It's hard work. But you'll learn lots."

"I like school."

They arrived at the children's school, which was a slim, multi-storey building. Yonah's father bent over and gave her a hug. Silently, Sayzia moved in to hug their father and they turned to walk into the school.

"Have a good day, my girls!"

"Bye, Pa!"

YONAH AND SAYZIA WALKED together back home after the school day was done. As usual, Yonah launched into what she had learned in her class while Sayzia listened. They dawdled along the way, taking a circuitous route through Kelab's markets to look around.

When they arrived home, their mother was folding laundry.

"How was school today, my little mice?"

"It was good," Yonah said, dropping her schoolbag to the floor. "We're learning how to subtract and we're reading a book about an adventurer!"

"That sounds wonderful. And you, Sayzia?"

Sayzia, who had been sneaking up the stairs, stopped and looked down at her mother and sister. "School was fine. I beat Jaren in a race. He said I couldn't do it, but I did."

"Congratulations on your win. I need both your help with dinner while Obi naps."

They were just setting the table when their father came home, a grim look on his face. Normally, he would burst through the door with his arms wide and shout greetings to his family, but today he quietly set his bag down and glided over to his wife.

"The rumours appear to be true," he said to her, keeping his voice low. Yonah gazed up at her parents, her hands drifting to a stop from their work.

"How can you be sure?" her mother asked.

"One of my co-workers knows someone in the party. Things will be coming to a head soon."

Yonah piped in, "What will?"

Her mother and father both turned to look at her as if they had forgotten she was there. Then her father quickly smiled.

"Nothing for you to worry about. Tell me all about your day!"

The family of five ate supper together. Once they had cleaned up, Obi went to play with his toys, Sayzia joined him, their mother began to read a book, and Yonah dug into her father's bookbag and pulled out a thick tome. She brought it over to him.

"Can we look at this one?"

He smiled and settled himself onto a floor cushion with his back against the wall. Yonah wiggled into his lap and opened the book across her legs. There were pictures and words all jumbled together across its pages.

"What are those?" she asked, pointing at a beautifully illustrated picture in the book.

"Those are mountains," her father replied. "They lie north of us."

"They look big."

"They are. They stand taller than anything you've ever seen before. And way up at the top, they're sometimes covered with snow."

"That's the white stuff that falls from the sky if it gets cold," Yonah said, remembering from previous lessons. She had never seen snow.

"Yes."

"Why don't we have mountains?" Yonah asked.

Her father paused to formulate an answer. "Well, we have other things instead. We have deserts and plains, a few rivers, a canyon. We can't have everything."

"Have you seen mountains?"

"I have, a long time ago. They were beautiful." Yonah watched her father's long fingers linger on the picture. "Maybe I can show them to you one day."

Yonah squirmed around so she could look up at her father. "I'd like that. Can we go see the canyon, too?"

His lips pulled wide into a grin. "I'll show you the whole world, if you'll let me."

YONAH WENT TO BED THAT NIGHT happy. Her mother sang softly to her once she was snuggled up in her bed, her voice smooth. Yonah quickly drifted off to sleep.

When she woke, it was still dark. There was shouting in the street. Yonah rubbed her eyes awake and peered out the window over her bed. Below, people were running. Others marched, not in unison, but with a great sense of purpose.

Outside her bedroom, she heard footsteps. Yonah hopped off her bed and stepped into the hallway. Her mother and father were whispering to each other in hushed and aggravated voices. Her mother saw her first and closed her mouth with a meaningful look at her father.

Her father turned to see Yonah watching them.

"My girl!" he said. "Why are you out of bed?"

"Why's everyone outside?"

He knelt in front of her. "I'm not sure, but I'm going to find out."

Her mother took a step towards him. "No! You don't need to go! What are you going to do? What's done is done."

"I'll just go to the university and back."

"You can't change anything tonight."

A wailing came from Obi's bedroom. Yonah's parents looked to their son's room and back at each other. Both were firm, locked in a battle of stubbornness.

"I'll be back soon," Yonah's father said, bowing his head in apology.

Fire lit her mother's eyes as she watched her husband walk down the stairs and out the front door. The shouts grew louder as the door opened, then were muffled when it shut.

Without looking at Yonah, her mother said, "Go back to bed, Yonah." She started for Obi's bedroom.

Yonah watched her mother disappear into the Obi's room, standing bare foot in the hallway. She went back to her bedroom, climbed onto the bed, and looked out her window again. There was still shouting, still running. Off in the distance, there were great fires sprouting up around the city of Kelab, bright orange against the black sky.

"Yonah?"

She turned her head and saw Sayzia standing in the doorway, her hands clutched into her chest.

"Come here, Za," Yonah whispered, waving her sister over. Sayzia ran to the bed and leaped onto it. It jostled as she clambered next to Yonah to peer out the window.

"The city's on fire," Sayzia said, her eyes wide. "What's happening?"

But Yonah had no answer for her sister.

Their mother's voice came from behind them. "No. No, no, no. Get away from the window. You should be sleeping."

Sayzia was making her way off the bed to return to her room. Yonah asked, "Why's Kelab on fire?"

"What are you talking about?" Their mother sauntered over to the bed and froze when she looked out the window, her mouth gaping open. Yonah saw small dots of orange reflected in her mother's eyes.

For a moment, their mother didn't speak. She stood staring out Yonah's window at the city. Yonah watched her mother's face for movement, for a sign, for a message. Suddenly, their mother's eyes flicked down to her daughters.

"To bed. Both of you."

"I can't sleep with the yelling," Sayzia grumbled.

"You will try. Yonah, lie down."

Yonah did as her mother told her and lied down on her bed, but once her mother and sister had left the room, she propped herself on her knees again to watch the outside world.

She could smell the smoke that billowed up into the sky. Someone far away screamed, followed by some yelling. Yonah watched a few more people running down the street. A loud bang echoed through the streets, and then cries from a crowd. Her body trembled in uncertain anticipation.

She wasn't sure how long she had been watching, but eventually, Yonah heard the front door open and shut, then the sound of her mother's footsteps passing her bedroom door and moving down the stairs. Yonah scrambled to her door and slowly opened it. Her parents were talking downstairs.

"I was so worried!" her mother said. "What's happening?"

"It's happened," came her father's voice. "The president and most of the government officials have been killed. "Althu took over."

"The military minister?"

Yonah crept over to the top of the stairs to get a look at her parents talking in the dark common room.

"They've set the schools on fire, all of them. The university is gone. They're executing the other ministers."

"Who's they?"

Her father shrugged and shook his head. "His supporters? There are people acting on his orders."

"Why? Why is he doing this?"

He looked into his wife's eyes. "He wants power, Va. And he doesn't want anyone to take it from him."

Before she could stop herself, Yonah said out loud, "So there's no school tomorrow?"

Her parents sharply turned their heads to look up at her, her mother with annoyance, her father with sadness.

"I thought I told you to go to bed!" her mother snapped.

But Yonah waited for her father's answer. She wished with all her might that her father would tell her he was only joking, that the fires hadn't ruined everything, that tomorrow would be normal. But his eyes spread their sadness through his face.

"No, Yonah. No more school."

Chapter Three

Yonah watched the masters talking and laughing, dressed in their fine clothes and jewels, eating quantities of food her family hadn't been able to afford in years, telling each other the lies that Althu had told them – that the slavery act was necessary, that it kept the country healthy, that the lower class needed watching.

Since their meeting in his bedroom, Naris had requested that Yonah be his personal wine pourer for the duration of his stay at Master Puru's.

"I'll have to bring in another worker from outside," Lari sighed, shaking her head at the news. She gave Yonah a quizzical look. "What did you even do last night if he didn't bed you?"

When Yonah had returned to the slaves' quarters the previous night, Lari had been ready with warm cloths, a poultice, and a drink of some sort, but none of the supplies had been necessary since all Yonah and Naris did was talk.

As Naris' personal wine pourer that night, Yonah was stationed at his table and wasn't required to traverse the entire hall to tend to the other guests. Once again, Naris was the sole stationary figure in the hall, letting people come to him if they wanted to speak.

There was only one man for whom Naris stood up to greet. He was pale, had brown hair including a thick beard, and looked to be in his twenties. Naris and the man warmly embraced each other.

"I wasn't sure you would make it all the way down here!" Naris said, leading the man to an empty chair next to his own. "How was your trip?"

"Oh, it was good enough." The man sat down. "And how are you?"

"I'm fine."

The man turned his chin down and squinted his eyes at Naris. "Are you sure?"

"Yes," Naris said forcefully.

The man's eyes shifted up to Yonah, who was standing next to Naris. "Did you bring this one?"

"No, she's one of Master Puru's." They spoke of her as if she wasn't there, which made Yonah's skin crawl.

"I'm surprised he can afford to let any of his slaves tend only to you." The man picked up a cup from a nearby table and motioned towards Yonah. "Please." Yonah stepped around Naris and poured wine into the man's cup.

"He likes me," Naris said with a shrug. "And he likes my wine."

The man spoke in a more hushed tone. "And do the slaves here seem to be under control still?"

Naris nodded. "In the immediate vicinity, yes. But if you talk to the other masters, they'll tell you stories of free folk and slaves rebelling."

"The buzzing of rebellion has long been heard in Jalid," the man said, "but never so aggressively as in Harasa." Yonah's ears perked at the mention of the country north of Harasa. It was possible that her sister Sayzia had been taken there.

"If you've heard whispers of rebellion for so long up north, then we have nothing to be worried about here," Naris responded.

"Ah, but what the masters in Harasa don't understand, Naris, is that we are far kinder to our slaves in Jalid than you are. Mine are not so unhappy as to revolt overnight. Meanwhile, I can feel the bitterness dripping off every slave I come across in the south."

Naris glanced at Yonah. "I find the population here rather intriguing."

The man leaned in closer, looking deeply into Naris' eyes. "You need to pay more attention, Naris." His voice was low and serious, so serious that Naris remained silent. "It's easy to tell what the slaves want. They're just like the rest of us. They want good food, shelter, a chance to put up their feet. But Harasan masters have never bothered to learn this."

"You don't think that being easy on your slaves will make it easier for them to rebel against you?" Naris asked.

The man shook his head. "I believe Master Rya's slaves rebelled not because they were slaves, but because they were unhappy." He patted Naris' knee and stood. "I think I'll turn in for the night. Until tomorrow, Naris."

Naris was too caught up in his thoughts to return the greeting. The man disappeared into the crowd. Naris suddenly looked at Yonah. "You are quiet."

"We are not to speak unless spoken to."

He stared unblinkingly at her as he drank from his cup. He then held the cup out for her to fill. As she did so, Yonah saw Naris look her body up and down. Her muscles tensed. He noticed.

"You are still anxious around me."

She didn't answer, despite Naris waiting for a long time, long enough that he finished his wine again.

"What do you think of Master Kejal?" He motioned in the direction the man had walked.

"He seems intelligent," Yonah answered.

"And what makes you say that?"

"He recognizes that his slaves aren't objects, but thinking and feeling human beings, and he's using that to his advantage." She heard a twinge of bitterness in her voice.

"But you still dislike him," Naris said.

Yonah didn't want to say anything that would get her in trouble if Naris shared. "As a slave myself, I dislike the fact that he has slaves." Her brother and sister had been stolen from her because of slavery. She had been without her family for years now because of the new slave culture that this corrupt government had instigated. She was trapped because of the people in this room, these people who had willingly accepted the slave culture because it worked to their advantage. They chose to ignore the humanity of their workers, to ignore any sense of morality for the sake of money and luxury.

"You must not think very highly of most of the people in this room," Naris said.

"They do not think very highly of me."

"What do you think of me?"

His look showed mixed emotions – intrigue, determination, even nervousness. Yonah wondered if he was just as puzzled by her as she was by him.

"I think a lot of things," Yonah told him. Naris waited for her to continue.

"I don't understand what you want from me. Any other man would have taken me to his bed last night."

"Would you have preferred that?"

Their eyes were once more locked together, windows to their souls open – neither one yet understood what they saw in the other, hard as they tried.

Before Yonah could answer, a woman sparkling with jewelry drunkenly kissed Naris on the cheek. "My dear boy, you are so beautiful! How is it you aren't married yet? If I were a younger woman, I would just eat you up!"

"Pahari, you are too kind!" Yonah could see Naris' discomfort.

The woman's face suddenly turned serious. She grabbed Naris' hands. "And how are you doing without your parents? Is it just you in that big house now? I was so sorry to hear of their passing."

"Thank you for your condolences." The polite smile on Naris' face was quickly fading away. His disposition was not one of grief, however, but a quiet anger.

"Let me know if I can be of any help to you," the woman persisted.

"It was nice talking to you, Pahari." Naris guided the woman away from him until she was forced to release his hands and stumble off towards another conversation.

Yonah stared after the woman. When she finally looked back to Naris, she saw that his brow was furrowed and his nostrils flared. His face was pointed towards the party, but his eyes weren't seeing it. His mind was far away.

Suddenly, Naris grabbed Yonah's wrist and pulled her down towards him so his lips brushed against her ear, causing the fine hairs on her neck to stand. "Come to my room again tonight."

She tried to stand, but he held her down next to him. "Yes?" he said.

Her heart rattled in her chest. "Yes." He released his grip on her.

She went to his room after she had helped clean up the evening meal. Her legs and feet ached as she made her way up the various staircases and down the massive hallways. Naris answered her knock on the door with a brisk, "Enter," and she stepped inside.

The room look much the same as the night before, including the messy bedsheets. Yonah assumed that Naris had already had a visitor this evening.

"I want to play chess tonight," he said. He was sitting at the games table. "Do you play?"

She said it plainly. "No."

He was not dissuaded. "I'll teach you. What will you drink?"

Yonah made her way over to the sitting area and said, "Wine is fine."

Naris smiled and stood up. "You liked it, did you? Good." As he poured her a glass he said, "I'm surprised your father didn't teach you chess."

"I was only ten years old when he was killed. A little young for chess." Even though his murder was nine long years ago, she could still see his bearded face, still hear his laugh, still feel that strong and unwavering love a little girl felt for her father.

"And how old are you now?" Naris set her glass on the opposite side of the table from him and sat.

She sat down across from him. "I'm nineteen."

"Old enough for chess."

She dropped her eyes, suddenly very tired. "I suppose so."

Naris did not seem to notice her change of mood, or he chose to ignore it. He was a master and she a slave, after all. Her job was to do his bidding,

41

no matter what she wanted or felt.

After a few minutes of his instruction, Yonah could not help but grow more interested in the game. It had been a long time since she had played anything. It had been a long time since she had learned something new. Yonah had always liked to learn. It was why she had enjoyed school so much. She had always listened ravenously to her teachers and to her father when they explained what was unknown to her. Learning a new game on this dark night lit a tiny spark in Yonah's soul that had remained dull and dark for a long time. She was not very good at first, but Naris was oddly patient with her. He taught her along the way where she had gone wrong, what he would have done in her place.

"You cannot be so conspicuous," he explained. "Build your framework without my knowing before you make your attack."

A yawn escaped Yonah's mouth. She quickly covered it with both her hands, but Naris had already seen. There was a smirk on his face.

"You are tired. You should go to sleep. I enjoyed our game."

Yonah stood up and paused. She didn't have to tell him, but she wanted to. "I did, too."

Naris' eyes were sparkling with hope. "Then perhaps you would like to play tomorrow night as well?"

She gave a minute nod. "If that is what you wish."

"Is that what *you* wish?" he countered.

They were caught staring at each other once more. Yonah didn't know how to appropriately answer Naris. She was still a slave. She had to remember that.

"Goodnight, Master Naris," she said, dropping her eyes to the floor and rushing out of the room.

As she made her way back to the slaves' quarters, she pondered over Naris. She had been so apprehensive about going to his room that night, even more so than the previous night, and it had turned out rather pleasantly. She had forgotten for a while who she was. She had felt like a child again, the child she was before everything changed. Even if she had felt a few moments happiness that evening, Yonah wasn't sure if it was acceptable that a master had been the root cause.

ON THE THIRD EVENING, Yonah entered Naris' bedroom and saw that the bed was pristine. Her muscles tensed and she became sure that instead of satiating his appetite with another slave girl, Naris was expecting to bed Yonah tonight.

He was sitting in his usual spot at the low games table, the chess board was set up for a new game, and a bottle of wine and two glasses sat on the table. "Should we review the rules first?"

Yonah tentatively sat across from Naris, ignoring the already filled glass sitting nearby. Naris, not noticing her discomfort, started reviewing the game with Yonah. She didn't hear anything he said, only watched him anxiously.

He took care of himself, she noted. His beard was trim, his teeth were white, no stench came off his body. Yonah had listened to her peers describe the men they had pleasured in exchange for money: dirty fingernails, bad breath. And sometimes they were violent, slapping the girls, holding their heads down, pulling their hair, hurting their bodies. Yonah wouldn't know if Naris was a violent one until it had already begun.

"Yonah?"

She gasped as her vision cleared and she registered Naris sitting across from her. He wore a look of concern.

"Are you alright?" he asked.

Her hands were shaking. She clasped them together to try to still them. "I'm fine."

"You don't look fine."

Yonah's fingers started to ache from holding her hands so tightly. "Will we be..." her voice faltered. She turned her head to look at the bed.

"I had been hoping so," Naris replied.

Yonah tried to remain composed, even though her insides started to shake.

"But I would rather you wanted to," he added. Her breath caught in her throat as she turned her gaze back to Naris. "Do you want to?"

She opened her mouth to speak, but no words came out. No, she didn't want to. But slaves were meant to do masters' biddings. In her three years as a slave, never had a master given her such autonomy.

Naris smiled softly. "Let's just play chess tonight."

"Why are you being so nice to me?"

Naris pursed his lips. He didn't speak for what felt like minutes and minutes. "Because I like you. White goes first."

They were quiet at first, until a game later when Yonah removed Naris' queen from the board – to his surprise – and a joyful laugh burst out of her. She moved her hand to her mouth quickly, surprising herself with her outburst. She hoped Naris wouldn't be offended.

But he was shaking his head and trying to hide the smile on his face. "That was very good," he said.

A warm sense of pride filled her up. She still lost the game, but she knew she was getting better.

"You'd better get some sleep," Naris finally said, standing up.

Yonah stood, too, and said, "That was fun."

His boyish smile lit up his face. Naris walked with Yonah to the bedroom door, but he placed his hand on the handle and left it there. He looked down at her with a softness in his eyes.

"Can I kiss you?"

A combination of delight and terror filled Yonah's chest. Surely it was wrong for a slave and a master to have any relationship beyond those roles. Yes, it was. But the gentle curiosity on Naris' face and the warmth of his lean frame close to hers had sent her skin trembling with anticipation.

"If that is what you wish," she whispered.

"No, Yonah. I'm asking you."

Naris remained frozen in place as Yonah watched him. He would wait for her answer. It was because of her own curiosity, and the fact that she knew Naris would wait if she told him 'no,' that Yonah finally, slowly nodded.

He leaned forward, his lips starting to pucker. She closed her eyes and met him halfway. When their lips met, Yonah felt as if her chest was glowing. The glow filled Yonah up. It was unlike the angry flame that normally burned within her. Naris' lips were gentle on hers. He smelled of thyme, slightly sharp but not overpowering.

He was pulling away. Yonah's lips tingled as she opened her eyes. Neither one of them smiled as they looked at each other. Instead, Yonah's mouth hung open in awe and Naris looked at her with confused wonder.

"Goodnight, Yonah," he said almost inaudibly.

"Goodnight."

Naris opened the door for her and she stepped out into the hallway. Once the door was shut between her and Naris, Yonah touched her fingers to her lips. She stood for a long time in the hallway, trying to remember the feel of Naris' lips on hers, smiling at the thought of enjoying her evenings with him, worrying over the fact that a master was making her feel this way.

HER PRESENCE IN NARIS' ROOM was once again requested the next day around noon. Yonah wasn't nearly so anxious about their meeting as she made her way there, although she was curious about why he had called for her midday. When she entered the room, she saw him standing on the balcony across from the door. His room was at the back of the palace, giving him a view of the green courtyards that fanned out below.

Naris turned when he heard Yonah enter and smiled at her. "Come take a look."

It was the hottest part of the day in the dessert region of the country. The heat reminded Yonah of the many times she and her closest friend among the outdoor slaves had gotten dizzy from heat exhaustion, and how they had to hide beneath the shade of the trees and bushes in the courtyard, all while staying out of view of Master Puru. But Yonah spent so little time outside since moving indoors that now, as she took a breath of the fresh air, she felt her chest balloon, grasping for the fresh oxygen, trying to hoard it for the next famine.

"Is that where you normally work?" Naris was pointing in the distance, to the edge of the estate property, at the huts where the outdoor slaves slept.

"That is where I normally sleep," Yonah responded. She pointed at the river outside of the wall. "And that is where I collect water," she then gestured to the courtyard, "to bring it in here."

"You're a gardener," Naris said. She nodded.

She watched the small figures meandering between the huts and the river and back to the courtyard. There were far fewer people out there than usual, ever since the sickness had swept through and killed so many of them.

Sorrow washed over her as she thought of her old life out there with her friends.

"What's wrong?" Naris asked.

Yonah started at the question. "I lost a very close friend during the fever." She kept her eyes turned to the courtyards. "I miss him."

Naris' voice was gentle. "I'm sorry to hear that."

A peculiar warmth glowed inside of Yonah. It was unlike the anger that burned when she thought of the cruelty of the masters and the Guard. It was soft and pleasant, but also unknown to her, which made her uncomfortable.

In an attempt to make the feeling go away, Yonah turned to her curiosity and said, "I understand you lost your parents."

Any gentleness in Naris' face turned hard. His eyes quickly filled with disdain. "Yes," was all he said.

Afraid of his sudden change of mood, Yonah left the conversation at that. The two of them stood in silence as they looked out over the courtyards. As the moments passed, the tension eased into a lazy contentment.

Finally, Naris broke the silence by asking, "Do you prefer inside or outside?"

Yonah recalled how grubby her skin got working outside in the dust and dirt, how her hair was always knotted and grimy, how her clothes were never clean. She thought of how the hot sun made her dizzy nearly every day. She thought of the laughter around the fire at night and how she took comfort in the sound of other people's breathing when they were all sleeping. Her nostrils flared as she inhaled the outdoor air.

"I'm used to the outside. It may be harder living, but I think I like it more."

"You don't like the palace?"

"It's beautiful." She traced her fingers along the silver encrusted railing of the balcony. Master Puru had so much wealth that he flaunted it anywhere he could, to sit and do nothing but look impressive.

She felt Naris step closer to her. "Do you think you could get used to living in a palace?"

"I suppose so," she said slowly. Her muscles tensed. He was standing so close that she could feel warmth coming from his body. "Why?"

He looked out at the courtyards and the outdoor slave quarters for a moment. "Because I was wondering what you might think of coming to live with me."

She looked up at him. He was still looking out, avoiding her gaze.

"What do you mean?" she asked.

He faced her. "I mean I want you to come back home with me and live there and be my…companion."

Yonah stood there, dumbfounded. He wanted to take her away from here. But Master Puru owned her. Was Naris planning to buy her from him?

Surely, she wasn't worth that headache.

"What would I do there?"

He smiled. "Absolutely nothing. I just want to be able to spend time with you, the same way we have over the past few days. You needn't work, inside or outside. You will be free to do whatever you like when you are not with me."

It sounded almost like freedom.

An idea came to Yonah. To use Naris' affection to her advantage. To convince him to do things for her. Maybe she could use him to find Sayzia and Obi even before her twentieth birthday. Maybe she could even free them and they could be together again.

Naris leaned in to Yonah, looking into her eyes. "Would you like that?"

She nodded. "Yes. I would."

Chapter Four

When sixteen-year-old Yonah opened her eyes, she saw her brother's sleeping form lying next to her, his cheek scrunched up between his nose and the ground. Yonah sat up and saw, on the other side of Obi, her sister Sayzia, also asleep, and beyond her, more children of varying ages. They were covered in tattered clothing, some in ratty blankets. The sky loomed vast above their heads, paling from the blackness of night to the grey-blue of early morning.

Yonah peered over the low wall of the rooftop, down to the street just three storeys below. There were only a few people out. She noticed a pair of men dressed in the black and red garb of the president's Guard as they stumbled out of a building, looking disheveled but satisfied.

Another group of Guards, looking much more alert, were coming down the street towards the pair. Yonah watched them meet, chat, and continue their separate ways.

One of the Guards turned his head upwards and Yonah ducked down beneath the low wall. Her heart pounded. After a few moments, she inched her eyes above the wall to see if the Guards were gone. They were walking down the street, away from their hideout.

Yonah nudged Obi and Sayzia awake. They moaned in protest, but Yonah whispered to them, "We should go."

She looked up. There was already a pair of children waking up and vacating the rooftop. While the orphaned children of Kelab tended to gather at night for security and safety, they dispersed during the day and kept to themselves. Yonah and her brother and sister had been using this rooftop as their place of rest for a few days now. They would soon move on to another spot in order to avoid the Guard, who were always on the lookout for potential slaves.

"Come on," Yonah whispered, continuing to nudge her siblings. "Let's go."

Obi rolled over and sat up, rubbing his face. At eleven years old, he was catching up to his sisters in height, though he wasn't quite taller than them just yet.

Sayzia's eyes opened up to the sky. She stared for a moment before sitting up. A hardness had grown into those eyes over their four years living on the streets. There was something familiar in them that Yonah recognized from her sister's serious personality as a young child, but now they also carried the burden of grief and survival.

The three siblings crept among the sleeping forms of the other children to the opposite edge of the rooftop. There was a hole there that led to an abandoned apartment inside the building. At night, the children used abandoned furniture to build a staircase up to the hole in the ceiling, and once everyone was inside for the night, the top pieces were withdrawn up to the rooftop so no one could climb after them. In the morning, the last children to leave for the day knew to bring those pieces back down with them so they could start over at the end of the day.

Now, Yonah, Sayzia, and Obi hopped down from the ceiling straight to the floor. It was a risky ten-foot drop, but one that they were now accustomed to.

There was a window in the apartment from which hung a rope made of different strips of cloth tied together. Obi and Sayzia went down first, then Yonah. She gripped the makeshift rope with all her might, afraid every time she used it that it would rip and send her careening down to a life-ending injury. The rope ended at the second storey window, which led to another abandoned apartment. From there, the children jumped to the balcony on the opposite building, slithered down the outside railing, and dropped down to the ground.

"What's for breakfast?" Obi asked.

"Same as usual, Little Bear," Sayzia answered.

The three of them walked through the city, past derelict houses, thriving storefronts, travelling merchants. Kelab was beginning to wake up.

Every time they saw a member of the Guard, or a flash of red, they hid around a corner, clung to a thick piece of crowd, kept their heads down. Drawing the attention of the Guard was the last thing they wanted.

Yonah smelled their destination before she saw it. The scent of freshly baked bread, cinnamon, and honey caused her nostrils to flare wide and her mouth to salivate.

They went to the bakery every morning. It was owned by a couple who had been friends with their parents. They had several children of their own and were unable to take Yonah and her siblings in when they were orphaned, but they happily gave the three of them a loaf of bread and some sweet pastries every day.

"Good morning!" the man said brightly. He already had a bundle of cloth ready for them. "How are my three friends?"

"We're fine, thank you, sir," Yonah said. She took the bundle. It was still hot. She withdrew the cloth that yesterday's bread had arrived in from her shoulder bag and handed it to the baker.

"What are you up to today?" he asked. It sounded like a harmless enough question to a passerby, but to the baker, Yonah knew, it was a question of how the children would survive.

"I'm going back to the laundry shop," Yonah answered. "Sayzia and Obi will try to find some work at the market."

The baker shook his head. "You had better hurry along and find something to do, then, before the Guard catch you. And stay away from the Yellow Square. I hear some of the vendors there are turning children in. I worry every day for you three."

Yonah smiled half-heartedly. "You say so every day."

His eyes held on to Yonah tightly. "I mean it."

She nodded to acknowledge his concern. "Well, thank you for the bread. We'll see you tomorrow."

"Be safe, children."

As they started down the street, Yonah flipped a corner of the bundle open to reveal the usual loaf of bread and a treat of three cinnamon rolls.

"That looks great!" Obi said, quickly snatching one of the rolls from the bundle.

Yonah held the bundle out for her sister, who took one of the rolls, tore a piece off, and popped it into her mouth. Her eyes widened briefly with pleasure. She nodded to Yonah. "They're good."

Yonah picked up the last roll. "Will you go back to the same lady you saw yesterday?"

Sayzia nodded as she chewed. She swallowed. "And if she doesn't have work for me, I'll try the tailor from the other day."

"And what about you, Obi?" Yonah asked her brother.

"Can't I take one day off?" he grumbled, licking his fingers clean, having already finished his roll.

At the same time as Yonah said, "Absolutely not," Sayzia was saying a resounding, "No."

"We need the money," Yonah explained.

"And what if the Guard saw you?" Sayzia added.

"Fine, I'll go back to the river," Obi said sullenly. He took the bread from Yonah and ripped off a third. At the river there was a man who sometimes hired the boys to go diving for shells and rocks.

Yonah took the remainder of the bread from her brother and held it out for Sayzia. Her sister shook her head and said, "For dinner." Yonah wrapped the bread and tucked it into her shoulder bag.

They arrived at the launderer, made plans to meet there at the end of the day, and Yonah waved her brother and sister goodbye before entering the shop.

It was sweltering hot and dimly lit inside. A woman wearing her hair up in a bun emerged from a door that led to the shop front.

"Yonah, good morning. Come in." She spoke briskly. "I need you to start with that pile over there."

Yonah walked over to the pile in question and began scrubbing and soaking them in the steamy hot water that the shop owner had already prepared.

It was hard and unforgiving work that left Yonah's hands red and sometimes blistered, but it reminded her of her mother, and it was a job she could count on.

Yonah normally kept to the back room, but sometimes brought an order to the front, giving her a glimpse of the client. She did so now and almost froze in fear when she realized a Guard was picking up his order. Avoiding eye contact with the man, she set the wrapped clothes on the countertop and started for the back room.

"Have I seen you here before?" the Guard asked. Yonah stopped in her tracks, tried to put on her most pleasant face, and turned around.

"I'm usually in the back," she replied.

"Huh." He stared at her for a moment. "And how old are you?"

Yonah's tight-bunned employer said, "She's twenty."

Although Yonah's face was open and relaxed, her insides were trembling.

"You do know," the Guard said to the woman, "that you could be fined or imprisoned for harbouring orphaned children?"

"Harbouring! Sir, she's just works here. And she's of age. There's nothing wrong with that, is there?"

"If she's of age, no." He picked up his package and said darkly, "Have a good day," and left the shop.

Yonah breathed out a sigh of relief. "Thank you. I know I've said it before, but thank you."

"The rules don't make sense," her employer grumbled. "The slavery act is meant to put idle people to work, well you're working! None of this makes sense. You'd better get back to work."

Yonah could just barely get away with lying about her age. If it had been Obi or Sayzia being interrogated today, they would have had to lie about their parentage, something the Guard could easily disprove just by following them home.

At the end of the day, Yonah stepped out of the laundry shop, gently rubbing her raw hands, her bag a little heavier with the ora coins she had earned. She had to wait a few minutes, but Obi and Sayzia eventually arrived at their meeting spot.

"How was everyone's day?" she asked them.

"Fine," Obi said, slapping a handful of ora into Yonah's hand.

"One of the fruit vendors is trying to get rid of his entire stock today," Sayzia said. "If we hurry, we could find some good stuff for cheap."

With Sayzia leading the way, the three of them ran to the vendor. Sayzia found the ripest fruit that was left and bartered with the vendor while Yonah and Obi watched from the other side of the road. Even though the vendor seemed to be fairly agitated with her, Sayzia held her own, remaining calm and unwavering as she bartered. Eventually, she returned to her siblings and passed them some fruit.

"We still have enough ora for some meat pies and then for saving," Sayzia said with a smirk.

"How do you do that?" Yonah asked. "I always feel so nervous bartering with them."

Sayzia shrugged in response.

They bought meat pies to finish off their supper and ate them in an alley out of sight of the thinning crowds. It was silent as they ate. Yonah had run out of questions to ask her siblings, Sayzia was normally quiet, and Obi was busy wolfing down as much food as he could get his hands on.

Once they had finished their evening meal, they started back to the rooftop they had been sleeping at as of late.

"I think tomorrow night we should find a new place," Yonah said. "I saw a group of Guards wandering around there this morning."

Sayzia nodded. "We've been there a few nights. We could try near the gully."

Instead of returning to the rooftop the way they had climbed down that morning, they entered one of the city's various abandoned buildings, took the stairs to its roof, and used the top of Kelab to travel.

There were other children up here. It was like a secret world, a secret roadway that only the orphans knew about set against the backdrop of the pale blue and yellow sky.

Once they had arrived at their rooftop from the night before, they relaxed. Some of the children were chatting with each other, swapping stories from their lives before they had lost their parents. Sometimes, they even shared tips for vendors and shops that were looking for workers.

Working meant contributing to society. And contributing to society meant a better chance at avoiding being sold into slavery.

Eventually, the sun set, the children tired, and the rooftop grew quiet except for the sound of gentle snoring. Yonah, Sayzia, and Obi whispered goodnight to each other and lay their heads down to sleep.

A SHARP SCREAM STARTLED Yonah from her slumber. She sprung up to her feet, Obi and Sayzia not far behind her.

There was chaos on the rooftop. Children running in every direction, leaping over still sleeping forms, trying to find alternative exits. At the opposite end of the rooftop, there was a flash of red on black. The scene reminded Yonah of the day years ago when their mother had been killed.

"Come on, Yonah!" Sayzia was saying, tugging on Yonah's arm. She led Yonah and Obi to the rooftop edge. They looked over. On the street, there stood more Guards. Some chased children as they spilled onto the street.

"What about that way?" Obi said. His sisters looked to where he was pointing. Some of the children were running to the side of the roof top and leaping – where they landed, Yonah didn't know.

She furrowed her brow. "Let's try."

They raced over to the edge. The handful of children gathered in the small area resulted in everyone being jostled about. One child was standing on the edge, looking out to his landing target.

"Hurry up!" someone yelled.

There was more jostling, someone bumped the child, he wobbled and fell. He tried to jump midway through his fall, but Yonah wasn't so sure he didn't fall to the street below where, if he was still alive and relatively uninjured, the Guards would pick him up.

Yonah grabbed Obi's hand to keep him close.

"I can do it myself," he said, trying to shake her off.

"Not now, Obi!"

Sayzia's voice called, "Yonah, let's go!" She was already pressed against the low wall, having snuck through the crowd battling for space. Yonah pressed through with Obi behind her.

"Go," she told Obi. "That balcony over there."

It was the second-floor balcony across the alley.

Without a word, Obi jumped, springing into the air like a frog and landing on the other side with ease.

"Go, Yonah," Sayzia said.

"No, you."

Sayzia roughly pulled her sister up to the wall. "Don't fight with me, go!"

Yonah tried to calm her breath as she climbed up. She looked at the target. Obi was ready with knees bent, prepared to spring to her aid if she needed it.

She bent her knees and pushed off the wall with all her might. For a split second, her stomach leaped up into her throat. She landed on the outside of the metal balcony railing with her feet on the base and her hands on the top. She climbed over and looked to her sister.

Sayzia was already up on the wall. As soon as Yonah turned to look, she jumped. Behind her, a Guard appeared and started dragging children away. Sayzia struck the railing with her body, fumbled for her grip, slid downwards.

Yonah screamed and reached for her sister. Sayzia was hanging by the metal bars of the balcony railing, her legs swinging beneath her.

"Grab her arm, Yonah," Obi said, taking Sayzia's other arm. Together, they pulled Sayzia up.

Suddenly, the door to the balcony flew open and a woman in light linen stood in the doorway, her eyes blazing.

"Get out of here!" she screamed. "Get out!"

Obi led the way, standing on the railing and leaping to the balcony next door. The three of them bounded from one balcony to the next until they reached the back of the building. They slid down the outside of the last railing and dropped down to the street, then started to run.

Some of the Guards noticed them, but were too far away to catch up.

"We should get up to the rooftops," Sayzia gasped as they ran.

"Just keep running," Yonah answered.

They rounded a corner where they were met by a dozen more Guards, a mass of red and black uniforms. A couple of them were mounted on horses and galloped towards the three of them.

"Stop!"

Yonah, Sayzia, and Obi turned around and ran down another street. The pounding of the horses shook the ground beneath Yonah's feet.

One of the horses caught up with her and the Guard riding it struck her with the back of his rifle. Yonah's head throbbed. She stumbled and fell to the ground, kicking up dirt.

"Yonah!" Sayzia screamed.

"Go!" Yonah called back. "Keep going!"

But when she looked up, Yonah saw that her siblings had stopped running, caught between saving her and themselves.

"Run!" Yonah screamed so hard her throat hurt. "Don't stop, run!" It was one thing if she was caught, but to let her brother and sister lose their freedom on her account was unacceptable.

She was being pulled to her feet by the back of her shirt. She watched her siblings. They started to run again, but it was too late. The same Guard that had struck Yonah down caught up to Sayzia, then to Obi. They both fell much like Yonah, rolling through the dirt.

"We all work," Yonah started saying to the Guard that had pulled her off the ground. "We contribute."

"And you'll contribute as a slave, too," the Guard said.

"I work as a launderer. This isn't right!" She tried to pull away from him. The Guard struck her face with the back of his hand and she doubled over in pain. He dragged her down the street to a wagon that was full of other captured children. They all wore manacles around their wrists.

Yonah and her siblings were outfitted with their own manacles and lifted onto the wagon. The wagon started down the street.

She saw a slight quiver in Obi's bottom lip. He looked as though he were trying very hard to look brave, but she saw his eyes flitting side to side, fearfully trying to figure out what would happen to them.

There was a resigned calmness about Sayzia. She stared straight ahead as the buildings of Kelab passed by. Yonah tried to hide the sorrow that was welling up inside her. She had failed Obi and Sayzia. She had failed their parents.

Chapter Five

Yonah and Naris left the following morning. Lari sent Yonah away wearing a pair of billowing brown pants, a cream-coloured long-sleeved tunic, and an orange, lightweight but long coat with a matching headscarf. She had no other worldly possessions.

When she arrived at the front of the silver palace, Naris looked Yonah up and down, disappointment on his face.

"You look so plain," he said. "Where is your other clothing?"

"I don't own any other clothing," Yonah said.

Naris sighed. "We'll have to buy you something in Kirash."

"Is that where you live?"

"No, that's the town near my estate. They call where I live Vaha. Now, we'd better go."

The caravan comprised of two carriages that were each pulled by two horses, two male slaves who drove the carriages, and four Guards that had been hired to escort them. Naris opened one of the carriage doors and motioned for Yonah to climb inside. She ducked her head as she stepped up into the carriage and found a seat on one of the blue velvet benches. Naris followed her and, after closing the carriage door, sat across from her.

They had been alone before, but they had never been in an enclosed space such as this. The notion sent a strange thrill through Yonah.

"Have you ever been in a carriage before?" Naris asked.

"First time," she replied.

Naris smiled briefly and gave the wall behind him two taps. With a jerk, the carriage rolled forward and they were on their way. Yonah looked out the small window as they left Master Puru's palace behind and drove deeper into the desert wilderness.

In a few hours, the carriage stopped and, when Yonah emerged from the confined space, she saw they were at a train station. Naris' bags and boxes were transferred by the slaves to the train and Naris led Yonah to a passenger car.

Yonah had learned about trains in school. She knew that its passengers could travel clear across the country in a couple of days.

A man (not a slave) came to their car once the train had started its journey offering food and beverages. Naris bought some fruit and bread and shared it with Yonah.

Yonah slid a berry into her mouth and bit down. As its juices exploded onto her tongue, her eyes lit up at the sweet flavour. Naris chuckled.

"Have you had those before?"

"Not for years!" Yonah popped two more of the berries into her mouth. "Not since I was living in Kelab."

"Are they your favourite?"

Yonah carefully held a single berry in the tips of her fingers. "When I was a child, cherries were my favourite. But I don't have favourites anymore. They're all," she pressed the berry through her lips, bit down, and smiled through her closed mouth, "delicious."

"We will have to always have fruit nearby for you," Naris said.

Yonah furrowed her brows. "I wouldn't expect you to do anything on my account."

"You are living with me as my companion, Yonah. I will do everything I can to keep you happy."

As they chugged along, Yonah watched the arid desert morph into light dirt. The air grew slightly thicker. Small shrubs turned into larger and greener bushes. The trees grew slightly more plentiful. While still hot, this area was lusher than the desert region.

They reached another train station, transferred the luggage to yet another set of carriages, met up with different slaves and Guards, and continued on their way.

The sun was nearing the horizon and painting the sky pink when the carriage rolled to a gentle stop. The carriage shifted when the driver hopped to the ground and opened the door. Naris climbed out first.

"Welcome to my home – Vaha," he said with a proud smile, holding his hand out for Yonah.

Yonah took his outstretched hand and stepped down into the sunlight. She blinked up at the palace.

Naris' estate – Vaha – comprised of a palace that was made predominantly of grey brick with white alabaster finishes. There were several towers of exterior stairwells wrapped in alabaster carvings, all attached to the windowed main building. A dome rose up from the centre of the palace and a glass ceiling peeked up on the left side.

But surrounding the palace lay the majesty of the estate. Greenery spread out across the land, rows and rows of it, creating an oasis among the plains. Yonah realized the greenery was vines on which grapes grew. There were many slaves working in the vineyard, wearing hats and scarves to cover their heads from the sun. Their copper collars glistened in the waning light.

"Come," Naris said, interrupting Yonah's wide-eyed gaze. "Let me show you where you'll be sleeping."

He pushed the imposing carved front door open and Yonah followed him inside. The interior of the palace was finely decorated with tapestries, pottery, and paintings. The ceilings rose so high that Yonah had to crane her neck to see them. There was a balcony that ran through the centre of the room, suspended between two large staircases. Naris led the way up the stairs, along the balcony to an enclosed hallway, and up another set of stairs.

Yonah's room was on an upper level of the palace, overlooking the vineyards. There was a wide balcony and large windows. The walls were white and the small floor tiles a sea of varying blues and greens and purples. There was a bed off to the left, large enough to fit at least four people, and a white and gold chaise and an aqua blue armchair in the centre next to a short wooden table. At the end of the wide room was a set of drawers, a full-length mirror mounted on the wall, and a door.

"We can dress it up more to your taste if you like," Naris said.

"It's lovely." She had never had so much space that she could call her own. She was normally cramped in tightly next to someone in the same bed, or the same piece of floor. Even her room in the basement of Master Puru's palace was still very small, though she hadn't been there very long.

"I have some business to attend to," Naris said, "but I'll come back for you shortly. I'd like to give you a tour."

With that, he closed the door behind him and left Yonah alone in the large room. Her room.

Yonah's first order of business was to open the door to her right. It revealed a small, tiled room with a large porcelain tub sitting in the middle. Yonah tried to remember what it was like to have a proper bath instead of being pummelled by water from the ceiling at Master Puru's, or dipping into the river like she did as an outdoor slave, or scrubbing her skin hastily with fountain water as a child living on the streets.

She closed the door and faced the main room, opened the double doors to the balcony, and stepped outside. Below her, the vines stretched out and slaves bustled between the rows and down the lengths, carrying baskets and picking grapes. Beyond the boundaries of the estate – Vaha – the land lay flat and covered in light grass and shrubs. Yonah's eyes turned to the road on which they had entered the vineyard. It split at the edge of the estate, one road heading eastward from where they came, and one heading west to a town. The distance of the town made Yonah think it was likely only a twenty-minute walk away. It must have been the town of Kirash that Naris had mentioned that morning. Yonah wondered what sort of news she could gather there, what kind of allies she could make.

She wasn't sure if she was allowed to leave her room. Yes, Naris had said she could do whatever she liked when he didn't require her company. After all, that was the reason she had agreed to come live with him when he asked, but she didn't yet know how much freedom she had. She bided her time watching the slaves working below.

A man below looked up and saw Yonah from her third-storey perch. She couldn't quite make out the expression on his face, though she guessed he was mostly curious as to who the stranger on the balcony was.

Naris came back several minutes later, bursting suddenly through the bedroom door.

"The vineyard is beautiful, yes?" he said.

"I was just admiring it."

He stepped beside her. "It produces the finest wine on the continent." He did not need a second opinion on that. "Come, let me give you the tour."

As they left the bedroom, Naris placed his hand on the small of Yonah's back, causing her skin to erupt in tiny goosebumps.

Their first stop was Naris' room, which looked very similar to his guest room at Master Puru's palace. Yonah, however, made no mention of that.

Naris showed her his games room, where he often invited his guests to relax. It had a chess board, puzzles, and a card table. They visited his office, which hosted a large table on which rested ledgers, bottles of ink, and a quill. A table off to the side held a bottle of wine and a set of glasses. He showed her the domed hall where he could host feasts for a large party. He pointed out the mirrors that hung from the ceiling and the pictures that depicted fables and legends that were painted into the dome. He walked her swiftly through the dozen guestrooms, the small dining room, and the various sitting areas. Where Master Puru's palace had flaunted his wealth through its silver ornamentation, Master Naris' palace had an airy atmosphere that was embellished with culture, as shown through paintings, murals, and décor.

As they walked along the second-floor balcony in the entrance hall, Naris motioned towards the end at an inconspicuous set of doors. "That's the library. Can you read?"

Indignation flared up in Yonah's chest. "Yes. I learned in school."

He paused at the top of the stairs. "You went to school?"

"Yes. Just like everyone else." Yonah couldn't help but add, "Before the coup."

Naris' face flickered before returning to its resting state of self-assurance. "I'd like to take you out back."

They walked down the stairs towards the backdoor, past a stairwell leading downward still.

Yonah asked, "Are the kitchens down there?"

"Yes. But you shouldn't ever need to go there."

Naris pushed the large doors open and led Yonah out onto a patio set two steps above the ground. Several feet away from the palace was a large circular fountain spouting out water towards the sky.

"This is where we'll take most of our meals," Naris explained.

They explored the vineyard, winding round and round. Yonah noted that there were no exterior lodgings in the vineyard like she was used to at Master Puru's and asked, "Do all the slaves sleep in the same place?"

"Yes," Naris answered. "Everyone sleeps in the basement. Except you, of course."

Eventually, they were on the main road at the front of the property.

"Is it Kirash that I can see from my bedroom? The town off in the distance?"

"Yes, it is. I'll have to take you there soon to buy you a few things." Naris eyed her long linen shirt and pants. "You must be terribly warm in those."

"Not terribly. But they were good for travelling." Yonah had felt rather naked in the cropped clothes the indoor slaves wore at Puru's palace.

Naris did not look convinced.

"I'd hate to take you away from your business," Yonah said hesitantly. "If it's more convenient, I could walk into Kirash by myself."

Naris flashed his charmer's smile. "Then how would I help you pick out your clothes, my dear?"

Yonah started at the intimacy of the pet name.

"But I will grant you permission to go to town on your own, as long as you check in with me each time. I don't want to call you for company and find that you're gone." He stopped walking and turned to face Yonah. "I want you to be happy here. Do you believe that?"

His golden-brown eyes looked earnestly into hers. He was standing very close to Yonah. Her breath caught in her throat as she looked on his face.

She said what he wanted to hear. "I believe you."

His lips curled into a smile. "No, you don't. Not yet." He glanced down the road and back up to his palace. "Well, I've shown you everything. You must be tired. I am. Why don't we have a drink?"

Yonah silently followed him back to the palace, to the patio. They sat and waited as a young woman wearing a slave collar poured their wine. Yonah had been in the same position as that woman only a yesterday. It felt strange to be sitting while others did work around her, especially the kind of work she knew she could easily do for herself.

The woman scowled at Yonah as she poured her wine. Naris did not notice. Slaves were invisible to him, except for Yonah. While she and Naris sat and talked, the woman filled Naris' cup and ignored Yonah's. Yonah didn't want to say anything, knowing exactly why the wine pourer refused to serve her. They both wore the same collar that bound them to servitude, and yet Yonah was defying the laws of her collar.

Once they had finished eating, Naris walked Yonah back to her bedroom, saying he was tired from the day's travel. At the bedroom door, he said, "If you ever need anything, there's a bell string on the wall and one of the slaves will look after you."

Yonah wasn't sure how smart it was for her to expect service from her fellow slaves. "Thank you," she said politely.

Naris looked as if he were about to leave, but then hesitated, looking at Yonah with a soft expression. He brushed her lips with his and whispered, "Goodnight, Yonah," before starting down the hallway.

Yonah watched him go. She could feel the similar glowing sensation in her chest.

With Naris out of view, Yonah entered her bedroom. The first thing she wanted to do was take a bath in that glorious tub. She stepped into the side room where the tub was kept and briefly looked around to see if anyone had happened to leave hot water in anticipation of her arrival. Yonah was not surprised when she found nothing, then noticed a string hanging from the wall.

If she could just get someone up here to ask how to fill her own tub, then she might not completely alienate herself from the other slaves. Quickly, as if going slower would give her time to talk herself out of it, Yonah reached out and pulled the string once. She waited. Then she thought it better to wait in the main bedroom and waited there.

After a minute or two, Yonah opened the bedroom door and peered out into the hallway, straining her ears for the sound of nearing footsteps. Silence. She closed the door with a sigh.

Too embarrassed to go in search of a bucket and hot water, Yonah resigned herself to going straight to bed. As she had no other clothes, she kept her shirt and pants on, placed her jacket and scarf in a drawer, and climbed into the massive bed.

She couldn't help but sigh and softly moan as she sunk into the mattress. Her bones melted into the softness and her muscles succumbed to relaxation. Her collar annoyingly pressed into the back of her neck, but that didn't stop Yonah from enjoying this moment of bliss.

She looked out the windowed doors at the night sky. If anyone were looking for her, how would they know she had been moved to Vaha? They would have to know to ask Puru. Yonah pondered over the possibility that Sayzia and Obi had faced similar circumstances and were in fact no where near where Yonah thought they might be. It made the prospect of finding them seem impossible.

In reality, Yonah didn't really know where her siblings were. As much as she told herself that she was going to eventually find them and free them, she didn't have any idea how to do that. All she knew was that Obi had been sold to a sea captain, and Sayzia had continued north from the place Yonah had been sold.

Telling herself to see what came of visiting the nearby town of Kirash, Yonah curled up beneath the light blanket, closed her eyes, and fell asleep.

Chapter Six

For four years Yonah and her siblings had slept in alleys, on rooftops, and in the abandoned homes of Kelab. They had lived off mediocre sums of money that were easily spent on one small meal to be shared among the three children. They had learned to read people, to understand after one short conversation whether they were a short-term friend or an immediate enemy. They had grown up faster than children with parents did, having seen death, felt starvation, and learned the value of work.

After four years of protection, Yonah had failed Sayzia and Obi.

When they were captured, they had been fitted with copper collars, marking them as slaves. Yonah remembered watching as the ends of the horseshoe-shaped copper strip had been heated over coals. She tried to quell her shaking body so she wouldn't get burned as the copper was carefully wrapped around her neck, and then the hot malleable ends twisted together to seal it. To finish the job, the blacksmiths poured some water over the collar to begin the cooling process. The sudden contrast in temperature made Yonah gasp in surprise. Most of the water landed on her front.

Then they were taken to market where members of the Guards,

merchants, traders, and on-lookers watched the selling of the slaves. They stood in rows, ropes binding their wrists and ankles together and leaving only enough slack between their feet to enable them to shuffle along. Escape was impossible.

All Yonah could do now was hope that all three of them would be sold. Not everyone was sold at every trade day. The rumour was that anyone who wasn't sold was taken to a camp run by the government where they were worked to death.

"Yonah, don't look so worried," Sayzia murmured without looking at her. "It makes you look sick." Sayzia also knew the importance of being bought at this point.

"I hope we can all go together," Yonah said.

Sayzia gave her older sister a stern look. "This is goodbye."

Yonah turned her head and the sisters exchanged battling looks.

"This collar is heavy," eleven-year-old Obi grumbled from the other side of Sayzia.

There was a little commotion at the front of the square. The Guards were receiving their first client. Yonah knew from the way the man was dressed that he was a sea captain. He was not from Harasa. His costume wasn't right for that. Instead of the usual loose linen pants and long tunic with sandals that Harasans wore, he wore leather shoes, fitted pants, a shirt, and a buttoned vest. Yonah wondered if he had slaves from all over the world.

As the captain wound through the rows of slaves, he would nod and a member of the Guard would pull them out of line. The captain was choosing many of the boys and men. Yonah knew her brother would be among them.

"Tell Obi I will find him," Yonah told her sister, keeping her eyes forward.

She heard Sayzia mutter to their brother, "Yonah and I love you. Be strong."

Yonah wanted to insist Sayzia pass on her real message, but she didn't want to spend her last few moments with her brother and sister arguing.

The captain was in their row. He nodded at a few more men. Yonah thought he had a kind enough face. There was no permanent sneer or grimace, just professionalism. Maybe Obi would be alright. The captain stepped in front of Obi and, as Yonah and Sayzia expected, nodded.

Their brother was taken from them without a word. He looked back at his sisters. They returned the gaze with hard faces.

Once the captain had looked through all the rows of slaves, he returned to the front of the square where he paid the required amount, exchanged the slaves' ropes for chains, climbed on his horse, and led his new workers through the archway that served as the main entrance to the square. The next client was welcomed and the remaining slaves were re-examined.

Yonah and Sayzia were both passed over by the next several clients. They stood together under the hot sun, their skin slowly burning, their eyes squinting against the light. Their shadows were growing longer as the afternoon wore on.

Finally, two lean men stood in front of the sisters, deliberating. They looked worn, their skin leathery and tanned. They were nomads. The world was their home, and the elements their master.

One of them shuffled sideways to get a better look at Yonah's right arm. "What's that on your arm, girl?" he asked.

Yonah had been waiting for it to come up. She was surprised it had taken this long.

"It's a scar," she said. "From a bullet graze." Each time her scar was mentioned, it brought with it the reminder of their mother's murder, but that didn't hurt so terribly as it once did.

The second nomad stepped next to his friend, looking at the scar with a frown on his face. "Well, no one is going to buy her for her looks, but we already knew that, didn't we?" The pair of them chuckled. Yonah face began to burn.

"Has it hindered your movement?" the first nomad asked. Yonah shook her head.

"Well, move it about so we can see," the second nomad said. Yonah bent and straightened her bound arms and lifted them above her head, showing the nomads that her scar had nothing to do with her capabilities as a worker. The nomads nodded to each other.

"We'll take these two," the second nomad announced. "I'm sure they'll sell up north."

The statement left much to the imagination. Harasa was large, spanning plains and hills and valleys, all covered in either sand, course dirt, or short grasses. It eventually led to a northern mountain line that stretched east to west.

As she was roughly grabbed by the shoulder and pulled towards the front of the square, Yonah glanced at her sister, who was being pulled alongside her. For now, all three of them were safe from the government's work camp. For now, Yonah could take comfort in the fact that Sayzia and Obi would live another day. That was her consolation for failing to keep them from the Guard and from slavery. She could not, however, know if their masters would be kind to them or if they would die under their employ.

When they joined the group of slaves at the front of the square, a pair of guards cut the ropes that bound their wrists and ankles. These were all slaves that were being bought for resale. The nomads would take them to other cities to be sold at other markets. Yonah wondered how many other markets it would take before she was sold to a master or sent to the government camp.

A few minutes later, the nomads had examined all the remaining slaves and taken their pick. After they had paid the Guard, the pair of them climbed onto their horses.

One of the nomads spoke. "Do not think that just because you are not bound to each other that you can try to escape. We have hired help to ensure you stay where you belong." He motioned to the four other men and women on horseback that were accompanying them.

"Come," the other nomad said to his comrade. "Let's ride."

Accompanied by the two nomads and the four other riders, the thirty newly purchased slaves ambled out of the square towards their unknown fate.

THE CARAVAN HAD BEEN walking for days. They had stopped at one more market near the edge of the city before setting out on their journey north. The days were hot, the sandy road beneath their feet hot, the sun beating down on them hot. They were given water whenever the horses were given water. They were fed when the horses were fed. Meanwhile, the nomads and their help drank water and wine along the way. Yonah watched with a burning in her chest as one of them merely wet his pallet with water and spat it out onto the sand next to his horse. He caught her staring, grinned maliciously, and gently poured a stream of water straight into the sand.

Occasionally, horse-drawn carriages would whip past the caravan and, off in the distance, Yonah watched a train glide between the sandy dirt hills and the pale blue sky. Her tired legs ached for respite on those trains and carriages.

A handful of slaves had died on the walk already. Each time, Yonah looked to the faces of the nomads. Their noses crinkled, their brows furrowed, and their mouths turned downward every time they examined a newly fallen slave. After the brief examination and confirmation of the slave's death however, they merely turned away and left the body to melt in the desert heat.

"What's up north?" Sayzia asked her sister one day.

Yonah tried to remember what she had learned in school and what their father had taught her before his murder.

"I know that Harasa goes as far north as the mountains, and that on the other side is a different country. I think it's called Jalid."

"Do they have slavery in Jalid?"

"I think so."

They walked in silence. Yonah racked her memory for anything she knew about the northern country. It was past the mountains. She didn't believe it was a desert and plains country like Harasa.

"What's a mountain?" Sayzia asked.

Yonah looked at her sister. Sayzia didn't joke. This was an honest question. It would have hurt their father to hear his now fifteen-year-old daughter ask what a mountain was.

"It's a gigantic rock," Yonah said. "It stands taller than anything. We don't have them in Harasa."

Sayzia nodded, satisfied with her sister's answer.

At every town and village the caravan came to, they stopped to be examined by masters looking for workers. Little by little, the caravan was picked away and the sisters were yet to be sold. Yonah often wondered when and if there was an end of the journey at which point the nomads would give up on them.

"There must be cities up north where there will be work for us," Yonah said as they were led away from yet another sale. "These towns just want hard labourers."

"There might be cities up north," Sayzia agreed. "And we might never be sold."

Her sister's matter-of-fact attitude made Yonah's insides twist.

They reached yet another market and held yet another sale. This one took place in the centre of a small town made up of squat buildings painted in light yellows and reds. The dozen remaining slaves stood silently as buyers wove through their ranks, examining them.

"What's wrong with her arm?"

It was a woman who spoke. Yonah looked up at her. The woman wore the same copper collar around her neck that they all wore, yet spoke to the nomads with the attitude of a free woman.

One of the nomads stood next to her. "It's just an old scar. It doesn't have any effect on her movement. Show her, slave."

Feeling like a dog asked to do tricks, Yonah circled her arm around to show everything was in working order.

"Hmm," the slave woman said. "Alright, I'll take her."

"You may have her for two hundred ora."

"One-fifty."

The nomad chuckled. "Please, you insult me. This girl is clearly worth at least one-seventy-five."

"She's hardly a beauty, so she's no good for companion work, and you've brought her skin and bone. I'll have to fatten her up to get any use out of her."

"Well, I can't sell her for one-fifty."

Yonah glanced at her sister. She wanted to be sure Sayzia was safe. Perhaps the woman wouldn't like the nomad's price.

"Then one-sixty," the woman said.

Yonah found herself blurting, "Perhaps she could get a deal in buying the two of us?"

The nomad struck Yonah's face with the back of his hand. She gave out a brief cry as her skin started to burn and her vision blurred.

"You will speak when spoken to, slave!" he hissed.

"Our master will have no use for one so outspoken," the woman said.

The nomad's face, already grim, turned darker. "You wanted to buy her, so buy her."

The woman did not back down. "We have no use for this girl."

The nomad grabbed the woman's upper arm and shook her once. "You will buy her for two hundred ora, slave."

She showed no fear, didn't back away. "I may be a slave, but I am not *your* slave. I can tell my master what happened here and he will see to it that you never set foot in Araha again."

Yonah made note of the town's name. Araha.

After a moment of the nomad and the slave woman glaring into each other's eyes, the nomad thrust her arm away. "Fine," he said. The woman walked briskly away. The nomad struck Yonah again. This time all she did was whimper.

"You cost me a sale, slave," he growled at her. "Never let it happen again."

Yonah cowered over as she held her hand to her face.

He bellowed at her, "Understood?"

"Yes!" she cried out.

The nomad strode away, leaving Yonah shaking. She slowly let her trembling hand drift away from her face.

"Is it bad?" she asked her sister.

"You're foolish," Sayzia replied.

Sayzia was the realist, Yonah the optimist. It had often led to disagreements while the three siblings had lived on the streets, but it didn't usually lead to Yonah feeling inferior to her sister.

"You need to be more careful," Sayzia added in a gentler tone. "You aren't valued for your education or even for being a human being. You're only valued for the work you can do."

"I just want us to be together. I'm going to make sure we all end up together someday. I promised I would protect you and Obi."

"Just stop, Yonah."

Yonah stopped. Sayzia grabbed her hand without looking at her.

"We're not going to end up together."

"We can—"

"You could have been safe just now." Sayzia looked at her sister. "Never put yourself at risk like that for me again. It's not worth it."

Sayzia's gaze was so intense that Yonah couldn't look away. Her little sister's deep brown eyes commanded her attention, insisted that she listen, demanded she obey.

And so Yonah obeyed.

At the next market, Yonah was bought by a slave man on behalf of his master for one hundred ninety ora. As she was pulled away, Yonah squeezed Sayzia's hand until the distance between them pulled their fingers apart. She looked back at her sister. Sayzia's face was hard but approving. She nodded at Yonah. Yonah had to fight not to cry.

She was placed in a wagon with another boy and they rolled away from the market. Yonah watched as her sister – the last bit of her old life – was gathered up with the handful of remaining slaves and led onward, further north.

Yonah swore she would find her someday.

She was still staring back in the direction of her sister when the boy sitting next to her said, "I'm Biono."

Yonah turned to look at him. "I'm Yonah."

"I've never been this far from Kelab."

She shook her head dejectedly. "Me neither."

Chapter Seven

The following morning, Naris strode into Yonah's room before she had gotten out of bed. She had been lying awake, staring at the ceiling, unsure of what she should do.

"My dear, have you eaten yet?"

"No."

He furrowed his brow. He pulled the call-bell string in the corner of the room, looked out into the hall, and called out, "Slaves!" In a moment, Yonah heard a pair of footsteps rushing towards Naris.

"Bring Yonah's breakfast to her immediately. If it is not up here in five minutes, there will be trouble."

"Yes, Master."

Yonah sat up in bed, a sense of apprehension spreading through her. The household slaves were already showing signs of resenting Yonah's position; Naris threatening them with punishment would not make them inclined to see Yonah's side of things.

The food arrived minutes later – an open-faced sandwich layered with meat and an egg. Yonah was halfway through it when she noticed the mold on the bread. She put down the rest of the sandwich.

"What's wrong?" Naris asked. He was sitting in the chair across the room.

Yonah shook her head. "Nothing. I'm just full."

Naris stood up. "Then let's go."

Yonah climbed out of the bed, hooked her scarf around her neck, and followed Naris down to the front of the palace. There were two horses waiting for them there, led by a man with a thick chest and a few wrinkles on his face.

"Do you ride?" Naris asked her.

Yonah looked at the majestic creatures, tall and strong. "No."

"Then you will ride with me." He took one of the reins and the man, with a limp in his step, led the other horse away. Naris nimbly lifted himself into the saddle. Once settled up there, he held a hand out to Yonah. "Grab on."

She looked from his hand to his head up in the sky, to the horse's big head, and back to his hand.

"You needn't be afraid. I won't let you get hurt."

And she believed him wholeheartedly. Yonah placed her hand in his. His hand over hers felt strong and capable, and made her chest swell. She placed her left foot in the stirrup and pulled against him to swing her right leg over the horse, until she was finally sitting behind Naris.

"That wasn't so bad, now was it?" he laughed.

She was acutely aware of how her front side was pressed into his back. Naris reached behind himself to wrap her arms around his torso.

"Hold tightly," he instructed. "Or else I might lose you!"

The fear of falling off a speeding horse outweighed Yonah's uncertainty with being so close to Naris. She clung on for dear life. Her copper collar pressed awkwardly into her neck.

Naris kicked the horse and clicked his tongue and they were off. They sped down the road towards the edge of the estate. Yonah held on as tightly as she could to Naris' body, burying her face into the back of his shoulder. She could feel the wind whipping her long hair wildly about, pulling her billowing clothes back and away from her. Humans weren't meant to move so fast.

"Yonah, you're missing it! Look up!"

She turned her head so she could open one eye. Through her whipping hair, Yonah could see the world bouncing up and down with the horse's gallop. The vineyard was whizzing by, a blur of green. Suddenly, the greenery disappeared and all that was there were the yellows and pale greens of the plains. It was a wide expanse flying by.

Now that she was accustomed to the rhythm of the gallop, Yonah lifted her head from Naris' back to get a better look. She would have liked to brush her long dark hair from her face, but she didn't dare let go of the only thing keeping her on this beast.

Riding horseback was different than in a carriage. On a horse, Yonah felt defenseless. There was very little between her and a hard fall, but it also meant there was little separating her from the world rushing past. She was intimate with it all, able to reach out to touch the air if she wanted.

The town crept closer and soon they were slowing to a stop. They entered Kirash on its busiest street, a long pathway of stalls and carts and crowds. While it lacked the mob-like business of Kelab, the town was bustling. There was a mix of free folk and slaves winding around each other. Pockets of Guards were scattered throughout the streets, some walking or riding in a military fashion, others browsing through stores and chatting with the locals. They all wore the same black and red uniform. Yonah avoided eye contact with them, trying not to draw any attention to herself.

Naris had his horse walk through the crowds until he found a stall selling clothing. He swung his leg over the horse's head and hopped off, then turned around to assist Yonah to the ground.

His hands were around her waist when she landed. "Did you enjoy the ride?" He grinned, looking down at her.

"After I got used to it," Yonah said breathlessly, "a little."

He laughed. "Come. Let's buy you some things."

Yonah noticed that a few people were staring at them – a rich slave owner laughing and talking intimately with a poor slave girl.

Naris browsed quickly through the stock, walking ahead of Yonah. She went slowly, taking in the beautiful colours, touching the different fabrics. They reminded her of exploring the markets in Kelab before the new government took over.

"What do you want, slave?" the man running the stall said. He glared at Yonah accusingly.

Yonah stepped backwards, away from the tables. "I'm sorry," she murmured. "I was just looking."

"Then just look. I don't want your grubby hands on my wares."

Naris stepped between Yonah and the man.

"Do not speak to her in that way," Naris growled.

The man looked between Naris and Yonah with a snarl. "Pardon me, sir. Is there any way I can help you?"

"Yes." Naris pointed to the various outfits he had chosen for Yonah that lay on a table. As he and the man gathered them together, Yonah drifted away towards a long royal blue dress that was hanging from the stall tent pole. It was made of two layers and had a cinched waist. The inner layer was opaque, sleeveless and had a low neckline, and the outer layer was sheer and had long sleeves and a neckline that would caress the wearer's collar bones. When Yonah walked around to the backside of the dress, she saw that while the sheer layer continued its high neckline, the opaque inner layer had a drooping back that looked like it might reveal the lower back of the wearer. The simple beauty of this dress awed Yonah. She imagined how she might feel wearing such a lovely garment – poised, graceful, remarkable, even beautiful.

"Yonah," Naris called. She turned to look. "Is there anything else you'd like?"

She looked up longingly at the blue dress. She didn't dare touch it after the treatment she'd received from the stall owner. Would it be too much to ask for something so extravagant?

Yonah took her chance and said, "I think I'd like this one."

Naris looked briefly at the dress with a raised eyebrow. "No, I think that one is too plain for you, my dear. You need something that shines as brightly as you! Is there anything else?"

Yonah looked at the pile that sat on the table between Naris and the stall owner. The fabric was brightly coloured and she could see jewels and metals shining among them.

"Those are fine," she said. She understood she was Naris' doll. He would dress her how he liked.

"Then why don't you wait with the horse while I finish up here?"

"Yes, Master." She strode out from the stall tent and stood next to Naris' horse. It turned its head to examine her, snorted softly, then paid no more attention to her.

Yonah scanned the crowd. Those who were free walked briskly, looking as if they were on important business. A few children raced between the adults. Only the slaves went at an easy pace, if they weren't with their masters, which turned out to be more common than Yonah had expected. The threat of capture by the Guard and the additional years of enslavement as punishment seemed to do the trick to keep slaves from trying to escape. And maybe they weren't treated too terribly by their masters after all. Yonah wondered if her brother and sister had been so lucky to have kind masters.

Naris stepped next to Yonah. "Ready?"

She noticed his empty hands. "Did you not buy anything after all?"

"Of course, I did. They'll be sending someone with the package later this afternoon."

"But I could carry it."

"Nonsense. How will you stay on the horse?" With a chuckle, Naris swung onto said horse and reached down for Yonah's hand. She took his offering and pulled herself on behind him.

SHE SPENT THE REST OF THE afternoon wandering through the vineyard. She would walk down one row from the palace all the way to edge of the estate, and down another row back to the palace. Occasionally, a slave would come bowling down the row and she would press herself as far out of their path as possible in the narrow aisle. For the most part, she felt quite alone.

She longed for the company of her brother and sister.

The shadows were long when Yonah meandered to the patio where she and Naris ate together. He wasn't there yet, although a slave standing there begrudgingly said, "Master Naris wants you to know your package is in your room and that you should pick out your favourite for tonight."

"Thank you," Yonah said softly. The slave only rolled his eyes and left. Yonah made her way to her room. The package sat on her bed. It was large, wrapped in layers of white cloth and twine.

Yonah pulled at one end of the twine and it unknotted itself. She unfolded the cloth, revealing a pile of clothing. She slowly lifted each piece, holding it out in front of her and examining it. Many were similar to what she had worn as a wine pourer for Master Puru, hanging with coins or inlaid with bright stones, covering little of her skin. Yonah had no favourites among these garments.

The last piece in the pile made her breath catch in her throat. It was royal blue, with a sheer overlayer. Yonah cautiously reached for the piece and held it up, letting the folds fall open.

It was the dress. The one Naris had refused to buy because he thought it too plain. It was certainly not as loud as the other outfits he had picked out for her, but this dress had an understated beauty that drew Yonah in. To her, there was no comparing it to the other pieces.

Yonah paused. Naris must have seen her disappointment at his judgment of the dress. And then he had chosen to surprise her with its purchase. She couldn't help but smile at his consideration. The strange glowing sensation warmed her chest.

She put on the blue dress and looked at herself in the mirror. Her mouth dropped open as she looked at the woman standing before her. Yonah's eyes shifted to her right arm. The scar there was just visible beneath the sheer sleeve.

Yonah had never felt embarrassed by her scar. It simply told the story of one of the most tragic days of her life. For her, it was a reminder of how quickly things could change.

Not that it didn't draw attention. When she was younger, Yonah had felt the glances and the stares from every person she spoke to. She sometimes took to covering it up in case the Guard recognized it.

Gazing at the scar now – an ugly piece of her history burnt into her skin beneath a beautiful image of what Naris wanted her to be – Yonah wondered what Naris' reaction would be to it if he noticed it.

She walked down to the patio at the back of the palace. Naris was standing with his back to the palace door, looking out towards the fountain in the middle of the vineyard. He turned at the sound of the door closing. When he saw Yonah, his jaw dropped and he stared. At the same time as wanting to run away, Yonah felt a thrill of pleasure at the look in Naris' eyes.

"You look wonderful," Naris finally said.

Yonah clasped her hands in front of her and turned her gaze away from Naris.

He added, "And you look very happy."

They sat together at the table and Naris motioned to the wine pourer. It was the same woman as before. She rushed to him and filled his cup.

"Thank you for—" Yonah didn't want to talk about how he had spent money on her in front of the woman, but of course the wine pourer would know how Yonah had come across this dress. "Thank you for buying it after all."

"I told you. I want you to be happy here." Naris took a sip of his wine. "But I must insist that you wear the other things I chose for you from time to time."

She smiled politely. "Of course."

It was a pleasant meal. The wine pourer filled Yonah's cup at the start, then ignored her, even while filling Naris' cup throughout. Yonah, however, had no intention of calling attention to it, not wanting to give the slaves further reason for disliking her. At one point, however, Naris paused mid-sentence and stared hard at Yonah's cup.

His voice was dark as he said, "Slave, you've ignored my companion's cup."

"I'm sorry, Master," she muttered, pouring wine for Yonah.

"Make sure it doesn't happen again," he said coldly. This seemed to put fear into the woman. Yonah saw her eyes widen and her head bow as she backed away into her corner.

After a moment of silence, Naris said, "We'll play chess tonight. Come, my dear."

The wine pourer's head remained bowed, even as Yonah walked past her into the palace.

Instead of leading Yonah to the games room as she expected, Naris led her to his bedroom, where he had an additional chess board. He invited Yonah to sit as he poured them each wine.

Since they were alone, Yonah thought this was as good a time as any to ask, "Would it be alright if I went back to Kirash tomorrow?"

Naris watched her for a moment as he formulated his answer. "Why do you want to go back so soon?"

She wanted to figure out a way to find her siblings. "I just want to explore. The only place I saw for three years was Master Puru's grounds."

Naris passed Yonah a glass. "Well, I'll need to catch up on some work tomorrow, so I suppose it'll be fine for you to visit town. Will you walk?"

"Yes."

"Oh!" His eyes flashed and he started for a nightstand. "Why don't you go see a dressmaker and have them take your measurements? You can open an account under my name." He withdrew some paper, a quill, ink, and a small cloth bag which jingled from a drawer in the nightstand. He scrawled a quick note, then brought it and the bag over to Yonah and handed them to her. "That should cover whatever deposit they need to open an account."

Yonah froze as she realized how much money she was holding. For years, the fear of not enough money had plagued Yonah and her family and now she held a small yet heavy bag of an unknown quantity of ora that could have fed them all several times over.

She read the note.

Dear sir or madam,

I wish to open an account at your shop. Please have my companion's measurements taken and saved for future transactions.

Master Naris of Vaha

"Will I need so much money?" Yonah asked.

Naris shrugged and sat down. "Shall we play?"

Chapter Eight

Breakfast the following day was brought in to Yonah's room by a woman not much older than her. The woman knocked sharply at the door and then strode into the bedroom, silently set a tray down on the small table in the middle of the room, and promptly left without giving Yonah a single glance.

Yonah hesitated before climbing out of bed, unwarrantedly fearful that the woman was waiting just outside her door to listen in on everything Yonah did.

Her bare feet padded softly as she walked across the tiled floor to the table. The tray was simply set with a spoon next to a bowl of cream and berries. Yonah's mouth gaped open in awe and joy, and she scarfed down the food, never bothering to sit down.

As she licked the last remnants of cream from her lips, Yonah's thoughts turned back to the household slaves. It would do no good for her to be ostracized by them. She needed to try to build a better relationship with her peers.

Yonah dressed in her travel clothes, placed Naris' note and the bag filled with ora coins into one of her jacket pockets, and picked up the breakfast tray to return to the basement. With a quick glance at herself in her mirror – this woman didn't look like her formative years had been ones of great hardship – Yonah left her bedroom and made her way to the entrance hall, where the stairs to the basement lay.

As she wandered along the floating balcony within the entrance hall, Yonah noticed the library doors. She ached to go inside. Not today. She walked down to the main floor, found the basement stairs, and continued downwards.

She was in the kitchen. Several slaves were busily working, some washing dishes and some preparing food. They all looked up to stare at Yonah.

"What do you want?" someone asked her.

The dirty looks she was receiving rendered Yonah temporarily mute. She cleared her throat and said, "I wanted to thank you for breakfast. And to save you the trouble of having to come get my dishes." She set the tray down on a counter. She wished she could say more, but didn't know where to start.

"How generous of you," another slave said, his voice dripping with disdain.

"Alright, all of you, get back to work." The woman who had spoken appeared to be in charge. "You," she motioned to one of the workers, "clear that tray."

"Why doesn't she do it? She doesn't do anything else around here."

"Yeah, make the pet do it."

"I'm in charge down here. You'll do as I say!"

Yonah spoke up. "I know I don't do traditional work around here, but I do want to be on good terms with all of you."

"We'll be on good terms when you start serving me!"

"Get out of here, Pet!"

The woman in charge said to Yonah briskly, "You'd better leave."

Defeated, Yonah trudged up the stairs and left the palace through its large front doors. As she started down the path that led to the edge of the estate, she tried to push down any feelings of embarrassment and frustration from her failed attempt to befriend the other workers. Instead, she thought of her plan for the day.

Kirash was bustling, loud, crowded, and alive. It reminded Yonah of home. She had vague memories of walking to school through streets like these. The store owners in Kirash were opening their windows, stalls were being erected, merchants from outside the city poured in, and Yonah wove through the business with ease and awe. She could smell cooked meats, spices, and sweat. There was a constant blanket of sound with everyone talking to each other.

Her first task was to find a dress maker's shop so she could finish Naris' errand. As she ambled along the main road, she read the shop signs and listened to the shouting of shop keepers. She passed the clothing stall from which her new outfits came – the owner did not see her go by. She gazed at the jewels laid out at a table, inhaled the scent of fresh bread and fruit, ran her hand along the side of a cow that trundled in front of her, smiled longingly at a pair of free children chasing each other through the crowd.

She finally found a dress maker's shop and stepped inside, trying to quell the nerves buzzing in her body. It was a calm place. Though Yonah's footsteps clicked slightly on the wooden floor, the sound was muted by the rolled fabric that sat on rows and rows of shelves. Yonah stopped in front of a headless mannequin wearing a fine green and gold short sleeved dress and a golden coat.

"Can I help you?"

A woman wearing her hair up in a tight bun and a pair of wire-rimmed glasses gave Yonah a sharp, yet not unkind look. She was wearing wide cropped pants and a short-sleeved shirt.

"Yes." Yonah handed the woman Naris' note. It took the woman only a few moments to read it. She looked at Yonah, her eyes quickly moving up and down her figure and stopping on the slave collar around her neck.

"Come with me." She led Yonah to the back of the store where there were three large mirrors standing to create a wall of reflection. In front of the mirrors was a foot tall pedestal.

"Take off your sandals. Stand up there, please."

Yonah did as she was told. The woman took out a measuring tape from her pocket and directed Yonah as she took her measurements. Then she brought Yonah to a desk where she started writing out information.

"Your name?"

"Yonah."

"I will need forty ora to open the account."

Yonah pulled out the money bag and started placing coins on the counter, counting out forty ora. The dress maker took the coins and placed them somewhere behind the counter.

"If I may ask," the woman said, "why does a slave need measurements at a dress shop?"

Yonah shrugged. "I don't know."

"Hmm. Well, that's everything. You can tell Master Naris he has an account with your measurements recorded at Lenara's Dress Shop."

"Thank you," Yonah said politely and left.

Yonah started down the street again, reading the signs as she went. She finally found a map shop that lay inside a square building three storeys tall. Yonah opened the door and stepped inside.

As her eyes adjusted to the dimly lit interior, she saw the shadows of barrels filled with scrolls and shelves lined with paper.

"Welcome," a man's voice said. He was tall and had broad shoulders and thick arms. Yonah smiled politely at him through closed lips.

"What are you looking for, slave?" He didn't give the word the bite Yonah had heard from the shop owner yesterday.

She thought for a moment. "Do you have any maps of the whole continent?"

"Topographical or political?"

Yonah had no idea what the word *topographical* meant.

"I want to know what cities and settlements there are."

He raised an eyebrow at her. "Are you on an errand for your master?"

"Yes," she lied.

The man walked over to a barrel and pulled out a long rolled up piece of paper. "How about this?"

She took the roll and unrolled part of it. She did not recognize the jagged edges of land that revealed itself.

"Do you have anything smaller?"

The man took the map, rolled it up, replaced it in its spot, and started leafing through the papers on a nearby shelf. He silently handed her a folded piece.

Yonah unfolded the map and held it up. There was Harasa in the middle, the island nation to the west, the country of Jalid north of it, and some place called Modeef to the south. It was much smaller than Harasa. Yonah scanned the map for Kirash and found it in the central west portion of the country. She saw that not too far from the town was a port city – Basee.

The man snatched the map out of Yonah's hands. "Alright, you need to pay up if you want to be looking anymore."

"How much?" She pulled out her much lighter money bag.

"Fifteen ora."

Yonah gathered the coins in her hand. She quickly counted their value.

"I only have ten."

"Then your master should have sent you with more money."

"Isn't ten enough, really?"

The man frowned. "Are you bartering with me? This isn't market, this my shop. You can leave your master's name and I can save that map for a fee."

Yonah had no intention of giving out Naris' name at a place where she wasn't supposed to be. "That's fine. I'll just come back another time with the right amount."

The map seller took a step towards Yonah. "Are you sure you're on an errand for your master?"

She started to back away. "Yes."

"Then just give me their name."

Yonah remained silent.

"Unless you stole that money from your master. Unless you're trying to escape. That would be putting me in a bad position. You'd be putting my shop at risk. I could get enslaved for helping someone escape."

She turned and fled. Yonah ripped the shop door open and raced outside.

The map seller followed her, yelling, "Guards! That slave! In the orange! She tried to get me to help her escape!"

Memories of her time living on the streets flooded Yonah's mind as she saw a pair of black-clad, red-sashed men run towards her. Instinct took over. She ran.

It was difficult maneuvering the crowded street. She brushed up and bumped into bodies as she tried to speed past them. Yonah turned a corner where the street wasn't so busy. She picked up speed. Her muscles were warm. Her mouth was dry.

Higher ground. That was how they survived on the streets.

Yonah looked up as she ran. Windows and short balconies scattered the sides of these buildings. She could work with that.

She jumped and grabbed the metal-supported edge of a decorative overhang. After swinging one leg up, she was able to pull herself over the edge. Keeping to the support edge so she wouldn't fall through the fabric, Yonah stood up. She could hear the Guards running closer.

Above her was a barred balcony. She jumped and wrapped her hands around two of the bars, then used a swinging momentum to hike her hands upwards until she could swing a foot onto the balcony edge and pull herself up the rest of the way.

The Guards were directly beneath her, yelling for her to come down. Yonah lithely jumped from one balcony to another, across and up. The blast of a gunshot shook Yonah's insides.

With another burst of energy, Yonah jumped across several balconies until she rounded the corner of the building out of the Guard members' view, then heaved herself over top of the building and rolled onto the rooftop.

She lay there for a moment, gasping for breath, shutting her eyes against the blinding sun. Then she peered over the edge. The Guards were below, stilling trying to see where she had disappeared to.

Content with her escape, Yonah scooted towards the centre of the rooftop so she wouldn't be seen from the ground and stood up.

Looking out over Kirash, Yonah saw that it was a shorter city than Kelab, and a little more green with trees.

"Who are you?" came a child's voice.

Yonah turned around, startled, and saw a group of five children staring at her. They hovered at the edge of the rooftop, ready to make an escape if necessary.

"Nobody," she said breathlessly.

"What are you doing up here?"

She motioned to the street. "I'm hiding from some people."

The oldest child – he was maybe twelve – said, "I've never seen a slave up here before."

"I used to be like you. Only I lived in Kelab."

"They caught you?" the smallest child asked.

Yonah nodded. "Been a slave ever since."

It was a sobering warning for the children. They stared at Yonah and Yonah stared at them for a moment. She finally said, "Look, do you kids know anything about Basee?"

They didn't answer at first, then the older boy pointed and said, "It's that way."

"Do you know how far?"

He shook his head. "Kids that go out there don't come back."

Yonah nodded in understanding.

"Why were they chasing you if you're already a slave?"

She wasn't sure how much she could really tell these children. They weren't friends. If someone were to offer them safety at her expense, they would tell her secrets without regret.

"No reason."

"Are you with the rebellion?"

Yonah started at the mention it. She hadn't heard much about the rebellion since serving at Master Puru's feast. "What do you know about it?"

The oldest boy chimed in before the others. "Like we would tell you."

Having been an orphan constantly trying to dodge the Guard herself, Yonah could understand the children's apprehension towards talking to her, but that didn't make it any less frustrating that every conversation finished at an abrupt dead end.

"Well, can you tell me if there's any place in town where I could get information?"

"Don't answer her," the oldest boy said. One of the other children whispered to him. He grimaced at the child and shoved his head away. "Nope."

Yonah pulled the money bag from her pocket and dug out five coins. She held one up so the children could see it. "One for each of you. Now do you know?"

"Put the coins there," the boy said, pointing to the ground halfway between him and Yonah. Yonah set the coins on the ground and backed away.

"Look," she said. "I'm just trying to find my brother and sister."

"Try The White Stallion," the boy said.

"Where's that?"

"The edge of town towards Basee." He prodded the smallest girl, who, quick like a mouse, skittered towards the coins, scooped them up, and ran back to the others. All the children disappeared over the edge of the roof, presumably to another shorter building. Yonah didn't bother looking to see where they went; if they didn't want her to follow them, they knew how to shake her off their trail.

After she had maneuvered her way back to the street, Yonah leaned against a wall, exhausted from the exertion. She would go back to Vaha for now. With only five coins left in her bag, she was unsure she would find any success in hiring help. She started back down the main road, keeping her eyes out for the Guard.

SWEAT WAS DRIPPING DOWN her neck and back by the time she reached the estate. Yonah was grateful to have her scarf over her head as a bit of shade from the sun.

She watched the slaves working as she passed by. Having been an outdoor slave for Master Puru, Yonah could imagine what they might be feeling now: sweat dripping down their faces and into their eyes, dry mouths that ached for water, heavy limbs that felt like melting into stillness with the rising heat.

"Do you remember what working is, Pet?" a slave spat at her as she walked by. She was a domestic slave, not blazing from the heat like the others. Yonah's heart lit afire in indignation.

"Yes, I do."

The slave woman, who had been rushing towards the back of the estate, stopped. She walked up to Yonah and shoved the water pail she carried into Yonah's arms. "Then you go get water. Help your 'fellow workers.'"

Maybe if she cooperated, she could win the other workers over. There was fire in her voice as Yonah said, "Fine. Are you filling this in the fountain?"

"Wow, you're a genius," the woman sneered. She followed as Yonah started for the back of the palace to the fountain.

Yonah dunked the bucket into the water to fill it and held it out for the woman.

"Hope that helps," Yonah said.

"You filled one bucket of water," the woman said, taking the bucket from Yonah. "That doesn't make up for the fact that you're taking advantage of the rest of us."

"I'm not," Yonah argued. "I'm not trying to. Master Naris brought me here to be his companion. I don't really get a say."

"Oh, poor Pet has to sit around all day while other slaves wait on her!"

"I'm not trying to make you wait on me." Yonah could feel anger coursing through her.

The woman spoke so emphatically that the bucket shook a little, slopping some water out. "Don't expect any sympathy from us, alright?" The look of disdain on the woman's face enraged Yonah further. "You're just like a master."

Yonah had no words as the woman stormed away. Her mouth hung open in shock. Comparing her to a master was ridiculous and unfair. Or was it accurate?

"Are you alright?" came a voice.

Yonah turned and saw a young slave man around her age standing nearby. He had a handsome face, with large eyes and a strong jaw line. His hair was shaggy and unkempt, and his body lean from labour.

Yonah gave an exasperated sigh and said, "I'm fine."

"I heard yelling," the young man said. He looked at Yonah's clothing. "So, you're the master's pet?"

Yonah stopped herself from rolling her eyes. "I didn't realize that was my nickname these days."

He shrugged. "I don't think anybody around here knows your real name." He held his hand out. "I'm Bana."

She shook his hand. "Yonah. The resident pet." He laughed. "Thank you. For talking to me, I guess. Nobody's been very kind to me since I've come here. Except Master Naris."

"We're all slaves. We have to do as we're told. Some of us are just luckier than others." Bana glanced over at the palace and said, "Well, I'd better get back to work. But feel free to come say hi if you're ever bored."

She nodded, and Bana walked back to his workstation. Yonah looked behind her and saw Naris standing on the patio, watching her. He looked regal in his light blue tunic and shirt. Yonah made her way towards him and saw that he did not wear his usual pleasant expression. Instead, his brow was slightly furrowed, his eyes thinking. His eyeline sometimes shifted to Bana and back to Yonah.

When she finally reached him, he said, "You've made a friend."

"We just met."

"What's his name?"

Yonah considered lying for a moment. "Bana."

Naris didn't respond for a moment, watching the slave man work. He then looked to Yonah and his expression softened. "I would like you to join me in the games room after dinner." His eyes shifted over Yonah's travel clothes. "And please wear something we bought for you in Kirash."

She wore her blue dress. It was the only thing Naris bought for her that she really liked.

The blue dress was the only thing Yonah had been wearing lately that let her scar remain visible. It wasn't until they were walking together up to the games room that Naris finally caught sight of it through the sheer sleeve and said, "What's this?" He ran a finger along the pink strip of skin on her arm. Yonah's skin prickled at his touch.

She turned her head and looked at Naris just as his eyes rose from her arm to meet hers. Their faces were just a foot apart. Yonah searched for meaning behind his question – a sign of whether he asked out of control or curiosity.

"It's from my childhood," she finally said.

Naris glanced briefly down at the scar again. "It looks like a bullet graze."

She stared defiantly at him for a moment, then gave him the smallest nod of affirmation.

"My father had one, too, from when he visited Kelab. He got mixed up in a big riot by accident. He was just walking when it broke out. When he showed it to me, he said, 'This is what happens when we let the lazy and the indolent take advantage of us.'" He opened the door to the games room.

Yonah felt hot as she entered, a different kind of heat than the usual glowing sensation in her chest. "How old were you?"

Naris shrugged. "Twelve or thirteen."

Naris was just a few years older than her. That would have put her at nine or ten years old. "My father was killed in a riot in Kelab. He was protesting how the upper class was taking advantage of the poor." She fought to keep her voice steady. "He was a hard-worker and a good man."

Naris' eyes dropped down to Yonah's scar again. She saw his eyebrows furrow and his eyes blink several times.

"Well," he said. Then he was silent. The room was still and it magnified the divide between the two of them. They were the children of a generation that had seen a massive shift, belonging to opposing sides.

He abruptly changed the subject. "I asked you here because I wanted to know if you liked any of these." He motioned to a table. Yonah looked and saw that across its surface lay necklaces, bracelets, anklets, rings, and earrings. Their metal shone, jewels glistened, beads demanded attention with their bright colours. There was so much wealth laying in front of Yonah, ready for the taking. They reminded her of Master Puru's celebrations, and the men and women who wore extravagant clothing and accessories. She thought she might be able to sell some of the jewels and use the money in Kirash.

"They're beautiful," she answered, her voice matter-of-fact.

"They're yours. Unless you don't like them. They belonged to my mother and I don't need them."

She looked at Naris. He was watching her again. This time not with a furrowed brow, but with wide, watchful eyes. This look didn't belong to a master, but to an unsure child. While this wasn't the first time Yonah had seen this look, this was the first time she was registering that it was a deeply intimate and vulnerable one.

"Thank you," she said softly, sincerely.

He smiled. "You like them, then?"

"You're being very kind to me."

He placed his hands on her arms, his thumbs stroking her skin. "I like you." He kissed her and she was once again temporarily lost in his embrace. But she felt his hand over her scar and thought of the days her parents were murdered and quickly pulled away.

Naris smirked at her. "I'm winning you over."

She was alarmed at the truth of this statement. She broke his gaze and looked down at her feet.

"Should we play a game?" Naris said. He took Yonah's hand and led her to a chair.

As they played, Yonah was fighting with herself, torn between the fact that she enjoyed Naris' company and wanted to explore their relationship further, and the fact that they both came from such different worlds. He was a child of privilege that was taught what she considered a huge misrepresentation of what the coup had done to the people of Harasa. The coup had left his life untouched, if not improved it. She had experienced it first-hand, through her family losing their first home, through losing her chance to go to school, through the deaths of her parents, through her separation from her brother and sister.

Sayzia and Obi. She had promised that she would find them and that they would all be together again. Even if she lived a life of luxury with Naris, it wasn't the life of love that she once had with her siblings.

Chapter Nine

Little Obi was roaring loudly as he, Sayzia, and Yonah walked through the streets of Kelab. Yonah, now ten years old, was burdened with a large basket full of freshly laundered clothing.

"Why are you roaring?" asked Sayzia, sounding slightly annoyed.

"I'm a big bear! Roar!"

With a small smile, Sayzia said, "No, you're a little bear. Big bears are as tall as houses."

"But I want to be a big bear!" he whined.

"You will be someday, Obi," Yonah said, hoping to stop him from throwing a tantrum. "But you'll always be Little Bear to us!" "Why?"

Yonah hitched the basket up so she could get a better grip on it. Sayzia said, "Because we'll always be your big sisters!"

"I'll be bigger than you one day," Obi replied, defiantly.

The houses they were walking by were bigger than the ones in their neighbourhood. They had proper front doors and windows. Yonah was reminded of their old home. But since the coup a year ago, their father wasn't allowed to teach and the family had to move into a smaller house.

The three children walked up to the door of one house with rich purple curtains. Sayzia knocked on the door for Yonah and stood next to her.

A woman dressed in a linen shirt, pants, and large, gold hoop earrings opened the door and looked down at the children.

"My mom, Valli, sent these for you," Yonah grunted, holding up the basket.

The woman smiled kindly at her. "Tell your mother thank you." She took the basket from Yonah and set it inside her doorway. Then she pulled a small drawstring bag filled with coins from her pocket and handed it to Yonah. "You children be safe, now. The Guards are always watching."

Yonah took the satchel, staring into the woman's eyes. The Guard worked for the new president of Harasa, the man who had forcibly taken over one year ago. Their primary job was to police the cities, which included capturing any homeless or disabled people, criminals, enslaved fugitives, rebels, or orphaned children for the newly founded slave trade. They personally were paid extra for every person they captured and sold, meaning they often abused their power and tried to sell other children as well. They were real-life monsters that Yonah and her friends whispered about.

As the woman closed the door, Yonah turned and led her siblings back home.

Their new house was considerably smaller than what Yonah had dubbed 'the big house.' It was just a few rooms crammed together on the ground floor of a larger building. Instead of wooden floors, it was packed clay and dirt. Instead of having her own bedroom, Yonah shared with her brother and sister.

Yonah could hear her mother singing even before they had walked through the rickety front door.

"Here, Ma," she said, handing her mother the bag of coins.

"Thank you, Yonah," her mother said, kissing Yonah on the head. "Hello, my little mice."

Obi roared in response. "I'm a big bear!"

"You're a little bear," Sayzia corrected him.

"Is Pa home, yet?" Yonah asked.

Their mother was stirring a soup over their small stove. "Not yet, Yonah."

As if saying his name had summoned him, Yonah's father strode through the door, wiping sweat from his brow. He spent his days traveling through the city to his secret tutoring appointments. Although the president had forbidden any sort of education among the lower classes, Yonah's father was adamant that it would be the only way the people could rise up and fight against his rule.

"Hi, Pa!" Yonah said, swiftly walking up to him and wrapping her arms around his waist.

"Hello, my girl!" he exclaimed and hugged Yonah back. Then he moved to his wife and said softly, "Hello, my love." They kissed.

"You're just in time," Yonah's mother said, ladling soup into bowls. Her father helped set the bowls out.

The family gathered at the round table. If the children were bigger, they would have been sitting shoulder to shoulder.

Yonah inhaled deeply with her nose over the soup. Its spices hit her and she smiled.

"What are we going to learn about tonight, Pa?" she asked as she picked up her spoon.

"It's just a short lesson tonight, my girls," he answered. "I have somewhere to be."

Yonah looked at her mother just in time to see her lips pinch together and release.

"It's fine, Va, it's a peaceful protest."

"I know," she said, her voice hard. "But things happen."

After supper, Yonah and Sayzia sat on the rugged floor while their father instructed them. Yonah gazed eagerly up at him as he spoke, soaking in as much knowledge as she could.

Eventually, her father's eyes flashed to the clock on the wall and he said, "We should stop there. I have to go." He set down the book he had been holding and started to put on a light coat. "Why don't you two read to Obi while I'm gone?"

Sayzia said, "Because his books are boring."

"It's not about you reading, Sayzia," their father said. "It's about you helping your brother. He would have started school this year."

"I'll read to him, Pa," Yonah said.

"You can both do it. Va, I'm going."

Their mother emerged from the other bedroom and wrapped her husband up in an embrace. "You'll be careful?"

"Of course. It's just talking. I'll be fine."

He kissed his wife and waved to his children before heading out the door. The four of them stared at the closed door for a moment.

Yonah finally grabbed her sister's hand and took her to the corner where Obi was playing with his toys. "Come on, Za." They sat down next to their little brother and began to read to him, as per their father's suggestion.

Later that night, when their mother had just put Obi to bed, there was a frantic knock at the door. She opened it. Yonah saw one of their neighbours standing outside, her eyes wide.

"The protest," she hissed. "It's all gone wrong. The Guard started shooting. Yaz just told me."

"Can you look after my children?" their mother asked. After a nod of confirmation from the neighbour, Yonah watched her mother throw a shawl around her shoulders and race out into the darkness. The neighbour woman stepped inside and gently closed the door.

"Hello, girls," she said, a pained smile on her face. "Your mother will be right back."

Yonah and Sayzia stared at the woman. They saw right through her false cheer. Her cautious demeanour set Yonah's body trembling. She was waiting for bad news.

With their mother gone, the house was oddly quiet. No mindless humming, or lullabies, or happy melodies. Yonah wanted nothing more than for the front door to open and for her parents to return home, but at the same time, she feared what else might happen once that door opened.

The neighbour tried to coax them to bed, but both Yonah and Sayzia refused. Yonah rubbed her eyes over and over, trying to stay awake. She was no longer reading the words in the book in front of her, just staring at the shapes the letters made.

The door opened and there was a flurry of movement. Three men were carrying a large mass between them, followed by Yonah's mother. They paused briefly, then one said, "The table," and they set the mass down on the round table.

Yonah realized it was a body when she saw its legs hanging off the edge. Her skin began to prickle. She looked to her mother; her eyes were red and raw. Her mother looked into Yonah's eyes and Yonah watched as her mother burst into fresh tears.

Yonah's chest clenched. She started for the table, but their neighbour scurried over to her and Sayzia and started ushering them to their bedroom.

"No," Yonah muttered. The woman grabbed her arm and dragged her away. "No! Is it Pa? I want to see Pa!" Tears were streaming down her face.

"Not tonight," the woman said, dragging both Yonah and Sayzia into their dark bedroom. Obi stirred but didn't wake. "You'll see him in the morning." And she closed the door.

Yonah grabbed the door handle and twisted and pulled and tugged, but the neighbour woman must have been holding onto the other side with a firm grip.

"Let me out!" Yonah screamed.

Sayzia grabbed her arm and said, "Hush! You'll wake Obi!"

Yonah released the door handle. "Don't you want to see Pa?" She was panting from the exertion.

"Yes," said Sayzia, her voice fading away with the word. "But it might be better if we don't tonight."

Yonah glared at her sister, angry at her for taking the adults' side.

Sayzia continued, "It sounds like he got hurt. Or worse."

Although they were standing in darkness, Yonah could feel her sister's presence in front of her, small but mighty. Yonah huffed out a puff of air and stormed off to the bed she and Sayzia shared, willing to listen to her sister, but unwilling to let herself fall asleep.

But she did fall asleep. And the next morning she woke up with dawn.

She wanted to go out to the kitchen, but something held her back from bolting out of the bedroom. Yonah gingerly got onto her hands and knees and whispered into Sayzia's ear, "Wake up. Za. It's morning."

Sayzia groaned and rolled over.

"I want to see Pa."

Her sister's eyes opened, alert. They looked at each other, both afraid of what they would find on the other side of that door. With a tiny nod, Sayzia sat up and followed Yonah out of bed.

They stood in front of the closed door. Yonah grabbed her sister's hand. Sayzia squeezed. Yonah reached for the door handle. It opened.

Someone had brought another table to prop up the body's legs. Their mother was sitting in a chair, her arms folded across her chest, her shawl still over her shoulders. Although her eyes were pointed at the body, they were unseeing.

She looked up at her daughters. Her face clenched and released. She held one of her arms out towards the girls.

They shuffled around the tables to their mother. She wrapped an arm around each of them.

"Oh, my girls," she whispered, her voice shaking.

Yonah now had a clear view of who was lying on their table. She had known before, but now it was undoubtedly true.

Her father's face was void of all expression. Eyes closed. No smile. Oddly pale. They had changed his clothes. Besides his colouring, it was almost as if he were sleeping. But Yonah could feel how he wasn't quite there, how this body was a shell of who she knew.

"What happened?" she asked.

Their mother sighed. "The Guard attacked the protesters. They shot your father."

Yonah slowly stepped towards the table. She reached for her father's hand. She gasped at its cold touch, but wrapped her fingers around it. She remembered holding his hand when they walked to school together before the coup.

"Why did they do that?" she said, her eyes still on her father's face.

Her mother's voiced was strained as she spoke. "I don't know."

Yonah's eyes welled up with tears and, for the first and certainly not the last time in her life, she wept with grief for the loss of a loved one.

Chapter Ten

Yonah held her arms, cradling her body as she sat on her bedroom balcony overlooking the vineyard that morning. The same woman who brought breakfast the day before had come and gone. Now she sat alone.

She had dreamed of her family, dreamed that they were all together, that the coup had never happened, that the Guard never existed, that they were happy. And when she had woken up, her cheeks were wet with tears.

As Yonah watched the slaves begin their work, she felt the pinprick sensation in her eyes, the threat of more tears. She ached to hug her father once more, to hear her mother sing again, to hold Sayzia's hand, to give Obi one more piggy-back ride.

Then she was sobbing. She was unabashedly wailing with anguish, letting the tears stream down her face, pulling her mouth into a horrible gaping hole, digging her fingers deep into her arms as if to prevent herself from breaking apart.

Her heart felt hollow. Its innards had been carved away and ripped out of her each time her family was ripped apart. It was a mish mash of scars from multiple injuries and re-openings. It was the reason everything hurt and it was also the reason she kept living.

Yonah wasn't sure how long she cried, but the tears slowly began to subside, the pain dulled to a low throb, and she sighed in exhaustion.

There was a knock at the bedroom door.

"Come in," she said, her voice cracking just a bit.

"Yonah?" It was Naris. She didn't want him to know she had been crying. She didn't answer his call.

Naris stepped onto the balcony and, when he saw the remnants of Yonah's tears, asked, "What's wrong?"

If only she could tell him. The corners of her mouth trembled as she tried to hide her frown.

Naris knelt in front of her and took her hand in his. He looked pleadingly up at her. "What's wrong?"

Maybe it was his kindness and its reminder of what home felt like that threw Yonah back into her sorrow. She closed her eyes and two more tears drizzled down her cheeks. "I miss my family."

Yonah knew that Naris didn't understand her sorrow. Even so, he wrapped his arms around Yonah and held her close to him. She could hear his heartbeat through his chest. She felt immediately warm in his embrace, like sitting next to the fireplace. Because everything about Naris' arms around her felt so comforting, Yonah returned the embrace, holding him close so that he wouldn't let go.

A few minutes later Naris relaxed his hold on Yonah and said, "You've reminded me of a place I'd like to show you."

He took Yonah's hand and led her out of the room, down through the palace, and out the back doors. They went past the fountain, through and beyond the vineyard. Yonah let go of his hand and took in a deep breath, closing her eyes and turning her face up to the sky.

"I think you like it outside," Naris finally said.

"I do."

"Why is that?"

Yonah looked around the grassy plain, a pale green beneath the blue sky. "I can escape in nature. It helps me to forget."

"Dare I ask, forget what?" His voice was trembling.

She paused before answering, wondering how wise it was of her to say what it was she wanted to say.

"My life. Where I am. What I've lost." She looked upwards again. "I get to be thankful for the miracles around me."

Naris was quiet for a moment. "Did you often play outside as a child?" he asked.

"Yes. Almost every day." She remembered how the gully had been a sort of sanctuary for her and the other children until the day everything changed.

"Did you have a favourite spot?"

"The gully." Yonah watched Naris as they walked. He was taught that slavery was right and that the upper class was better than the lower. She could show him what that really looked like.

"Would you like to hear the story of how I got my scar?" she said.

She could feel the air around them buzz with tension as Naris silently walked with Yonah. "Would you like to tell me that story?" he asked, his voice dull.

"I would."

Naris did not respond, which Yonah took as an opportunity to begin.

"We were at the gully. Our favourite spot to play. The Guard ambushed us there. They were firing their guns at us. A bullet grazed my arm as I was running away. One of them followed my siblings and me home." Her insides trembled at the memory. "He wanted to take us away, but my mother wouldn't let him. He shot her. For no reason. He turned us into orphans, so he could make money off our loss." Her voice shook with rage. Thinking of that day always filled her with a dark sadness that made her wonder about all the what-ifs in her life.

The air around them felt heavy with discomfort and anticipation.

"I'm sorry to hear that," Naris murmured.

The bitterness that sometimes crawled around inside Yonah was active. "We were supposed to be safe." She tried to push the bitterness away. "We were a family. Even if we were already broken."

She thought of reading with her father, of playing with her brother and sister, of helping her mother around the house.

"But why did the Guard chase you?" Naris asked. "Why did they attack you when they knew you weren't orphans?"

Yonah snorted. "You don't think the Guard will do anything to make some extra money? Including selling children who still have parents?"

There was another moment of silence during which Yonah assumed Naris was trying to comprehend the information she had just passed on to him.

"What about your parents?" she asked. "What happened to them?"

"They died during the sickness."

Yonah was taken aback. The way Naris strutted around, she thought he had been running this vineyard for years, not a few weeks.

"I'm sorry about that. That's just a short while ago."

"Don't be." His voice was dull. "They weren't very kind."

Whether she was truly curious or spurred on by the resentment of her own family history, Yonah pressed on. "What makes you say that?"

He was silent as they continued walking.

"We're here," he said. They were at a tree that stood alone on a low hill.

"Where are we?" Yonah asked.

"It's my tree house. You can't really tell from here."

"A treehouse?" Yonah had never heard the term before.

"The tree was a gift to my grandfather. This species doesn't normally grow around here. He had a treehouse built into it for his children, and I inherited it from them when I was a child. Would you like to go up?"

Yonah looked up at the looming tree. "Is it safe?"

Naris chuckled. "Of course! Come on." He began climbing up the fanned-out branches that created a natural ladder up to the top. Yonah tentatively followed.

Her body was very accustomed to climbing. She remembered climbing the rocks and trees at the gully. She remembered scrambling up broken brick walls in Kelab when she and her siblings lived on the streets. She remembered climbing rooftops in search of a place to sleep for the night – up above the adults, there was a world of orphans.

As she neared the top, Naris reached an arm down to her. She took his wrist and, together, they pulled her up to safety.

It was a very private space, surrounded by the leafy branches. The treehouse had walls on three sides, and the fourth side had a waist-high wall that allowed for looking at the view. The wall closest to the palace had a small window for peeking at the vineyard.

"So, this was my favourite place as a child," Naris said. "I spent as much time as I could out here. When my friend visited, I would always bring him here." He sighed and spun slowly around to take in the entire room. "I have many good memories in this place. I haven't been up for years."

"This would have been a wonderful place to play," Yonah conceded.

He grinned at her. "So, you like it?"

His eagerness to please her surprised her. "Yes. And the view is beautiful." She rested her elbows on the shorter wall and gazed out over the plain. Shrubs and bushes scattered the ground. Birdsong tinkled through the air.

Naris stood next to her. "It's even better at night with the stars out. I'm glad I could share this with you."

They looked out for a while, listening to the breeze rustle the leaves.

"Didn't you like your parents?" Yonah ventured.

Naris looked at Yonah with wide eyes. She worried she had pushed him too far. Then his lips curled into the slightest smile.

"No, I didn't," he said. "And they didn't like me. I suspect the only reason they had me was to take over the vineyard."

Yonah felt her chest heave at the thought of her parents finding value in her only for business. "And no brothers or sisters?" she asked.

"No. Although I wish I had. When it was just me and my parents, I always felt like I was being judged. I wasn't ever good enough. Not good enough company. Not a smart enough boy. Wasting my time with anything that wasn't learning the business." He stopped abruptly. His voice had started shaking.

They listened to the wind in the tree for a moment.

Once he had recovered, Naris said in a softer voice, "It would have been nice to share some of that burden with a brother or sister." He turned to Yonah. "You mentioned you had siblings?"

"Yes. A little brother and sister."

"Did you like having them around?"

"Yes," she answered slowly. "We were very close."

"What were their names?"

She didn't want to say at first. But Naris had been so kind to her that morning, and so sincere. "Sayzia and Obi."

"Do you miss them?"

"So much."

She looked at him. Naris was looking out at the plain with hard eyes. He said in a soft voice, "I wonder what it's like to feel loved by so many people."

Yonah's own sorrow gave way to a curious sadness for Naris. She watched his still face, his clenched jaw, his furrowed brow, his sad eyes. The love she shared with her own family was what made her strong and gave her purpose. Without them, Yonah was lost.

She wasn't sure if she did it of her own free will or if something else compelled her to place her hand on Naris' arm, but when she did, he looked down at her hand in amazement and she felt a warmth between them that grew from their shared sense of loneliness.

They didn't say anything. They only let the warmth of that touch linger as they listened to the sounds of nature surrounding them.

Chapter Eleven

The next morning, Yonah resolved to go to Kirash to visit the place called The White Stallion, as the orphaned children that she had met suggested. But, as she walked through the halls of the palace towards Naris' office, there was a struggle within herself.

She was falling for Naris.

He was kind to her, reintroduced pleasure to her, made her feel safe.

But he was her master and he was standing between Yonah and finding her siblings.

He would likely hurt her if, and when, he found out Yonah was using him, but that couldn't matter to Yonah. She had to remember that masters were the reason for her circumstance and that Naris was one of them.

She found him in his office. He didn't notice her lingering in the open doorway.

Yonah watched as he wrote. A lock of his dark hair fell over his forehead as he looked down at his writing. As he rested one elbow on the arm of his chair, one of his hands was mindlessly playing with his curls. His face was calm. Yonah's eyes followed the lines of his beard and moustache to his soft lips. She longed to feel those lips on hers again.

Naris looked up suddenly, a puzzled expression on his face. Yonah started, worried if he knew she had been staring.

"Do you need something?" he asked.

"I'm sorry for disturbing you, Master. I was wondering if I could go visit Kirash this morning."

It took him a moment to process her request, but eventually he smiled and said, "Of course. I'll be working today."

"Thank you," she muttered, leaving the room.

"Yonah," he called. She looked back into the room. "Call me Naris."

Her heart fluttered with excitement. She nodded and left.

Yonah had tucked several pieces of the jewelry Naris had given her into her travel coat. With only five ora left from her previous visit to Kirash, she figured she could barter with the jewelry instead. Because Naris had given her such an exorbitant amount, she was sure he wouldn't miss them.

She knew better than to return to the same map seller, so Yonah spent some time meandering down the main road in search of someone else.

She eventually found a map seller at the far end of the main street. The shop was only a small, square tent, bursting with maps rolled up and tied with twine. An elderly woman sat on a stool at the tent's entrance. Her eyes and lips were puckered with wrinkles, and her hands were bony and angular. She said to Yonah, "What is it you're looking for, girl?"

Yonah did her best to sound confident and assertive. "I need a map of the towns and estates of the continent."

The woman slid off her stool and shuffled over to a basket. She ruffled through the tags that labelled the maps, pulled one out, and handed it to

Yonah. "You can look, if you like."

Yonah pulled the string loose and unrolled the map. It looked very similar to the one she had examined in the other shop. It would certainly do.

"Thank you," she said. "I'll take it."

"That will be fifteen ora."

"Do you take," she paused, unsure of what the elderly woman's reaction would be, "other forms of payment?"

The woman squinted at Yonah. "What did you have in mind?"

Yonah withdrew a plain gold bracelet from her coat and held it out for the woman to see. The map seller leaned forward to take a closer look, then eyed Yonah's coat. "What else have you got in there?"

"Nothing," Yonah lied.

"Then I don't take anything other than ora coins."

Yonah stood defiantly watching the woman for a moment, but when the woman didn't budge, she reached into her coat again and pulled out two jewelled rings.

"Ah, yes," the woman said. "That should cover the cost." She took the bracelet and rings from Yonah's hand and began to slide them over her bony fingers.

"Thank you for your time," Yonah said stiffly.

"Thank you, my dear," the woman grinned. "Come back any time."

Yonah walked out of the tent, unhappy with the exchange. But she knew she had little leverage as a slave. There was always the threat of the Guard or a master being called. There was always someone to answer to, and always someone to throw you to their mercy.

At the far edge of town lay The White Stallion. When Yonah slipped into the white clay building, she realized it was an inn and dining room. Despite the hour, it was already busy. There was a bar at which several men sat and most of the dozen tables had at least one person seated at them.

Yonah found an empty table and unrolled the map over it. She easily found Kelab and pressed her finger to it. Following a red line on the map, she drew her finger north through several towns until she reached a place called Sintash. That was where she had been sold to Master Puru. From there, she had been taken southeast to his estate, which was on the map as Puruha. Yonah saw that Vaha was west of Sintash, and further west from there was Kirash, and even further west, all the way at the ocean, was Basee.

A barmaid stood over Yonah's table. "Careful with that. People might think you're up to something."

Yonah looked up at the barmaid. She guessed that she was a few years older than her. Her black hair hung down in long waves to her upper back, where it met the top of her gold-coloured shirt. One of her hands was fingerless but for the thumb. Even without looking for the tell-tale collar, Yonah knew from her disability that this woman was a slave.

The woman smirked down at the map in interest with eyes lined heavily in black. Then she looked at Yonah and asked, "Are you up to something?"

"Just learning."

"Nothing is 'just' anything when you're a slave. What can I get you?"

"What do you have?" Yonah asked with uncertainty.

The barmaid smiled kindly. "I'll get you some wine."

As the barmaid returned to her work, Yonah returned to examining the map, working to memorize the different towns and roads and estates and port cities. She wanted to get to Basee, but she had no idea how long it would take to get there on foot.

She looked up to watch the barmaid. She was a personable woman, seeming to strike up friendly conversations with all of the customers, free or not. Yonah wondered how much people spoke to her, how much information she managed to gather.

When the barmaid returned to Yonah's table with a cup, Yonah asked, "How long have you been here?"

The woman gave Yonah a puzzled look, but said, "Nearly a year now. Before that, I was in Basee."

"You've been to Basee? What's it like there? Are ships often coming in?"

"Well, yes, it's a port city."

Yonah could hardly contain her eagerness. "Could a person walk there from here?"

The barmaid thought for a moment. "Sure, but it would take about an hour."

Yonah's heart fell. She wasn't sure if she could risk such a distance without asking Naris for permission and that would draw too much suspicion. "Do people from Basee often come to Kirash?" she asked instead.

"Sometimes." The barmaid furrowed her brow at Yonah. "Why are you asking all these questions? You're going to get yourself into trouble."

"I'm looking for somebody. He's a sailor."

"Well, you'll likely find him in Basee sometime, whoever he is."

Yonah hesitated. She wasn't sure how to proceed. "If I described him for you, would you be able to look out for him for me? And I could come here once in a while and see if you've seen him?" When she saw the barmaid's face draw into an expression of disbelief, Yonah added, "I could pay you. I have these…" After a quick glance around the pub, Yonah held one side of her coat taut and pulled some of the jewelry out of her pocket. The barmaid squinted at her.

"Won't your master mind?" the barmaid said.

"I don't think he'll notice."

The barmaid still looked apprehensive. "Where did you get those? Are you with the rebellion?"

"What? No! I'm only looking… It's my brother. I haven't seen him since we were captured by the Guard. That was three years ago now."

The barmaid looked at Yonah for a moment with her furrowed brow. "What's your name?"

"Yonah."

"It's nice to meet you, Yonah. I'm Meerha." She placed her fingerless hand on the table and leaned against it. "I can't really do much with all that fancy stuff, though."

"I can trade it for something else," Yonah said. The closer she got to her goal, the more desperate she felt. "What do you want? I'll trade for it. If you can keep a lookout for my brother."

Meerha's eyes scanned the pub. "Hold on, I need to look after the other customers. Do you have time?" Yonah nodded. "Then wait here."

Yonah waited in her spot as Meerha continued working, moving from customer to customer with a relaxed smile on her face. Yonah sipped from the cup Meerha had brought her. She instantly recognized Naris' wine.

Meerha eventually came back and said quietly, "I'll keep an eye out for your brother. As payment, I want you to bring me some beauty wares."

"Some what?"

"You know, creams, soaps, face paints. Things that will make me feel a little more human."

Yonah nodded. "I can do that. Where do I get some?"

Meerha raised her eyebrows. "You don't have any money?"

"Only a little," Yonah replied. "And I'm not sure if I can get more."

The barmaid said, "There's a square south of here. In the corner stall, a man and a woman sell candles. If the man is out, ask him what their finest scent is. No matter what he responds with, you must answer, 'I prefer roses.' If the woman is out, say to her, 'The sand burns my feet at night, but candles keep me warm during the day.'"

Yonah gave the barmaid a quizzical look. "Do you mean 'the sand burns my feet during the day?'"

Meerha returned Yonah's look with one of annoyance. "No. It's a code. Now, say them back to me."

"'I prefer roses,' and 'the sand burns my feet at night, but candles keep me warm during the day.'"

"Good." Meerha leaned in closer. "Now tell me about your brother. Does he look like you?"

YONAH RETURNED TO VAHA with a lightness in her step. With Meerha watching out for news of sailors and potentially her brother coming into Basee, Yonah felt as if she were on the right path towards reuniting with both her siblings.

As she walked through the vineyard at Vaha, Yonah heard someone calling her name. She turned towards the sound of the voice. It was Bana. He strode over to her with his long legs.

"Off on another adventure?" he teased.

She made a point of leaving enough space between them so their conversation couldn't be interpreted as intimate. "I was just exploring Kirash."

"You were there not long ago, weren't you? What's so interesting there?"

"There's lots to see." She didn't elaborate. She didn't know Bana very well, but even if they did become good friends, there were some secrets that she knew she could only entrust to herself.

He seemed to understand. "You can keep your secrets. It's a gift to have one." He had started to turn to return to his work when he added, "You know, I meant it when I said you could come by and visit."

Yonah found herself smiling. "I'm not sure Master Naris would like that. He didn't seem too happy when he saw us talking the other day."

"What, he's the only person you're allowed to talk to?"

She shrugged. All she knew was that the look on Naris' face the day she and Bana had first spoken made her uneasy.

With a playful look on his face, Bana whispered conspiratorially, "He doesn't have to know."

Yonah laughed softly.

"Besides," Bana added, "I bet you and I have more to talk about than you and him."

"Well," she said, "we certainly have more in common."

Bana gave her a quizzical look. "Well, the invitation stands. I hope to see you soon, Yonah," and he turned back to his work.

Chapter Twelve

For the first time since arriving at Vaha, Yonah wore a sleeveless shirt to dinner with Naris. The outfit was pink and featured long billowing pants and a cropped shirt draped in coins, not unlike what she wore at Master Puru's when she had been called to work with the indoor slaves. When Naris saw the outfit, his eyes briefly flickered over her scar, and then he chuckled softly to himself.

"Somehow, my dear, when I compare this to your favourite dress, these clothes lose just a touch of their appeal."

"Then I can get rid of these and buy more clothes to my liking?" she said in a teasing tone.

He laughed. "I don't think so. They may not compare, but I still like them enough." For a moment, he simply watched Yonah from his seat, his eyes wandering over her body. Yonah felt naked under his stare. "But, of course, we can get you more clothes to your liking as well."

The combination of Naris' hungry stare and his offer to ensure her happiness left Yonah feeling a mix of uneasiness and gratitude.

She waited until they were upstairs in Naris' bedroom before asking what she had been wanting to ask all afternoon.

"Do you travel for your work?"

Naris looked slightly taken aback by the question, then answered, "I plan to. We'll be going north before the mountain passes close for the winter." He began to pour two glasses of wine.

"We?"

"Yes, I plan to take you everywhere with me."

Excitement lifted Yonah's heart. "Do you know where we'll visit on our trip north?"

"There are plenty of major estates on the main road to Jalid." Naris handed a glass to Yonah and sat down next to her. "And my closest friend lives in Jalid, so I would like to stay there for a few days."

Maybe she could find Sayzia on the journey. Maybe she could convince Naris to buy her from her master, too.

"What's your friend's name?"

"Kejal. You would have seen him at Puru's feast."

Yonah pictured the only guest at Master Puru's to whom Naris showed affection. The man who had warned Naris of the slaves rebelling in Harasa.

"When will we go?" she asked.

"After the harvest. Then I'd like to plan some excursions to the south during the winter. Why so many questions?"

She quickly said, "I used to read books with my father about all the wonderful things that you can see on the continent. He told me he would take me to see them all."

"Well, now I will take you to see them all," Naris said with a smile. He stroked the side of Yonah's face, sending a warm sensation to the parts his fingertips touched. "Let's go outside." He stood and took Yonah's hand.

The view from his balcony was very similar to Yonah's, looking out over the greenery of the vineyard, his greatest treasure.

"Look at that moon," he said, his eyes gazing upward.

Yonah looked and saw it, round and shining proudly upon the night, its silver glow radiating gently outwards. "She's beautiful."

Naris looked at Yonah. "Her beauty is nothing compared to yours."

She had not anticipated a comment like that. Yonah knew she wasn't traditionally beautiful. The masters had made that very clear. It was why she had started as an outdoor slave.

"You're the only person to think that," she finally said.

"How is that possible?" Naris seemed sincerely puzzled by the notion.

Yonah took a subtle step away from him. "Beautiful girls are the first to be bought by masters. Master Puru only let beautiful girls serve indoors."

"You served indoors."

"Only after all of the other girls died from that sickness."

"Making way for progress."

Yonah did not know any of the indoor girls who had died from the sickness, but they were girls just like her. They had once had dreams, worried for their families, felt fear. Yonah knew they were deeply cared for by the others, just as she had cared for her friends among the outdoor slaves. But they were not human to Naris.

She chose not to say anything, so as not to accidentally insult him.

"Yonah, are you happy here?"

She didn't look at him as she said, "You've been very kind to me."

"That's not what I asked."

She gazed out instead at the view. She spent most of her time taking in this view, in the early mornings when most of the household was getting ready for their day's work, late at night if she couldn't sleep. She stared out over the vineyard and beyond into the plains, remembering her past, thinking about her present, and dreaming about her future. "I miss my family."

"Then turn to me. Let me be the one you miss."

"Naris, I—" She stopped when she saw the look in his eyes, gentle, pleading, vulnerable. Those eyes made her heart melt with affection. Something in those eyes prevented her from lying to him in this moment. "I can't. Not even if I want to."

"Do you want to?" He grabbed her hands. His touch was warm and strong. "I hope…" He struggled to say the words. "I hope you will someday love me."

The scenario played in her head. A master with an estate filled with slaves, one slave girl on whom he doted and bestowed with rich gifts, the slave girl returning his affection only with her infinite time, the slave girl being mocked by the other slaves, the slave girl foolishly believing she was an equal to her lover, believing his love was real, living a life that was a facsimile of love. She couldn't let that happen. Though she was Naris' slave in body, she couldn't let herself become his slave in mind. She had to reserve all her thoughts for finding her brother and sister and reuniting them once she was freed.

"That's not possible," she whispered. She pulled her hands away from his.

Naris frowned at her. "Not possible? Yonah, you're already falling for me, I know this. I've felt it."

"But I am your slave," she snapped. "How can a slave love their master? You can hurt me if you want and there's nothing I can do about it. How could I possibly love someone who has that kind of power over me?" She wasn't sure if she was talking to Naris or herself.

"I wouldn't use that power over you," he said gently.

"You already do. I must ask permission to leave the estate. I must come when I'm called. You still treat me like a slave because that is what I am to you."

Naris reached for her hands again, but she dodged away from him. "But you're different. I treat you differently than the others. I let you do what you like. You do no work around here. You are practically free."

Her mouth dropped open. "Free? Is that what freedom is to you?" She could feel anger boiling inside her. "You are so far removed from all of us. You don't understand what we have lost." Her eyes began to well with hot tears. "I've lost my entire family because of people like you! People who can't be bothered to look after themselves. It's because of people like you that children are turned into orphans and torn away from their only family and traded like they're animals and forced to live a life they never asked for!" The tears rolled down her cheeks. Years of frustration and solitude and loneliness caught up with her. "It's not my fault people like you are lonely, because you surround yourself with people who resent you. It shouldn't be my job to make you feel better. But I *know* it's not my job to get tricked into thinking I could love someone like you!"

Naris' face had morphed into a dark grimace. Quick like a snake, he lashed out and grabbed Yonah's wrist. His grip tightened, his fingers pressing so hard Yonah was sure her bones were bending beneath them. His eyes glared at her with the anger she had only seen glimmers of when he reprimanded the other slaves, the glimmers that frightened them so much.

His voice was deadly quiet. "You do not speak to me in that way."

She stood there defiantly, trying not to wince at the pain in her wrist, trying not to panic at his strength.

"Yes. Master."

Their eyes were locked in a silent battle. He tried to will her to bend. She refused. After another moment, Naris threw her arm away from him. "Get out."

"Yes, Master." Despite her cool response, Yonah's heart fluttered violently as she strode inside to his room and out the door to the hallway. She didn't pause in the hallway to think, as she often did after her meetings with Naris, but walked as fast as she could back to her room.

Once there, she stood in the middle of the room, her body shaking with adrenaline. She cradled her wrist with one hand. It throbbed slightly from Naris clutching it so tightly.

Trying to ignore her shaking body, Yonah pulled her map out of one of her drawers and set it on the table in the middle of the room. She found the main road that travelled through northern Harasa, through the mountain pass, and into Jalid. She could not tell from any of the names where Naris' friend Kejal might live. But it was possible that Sayzia was on one of those estates.

Yonah folded up the map and stuffed it underneath the mattress, then changed into her travel pants and shirt for the night and climbed into bed. When she closed her eyes, she saw Naris' dark look, felt his hand on her wrist. Slowly, her trembling stilled, and her fear gave way to sleep.

YONAH WOKE TO THE SOUND of the door opening. She opened her eyes and, after a moment of blurriness, saw that the woman who normally brought her breakfast was rummaging through her drawers. Yonah snapped upright and said, "What are you doing?"

"The master wants some of your clothing returned to him," the woman said unfeelingly, not bothering to look at Yonah.

Yonah clambered out of bed. "Why?"

The woman shrugged. "Not sure." She held the beautiful blue dress balled up in one hand and had the orange travel coat and scarf hooked over the same arm. For the first time ever, she looked at Yonah. "He wants those, too," she said, pointing to Yonah.

Yonah defiantly folded her arms across her chest and stared at the woman, trying not to reveal how strangely devastating it was to be losing these items.

"Unless you'd like to take it up with the master yourself?" the woman said.

Memories of the previous night flooded Yonah's mind and she began to remove her shirt and pants.

"You two get into a fight or something?" the woman asked.

"Does it matter?" Yonah asked grumpily, handing over her clothes.

"It matters to some of them." Yonah knew the woman was referring to the other slaves. The woman nodded towards a tray on the table. "That might be the last meal I bring up to you in a while." Then she left, closing the door behind her.

Yonah kept to her room that day. She had no wish to stumble upon Naris, although it was more than likely that he would stay cooped up in his office all day, but she didn't want to take any chances. Instead, she spent her time with her newly purchased map. She tried to memorize the roads and towns, the mountains and the small lakes, anything that would help her better understand the country so she might find her sister.

It was only in search of food late that afternoon that Yonah left her room. The moment she arrived in the kitchen, the more outspoken slaves yelled names at her, shoved her, toyed at the coins on her shirt. Not all of them yelled at her, but they sat quietly at the communal table, not bothering to step in. The only food that was offered to Yonah were scraps, and the slaves threw it to the ground. "You're a pet. Pets don't eat from dishware."

Yonah stoically searched the kitchen for a bowl and, ignoring the jeering around her, scooped up the left-over meat and bread. Even though they were afraid of Naris, knowing that Yonah was not currently on his good side made the household slaves brave, especially in the kitchens where he never ventured.

"Have a good day, Pet," someone sneered loudly, starting up a new wave of jeers. Yonah turned with her sad bowl of food and began making her way back to the staircase up to the main level when she felt something soft hit the back of her head. She froze and tried to contain her reaction to just that. There was uproarious laughter.

She was stuck between two worlds, belonging to neither. The slaves didn't respect her because she didn't technically work. Her master couldn't truly care for her because she wasn't free. Trying to rise above the unfairness of it all seemed useless.

Yonah was steeling herself to walk up the stairs without a fuss when she heard someone yell over the laughter.

"What's going on in here? What do you all think you're doing?"

She knew from the sound of his voice that it was Bana. She turned to look at him.

He was standing in the middle of the kitchen between Yonah and the rest of the slaves. Everyone stared silently at him, some with shame, some with confusion, and others with disgust.

"She's a slave just like you," Bana shouted. "Her job might look a little different than yours, but it's still a job."

"She gets to have free reign of Kirash whenever she wants!" someone called, stirring up a grumbling agreement from the group.

"And she also has to sit with the master every day and not upset him in any way. You all know how he is."

The slaves shifted and glanced around uncomfortably.

Bana frowned at them. "Shame on you all." He promptly began to gather some food in his arms, turned to Yonah and said, "Shall we?"

She nodded and followed him up the stairs and outside to the fountain in the back courtyard. He sat on the lip of the fountain and spread out the makeshift meal.

"Don't you have work to do?" Yonah asked. "I mean, won't you get in trouble?"

"I'll be quick. But I just need to make sure you're alright."

Yonah's face twisted as she tried to hold back the tears that suddenly wanted to erupt.

"Thank you for helping me." She looked down at the ground.

"What are friends for?"

Friends. It felt like ages since she had someone to consider a friend. It was a wholly welcome surprise. Yonah looked up at Bana. "We're friends?"

He shrugged. "I'd like that."

It was a pleasant thought. Yonah sat down, leaving room for the meal between her and Bana.

"And thank you for bringing this. My first day here I had mouldy bread."

"I'm sorry about them. They're more upset about this than I thought." He handed Yonah a piece of bread.

As she took the offering, Yonah said, "I guess I can't blame them. They're right. I don't do any work. I'm just a pet."

"Doesn't make it okay for them to treat you the way masters treat them," Bana said with a look of disgust. Yonah simply continued gnawing at the bread. Bana leaned towards her. "Just don't let them get to you too much, alright? After all, they're just jealous."

"Tell that to my stomach."

He smiled. "Well, I tried to grab enough to last you a few meals there, so pace yourself." He stood. "I'd better get back to work. You come visit me, alright? I can talk while I work."

Yonah smiled softly. "Thanks. I'll do that."

FOR THE FIRST TIME SINCE their arrival at Vaha, Yonah did not join Naris for dinner. Instead, she ate both dinner and breakfast the following day alone in her bedroom, eating from the stash Bana had managed to quickly gather for her.

Yonah decided to explore the house a little bit more, less afraid of running into Naris now that he had had a day to cool off. She found the large dining hall. She imagined it had seen many feasts and dances. The floor was decorated in swooping lines of silver and gold on a blue background. When she looked up to the domed ceiling, she saw images of horseback riders racing towards each other with swords drawn, a woman with magical powers on a cliff-face at the edge of the ocean, a great whale with a monstrous tail, and more. She didn't understand what they stood for.

There was an image of a bear that reminded Yonah of her little brother. She remembered the song their mother had made up for him:

"Stop hiding, Little bear.

I know you're here. I see you there.

We'll dance and play and catch some fish.

Sleep 'neath the stars, that's my one wish."

After which Obi would either spread his arms wide from his covered face or jump out from his hiding spot and yell in his small child's voice, "ROAR!"

It was the library she wanted to visit. She found the door at the end of the floating balcony in the entrance hall, but when she tried to open it, it didn't budge. Fiery frustration spread through Yonah. She would have to ask Naris to open the library door for her, which meant she would have to get on his good side again.

That afternoon, Yonah took Bana up on his offer and went looking for him in the vineyard. He was at the front side of the estate, continuing his care of the plants. He was removing the leaves next to the ripening grapes. A smile lit up his face when he saw her.

"I was wondering if you'd ever visit," he said. "What have you been up to?"

"I've been exploring the house. The great hall is beautiful."

"I've never seen it. What's so great about it?"

"Well, first off, it's just so big, which is always impressive," Yonah said, absent-mindedly reaching out to touch a vine. "But I like the colours. And there are pictures on the ceiling."

"That's a strange place to put pictures."

"Maybe," Yonah shrugged. "But they're nice to look at. Can I help?"

Bana stopped his work to look at Yonah. She saw him glance at the scar on her arm and looked back up to her face. "You want to do some hard labour? Worried the master will abandon you?"

"You don't need to make fun of me," Yonah said, light-heartedly. "I used to do labour at my last place."

"Well, if you're sure you want to help, just take off the leaves close to the bunches. Just the ones on this side."

Yonah began to feel her way through the vine.

"How did you end up here?" Yonah asked.

"Working here? I've been here since I was a kid. The Guard rounded up a bunch of us."

"You're an orphan?" Yonah asked. Bana nodded. "Me, too."

"But I'll be free in a couple years. I can hold on until then."

There was a moment of silence as the pair of them worked at plucking the leaves from the vine. Bana broke the silence by asking, "Did they have a vineyard at your old place?"

"No. My job was hauling water and tending to the plants in the courtyard."

"Do you miss it?"

"The work?"

Bana nodded.

Yonah focused on the bunch she was working through, trying not to let her grief for her friends show too much. "I miss the friends I had. We were a family at Master Puru's. You probably are here, too."

"We are. I'm sorry you're not being welcomed into it."

"I understand why," Yonah said. The work of tugging at the leaves was satisfying. "But it's fine." She watched a handful float down to the ground. "It just makes me want to find my own family more."

"What are you talking about?"

Yonah looked at Bana, her eyes wide. "I mean, it just makes me miss my family more."

Bana didn't look convinced. "Is that what you've been doing in Kirash? Looking for your family?"

"No," Yonah said. She backed away from the bush. "I just don't have work to do, so I have to find new places to explore. Kirash is one of them."

"Okay, okay," Bana cut in. "Don't worry. I believe you."

She turned her eyes downward. "I'd better go."

"Sure. You know I won't tell anybody about Kirash?"

"There's nothing to tell." She turned around and started walking back to the palace. It was then that she saw Naris' face above in the window of his room, looking down moodily at them.

Chapter Thirteen

That evening, a slave came to Yonah's room to tell her that Naris requested her company at dinner. She could only assume that it had to do with his seeing her with Bana that afternoon.

They ate in the back again. The usual woman was their wine pourer. Yonah could feel the dry pride coming off her.

For a while, neither Naris nor Yonah spoke. Instead, Yonah gazed at the mosaiced floor and Naris' eyes went from looking out over his land, to Yonah, and back out again.

"I noticed," he finally said, "you spending time with that slave in the vineyard. What was his name again?"

Yonah met his eyes. She had told Naris the name only a few days ago. "Bana," she answered with a biting tone. Naris didn't respond, though his eyes remained watchful on Yonah. Her whole body was on alert, each muscle ready to react if Naris' temper went off again.

He sighed and rested his chin in his hand, his eyes wandering, as if a safe conversation topic might be hanging in the air.

At last he said, "I have been experimenting with a new recipe." When he was met with silence, he added, "Would you like to try it?"

Yonah was now required to answer, as she had been asked a direct question. If she wasn't a slave, she would have answered that no, she did not want to try out his new wine recipe and that she had no interest in his business. But she was a slave, and the only reason she lived the life of relative luxury that she did was in exchange for her companionship.

"If that is what you wish," she finally answered, compromising between wanting to end the conversation and not throwing her master into another rage at her insolence.

Naris snapped in the direction of the wine pourer. "Find Lucine."

The wine pourer set her pitcher of wine on the table and began to leave when Naris said in a dark tone, "My cup is near empty."

"Pardon, Master," she said, rushing back to pick up the pitcher and fill the young man's cup. As she replaced the pitcher on the table, Naris said, "And Yonah's."

The woman paused so briefly that Yonah wasn't sure Naris had seen it. But she filled Yonah's cup to the brim, and finally turned to fetch the new wine.

"I understand you are not favoured among most of the household," Naris said.

Yonah started at the unexpected topic. "Who told you that?"

"My business advisors. Information works its way up to me one way or another."

Naris was more in tune with the goings-on of his home than Yonah thought. She had assumed that he was ignorant of his slaves' feelings towards her.

"They don't like the special treatment I get."

"That is not their concern."

Yonah shrugged. "They're allowed to have feelings." She added, "That is one thing the masters can't control."

She saw Naris' jaw clench and release, though he kept his face calm. Yonah felt brief relief that the dig at their argument hadn't set him off.

"Well, they are not allowed to act on their feelings, at least." His face was hard. "Everyone in and outside of this house should treat you as my guest – no less. And no more."

She heard the subtle reference to Bana's kindness.

The wine pourer returned carrying a clear glass bottle and two clean cups. Inside, the wine had a pinkish-orange tinge to it. The woman set the cups on the table, uncorked the wine, and poured. Yonah watched as Naris grumpily eyed the woman.

When the new wine had been poured, Naris picked up a cup and held it out towards Yonah. She picked up the other cup and tapped it against his. Naris took a long whiff and a large gulp of the wine. Yonah lifted her cup to her face to smell it.

A combination of spices hit her and she was taken back to her small home in Kelab. She was playing on the floor with her brother and sister and the house was hot from her mother's cooking. She could see her mother's dark hair tied into a thick braid running down to her lower back, her ears glittering in studs and hoops, her hands white with flour as she made flatbread to go with the soup. Her soups were delicious, and she always smelled like the spices she cooked into them. Yonah liked how her mother sang while she cooked, starting softly at first, as if she didn't want to disturb her children, but eventually growing louder until her voice rang out to the street, and Yonah and her siblings danced and clapped to her song.

Yonah tried to hide the happy memory, keeping her face still.

She took a sip. She was jarred by the coolness of the wine, half expecting to take in some of her mother's soup. The cool liquid with sharp spices was an unexpected, though not unappetizing combination.

"What do you think?" Naris asked, interrupting her thoughts.

Yonah looked up at him. She hesitated. "It reminds me of my mother."

He looked puzzled. "Why is that?"

"It smells like her." She took another sip.

"And you have fond memories of your mother?"

Without realizing, Yonah smiled softly. "I do. I remember her singing in our house. She had the most beautiful voice." She laughed at the memory of her family singing together.

"What is it?"

Yonah's laughter died as she realized it was not only Naris who witnessed this intimate moment, but the wine pourer and the hired guards who were always hovering around.

"It's nothing," Yonah muttered, turning her attention to her food. Her memories of happier times did not need to be shared with strangers. Her memories were something she knew she could keep safe, if nothing else in her life.

"May I ask your mother's name?" Naris said.

Her food had to work past a large lump in her throat as she swallowed.

"Valli." She kept her eyes turned downward as she said it.

"Then that is what I shall call this wine."

Yonah froze. Her mother's name. She had given it away and now Naris was taking it. She looked up at him, pleadingly. He saw her face and hurriedly added, "To honour her."

"You didn't know her."

"But it's for you to remember her by." He raised his cup. "To Valli."

Yonah raised her cup to appease Naris. As he drank, she absent-mindedly cradled the cup to her chest, trying to hold her heart together. She knew it was meant as a kindness, possibly even as a way to make amends for the tension between them the past few days. It was sudden. Yonah had almost thought that her mother was there, as the memory of her had come on so quickly. And now they toasted to her memory.

To prevent herself from spiralling deeper into her emotions, Yonah suddenly lifted the cup to her lips and emptied its contents. As she set her cup on the table, it clicked lightly. Naris' gaze went from the cup to the wine pourer, who made no move to fill it.

"Slave!" Naris snapped. "Do your job."

The wine pourer jumped and bustled over to the table.

As the wine pourer served Yonah, Naris asked with a suddenly calmer voice, "Are you pleased?"

"Yes," Yonah lied. "Thank you." She caught a glimpse of the wine pourer's lips pulling into a scowl. The more kindness Naris showed Yonah, the more repugnant she seemed to the rest of the household. "Will your business advisors question the name?"

Naris shrugged. "I won't tell them what it means. And I get final say on what goes on around here."

The wine pourer moved back to her position against the wall. Yonah noticed that a drop from the bottle had fallen onto her pants. If the wine pourer had spilled on Naris, she would have been viciously berated for it.

"I don't want to affect your business," Yonah said. "My only job here is to be your companion."

Naris did not respond immediately. He looked at the wine pourer. Yonah saw the woman stiffen. Nervously, Yonah drank more of her wine.

"Slave," he said.

"Yes, Master." The wine pourer stepped forward.

"What is your job here?"

"To keep the cups filled, Master."

"And is it to have an opinion?"

She hesitated. "No, Master."

"So do you have an opinion on the name of my new recipe?"

"No, Master."

"And do you have an opinion on Yonah's job?"

"No, Master."

Naris leaned back in his chair and looked at Yonah. "You don't need to worry."

Yonah feared that he had only made matters worse rather than fixed anything.

They continued eating quietly. Yonah felt uneasy as she did so.

"What did you like about your mother?" Naris asked.

Why did he insist on taking ownership of her memories, too?

"You say she gave her life trying to protect you. Was she normally so maternal?"

Yonah looked at him, trying to read the expression on his face. He didn't show any signs of distress or anger. There were no subtle emotions to reveal what he meant by his question.

"She was very kind," Yonah answered. "She loved my siblings and me."

"How do you know that?" Naris was casually chewing on his food as he asked the question.

Her mother showed her love for her children in so many ways – in the way she laboured over their meals every day, in the way she sang lullabies to them, in the way she called them her little mice, in the way she had so unselfishly protected them, in the way she had begged for their lives. Yonah remembered the day she became an orphan, how her mother had tried to fight that member of the Guard, how broken she looked crumpled up on the floor with blood pooling around her, her songs gone forever.

Yonah's eyes strained as she tried not to let tears well up in them. "I just know." She took a large gulp of her wine, the one that smelled like Valli. "Why don't you tell me about your family?"

"Well, you and I had very different childhoods." Naris was growing moody.

"In what way?"

"You already know what it was like growing up with my parents."

Without any further explanation, Naris continued eating. Whether she was honestly curious, or she just wanted to needle Naris, Yonah said, "They must have loved you a little."

"This isn't the best place for this conversation," Naris murmured. He finished his cup of wine and set it loudly on the table. The wine pourer promptly strode over to refill it. Naris' face had turned inward and grown dark.

As the wine pourer walked away Naris yelled, "Slave!"

She turned.

"You did not fill my companion's cup!"

"Pardon, Master." She rushed over to Yonah, but Naris roughly grabbed her wrist, sending the bottle crashing down on the mosaiced floor, causing Yonah to start.

"What is your job here?" he hissed at the woman.

"I'm the wine pourer." Her voice had gone thin and high-pitched.

"Yet I'm always having to jog your memory."

"I'm sorry, Master! It won't happen again." She tried to pull away, but Yonah knew how strong his grip was.

"How can I be sure of that?" He nodded at the two guards and they came forward and grabbed the woman's arms.

She shrieked. "Please! I'm sorry! I promise I'll do better!"

"Give me your knife," Naris said to one of the guards. A knife was procured and Naris took it. The woman was openly sobbing. Yonah was frozen in her chair.

Naris grabbed one of the woman's hands and held it in front of him, palm facing up. "Now, I know I specialize in white, but perhaps if your hands run like red wine, you'll remember what is expected of you." He took the tip of the knife to her hand and dragged it along the palm.

The wine pourer screamed as Naris covered her hand in cuts, as he dragged the knife along her fingers, as he reached for her other hand to do the same again. Blood ran over the woman's skin and dripped slowly to the floor. She tried to pull away from Naris as he brought the knife to her skin over and over, but the guards held her, and she slowly sank to her knees. Naris held her hand, focussed on his work, ignoring the woman's pleading. Finally, he released her and stepped back.

The guards let go and the woman sat crouched, holding her hands in front of her. They were red and swollen with patches of skin that hung on by small fibres threatening to peel away completely. Her head was turned downward and her screaming sobs had gone soft. Yonah wanted to go to her, to tell her they would fix her broken hands, but her fear of Naris' anger kept her in her chair.

"Take her to the slaves' quarters," Naris said quietly. He stood still, staring at the small area of blood spatters on the floor as the guards grabbed the woman once more and disappeared into the palace with her.

Naris turned to take his seat at the table, but stopped when he saw Yonah. He looked at the knife in his hand, its tip still wet with blood. Yonah, too, was still, incapable of finding something reasonable to say or do.

"Just go," Naris finally said, his voice dull.

Yonah still couldn't find a way to make her legs move.

"Go!"

She jumped up suddenly and raced to her room.

SHE WAS GASPING FOR breath as she rushed through her bedroom to the balcony. The image of the wine pourer's hands filled her mind, and how the woman writhed in pain, trying to pull away from Naris and his knife. Naris had been so cold in his punishment. He had run the knife along the woman's skin not as if she were a human in pain, but as if she were a piece of wood into which he was determined to carve an intricate design. His ears had been deaf to her screams, while Yonah couldn't get them out of her head.

Yonah remembered Naris' grip on her a few nights ago. She remembered his anger at her. She had been so close to facing his full wrath, but he had somehow kept his anger in check with her that night. She wasn't so sure he would always be able to do so. There would be a time when he punished her for displeasing him.

Her breathing was not slowing. Her hands were shaking. Despite being outside in the cool evening air, Yonah felt hot and claustrophobic. She was trapped. She had to leave Vaha, but attempting to do so would put her at greater risk. The Guard would be on the lookout for her. And what would happen if she got caught and was brought back to Vaha? Would Naris cut up her hands, too? Her mind was growing fuzzy, and the world outside was tipping and dimming.

On weak legs, Yonah reached out for the palace wall and rested her side against it. She sunk down to the floor and closed her eyes, her tipping vision making her dizzy.

She turned her mind to better things. To her mother. No, that only reminded her of the evening's events. She thought of singing and playing with Obi and Sayzia. She found herself singing softly:

"Stop hiding, Little Bear.

I know you're here. I see you there.

We'll dance and play and catch some fish.

Sleep 'neath the stars, that's my one wish."

Yonah gave a long sigh. She had to find Sayzia and Obi.

There was a knock from inside and the door opened. Yonah remained where she was, curled up on the floor of the balcony, half hoping that Naris would think she hadn't gone back to her room after all.

"Yonah?" he called.

She squeezed her arms around herself. "I'm here."

Her eyes still closed, she heard Naris' feet pad across the floor until they were right in front of her.

"Are you alright?" He sounded alarmed.

She slowly opened her eyes. He was standing above her, looking nothing like the angry monster she had seen only a few minutes ago. Instead, his face was soft with concern. His hands were clean.

"I just need a drink of water." Yonah started to stand, and Naris reached for her. She flinched at his touch, but his hands on her shoulders were gentle.

The two of them made their way inside and Naris led Yonah to a chair. She sat down and watched him stride over to the low-standing cabinet and pour some water. He returned with the full cup. Yonah took it from his hand, careful not to let their fingers graze. "Thank you," she muttered.

Naris sat down in a chair across from her. He looked intently at her, running his hand along his short beard. They both felt the heaviness in the air; the weight of it made simply sitting together a struggle, let alone speaking.

"I'm sorry for what happened," Naris finally said. "I just wanted you to know that I would never do something like that to you."

He knew exactly what she feared. But his words couldn't make that fear go away.

Naris continued. "Because I don't think of you in the same way."

There still wasn't an answer required of her. She only sipped at her water.

"I know what I'm asking from you is...unheard of, Yonah." His gaze turned to his hands. "But what I feel is unheard of, too."

This would be a repeat of their conversation a few nights before, but Yonah had learned her lesson. She wouldn't be sharp with him. She would be gracious. She would keep him pleased. She would protect herself. Still, she could remain silent.

He looked up at her again. "I don't think of you as my slave. I think of you as my friend. And I don't want you to think of me as your master." He paused. "Am I your friend?"

She reminded herself to be cautious. "In a way." Naris waited for her to say more. "I've enjoyed learning chess with you. They make the evenings pleasant."

He relaxed a little. "I would never hurt my friend, Yonah. So, I would never hurt you. Do you believe me?"

He refused to see the world for what it was. As much as he wanted to claim they were friends, she was a slave and he was her master.

"I believe you believe that," Yonah said.

"Then how can I convince you?"

Now it was Yonah's turn to shift her eyes away. "You can't."

"Surely I can persuade you."

Yonah wrapped her fingers around her collar and looked pointedly at Naris. He pressed his lips together, as if trapping whatever it was he wanted to say inside his mouth. He stood.

"Perhaps this would be a good first step." He walked over to the table where there sat a package. He must have brought it in when he first arrived. Now he opened the package and revealed Yonah's old clothes – the travel coat and her beautiful blue dress. Naris looked pleased with himself. Yonah's reaction must have seemed underwhelming to him because he said, "Your favourites! They're yours again!"

Yonah stood. "Thank you." She was happy to see her favourite garments again. They made her feel like herself, more than any of the other clothes Naris had picked out for her. She reached for them so she could put them away.

Naris held them just out of her reach. "Does it help?" he asked.

She was standing unusually close to him, which made her feel uneasy. She knew he wasn't obliged to return the dress and the coat to her. He was her master. But the fact that he worked so hard, although with trouble, to please her was touching. "Yes," she said, not sure if she was lying or not.

Slowly, Naris place his finger underneath Yonah's chin and turned her face up towards his. Yonah's heart started to pound in her chest. She could feel it throbbing in her ears. Naris' face was coming closer to hers. She had to remind herself to close her eyes. She wondered if he would feel her lip trembling.

His lips pressed against hers. She had to think hard to make herself kiss back, as she was still in shock by what had happened downstairs.

Naris pulled away. "Are you alright?"

She only nodded quickly.

"Are you afraid?"

"A little."

He smiled softly. "You don't need to be. I would never hurt you."

Visions of the horrific scene downstairs came back to Yonah. At the same time, Naris returned to kissing her. The woman's screams. Naris' still face. He reached for her hands and placed one on his chest and one around his waist. The wine pourer's hands dripping with blood, spattering the mosaic beneath her. Naris' hands were in her hair and on her hip. She wished she were more covered up. The woman had looked so broken after it was all done, it hurt Yonah to watch. But this was why she was here, to please Naris. She had to be strong through this. She had to convince him that she would be his companion. He gave her opportunities that she would have no where else as a slave. That poor woman's hands. Yonah wondered if she would be able to work again. She trembled in fear at how easy it was for Naris to switch from his charming self to a cold monster. When would he hurt her?

She opened her eyes suddenly as she felt a tear fall from each of them. She rushed to wipe one of the wet trails away from her face, hoping Naris wouldn't notice. He pulled away from Yonah and saw the remaining tear line.

They were still, their hands still on one another. Yonah waited tensely for Naris' reaction. He watched her tear drip off her jaw to her collar bone. She swore his eyes rested on her slave collar.

"Goodnight, Yonah," he said. "Get well." He turned and left Yonah alone in her room.

She stood there for a moment, waiting to see if the danger was really gone. Then, with one sharp exhale, she stooped and cried. She didn't believe she had any more power within her to maintain control of herself.

Yonah sat down on her chair again and waited for her crying to subside. She had never felt so confused and alone as she did now.

The bedroom door burst open and Naris strode back in again.

"Have I been unkind to you? Have I ever hurt you?" He was restless, his voice louder than necessary. His shadow loomed in the doorway. "What reason do you have to be afraid of me? You yourself told me that we're on friendly terms. And you knew that I was expecting you to be my companion. You can't have thought that I would never want something physical from you." He paused and panted. The frustration that had driven him back here was waning to a quiet confusion. "So, what is the problem? Speak!"

Yonah flinched at his barked order. "I know something physical would be expected of me. I'm sorry for...ruining it. It won't happen again." She didn't have any fight in her for the time being. She just wanted to sleep and dream of some other life where there was no threat of corporal punishment and no solitude from any real friendship.

"And how will you make sure?" Naris said.

"The same as any other girl I suppose." Yonah remembered Lari's advice from the first night she and Naris met. She had said to think of happy things.

Naris' brow furrowed at that. He stared at Yonah for a time, taking in her sad and cold face. While she had feared the emptiness of emotion from his face only minutes ago, now he thought she was the one who was beginning to look emotionless.

"You are to spend all of your evenings with me, whether or not I call for you. We will eat in the usual spot."

Yonah's gaze had drifted downward. She nodded to show she had heard Naris.

"And you are not to speak to that man in the vineyard again."

The near snuffed-out embers in Yonah's chest flickered into a small, painful flame. "What?" she breathed, staring up at him.

"If I see you two talking, he will be punished."

"That's not fair." Her voice trembled angrily.

"What's not fair is I have been nothing but kind to you and you repay me by flirting with another man!"

"Flirting!" was all Yonah could sputter in her shock and anger.

"Yes, flirting! You are mine, Yonah!" Naris stood in front of her and leaned over so he was shouting into her face. "We could have something special! I treat you like a queen, better than any other girl I've met. Because you're special! But you're not respecting that. You treat me terribly."

Yonah's lip was trembling. She tried not to shrivel away from Naris' angry face. As much as she wanted to scream at him just how truly terrible he was, fear kept her quiet.

Naris looked deeply into her eyes, trying to puzzle out what she was thinking. Yonah saw the struggle on his face, and the desperation.

He stood up straight. "You will not speak to him again. Understood?"

She dropped her head in defeat. "Yes, Master."

"And you are not to call me that!" he said sharply. He contained himself before adding, "You will call me Naris."

Yonah didn't answer.

"Goodnight, then," Naris said. He stood in the doorway for what seemed a long time. "You may go to Kirash tomorrow if you like. I know you haven't been there in a few days." Yonah didn't address him. "I hope you can eventually forgive me, Yonah."

The room was plunged into a sorrowful silence that made a chasm between the two lonely souls that inhabited it.

Naris was about to leave when Yonah finally said, "If you were me, and I were you, would you forgive me?"

This time Naris was the silent one.

Chapter Fourteen

Yonah didn't sleep much that night. Her mind raced from her brother and sister to the wine pourer's bleeding hands, to Naris' monstrous face. Her stomach contorted throughout the night, writhing away from the passing moon and any light it shed.

When night was finally starting to fade and the dim white light that filled Yonah's room had gone blue-grey, she dragged herself out of her bed and dressed in her travel clothes. They were freshly laundered. Yonah took a moment to feel the fabric caressing her arms and legs, all the way down to her wrists and ankles. She filled her coat pockets with some of the necklaces, rings, and bracelets Naris had given her and left her room.

The palace seemed quiet, although Yonah knew that downstairs in the slaves' quarters there was much activity. There were chores to be done, breakfasts to be cooked, preparations to be made. Yonah bypassed all the activity and walked straight out the front doors of the palace.

Not even the slaves who tended to the vineyard were out yet. The walk down the lane through the bushes was somewhat eerie with nobody around, although Yonah was grateful to not be disturbed on her walk. She could take in the beauty around her and dispel any thoughts about the previous evening. The only good that had come out of it was that Naris had granted her permission to go to Kirash and she wasn't foolish enough to miss out on that opportunity. Being away from Vaha felt like times gone by.

By the time Yonah arrived at Kirash, the town was beginning to wake up. The energy in town felt crisp and buzzy. Everything felt fresh and brand new.

Yonah marched to the west end of town to The White Stallion, the pub where she had met the barmaid Meerha. From there she turned south as per Meerha's directions.

As Yonah walked, the stalls petered out, giving way to residential buildings. There were fewer adults and more children playing in the street. Dogs barked and played emphatically with whoever they could find. Elderly men and women sat on stoops with their curved backs arching into the sky. Yonah didn't see any other slaves in this area of the town. It was quiet and calm compared to the bustling main street.

She figured she had been walking for twenty or thirty minutes when she finally came upon a square. At the centre of it was a large well. Stalls were spaced along the perimeter. A row of trees had been planted along one side of the square, creating a length of shade beneath the already hot sun. The square wasn't nearly as busy as the main thoroughfare that Yonah spent most of her time on. It was populated mostly by, Yonah assumed, locals to the area who didn't want to go all the way to the main street. The stalls here lacked the frivolity and luxuriousness that the ones on the main road had, selling mostly food, home goods, and more practical clothing than what Yonah generally wore.

Across the square, Yonah spotted the stall she had been directed to. There was a woman, her neck free of a collar, standing behind a table that was scattered with candles in a variety of sizes and colours. Yonah strode straight across the square, veering only to avoid the fountain, until she stood in front of the woman.

"How can I help?" The woman looked old enough to be her mother. Her deep brown hair along the sides of her head had been twisted and pinned up before it was pulled back into a low bun. Her lips were painted a bright red and her eyes rimmed with black. Her features were sharp – her cheekbones, nose, and chin. She wore black linen pants and a plain white tunic, but her body was laced with rings, bracelets, and necklaces.

Yonah remembered Meerha's instructions and said, "The sand burns my feet at night, but candles keep me warm during the day."

Without missing a beat, the woman asked, "Who sent you?"

"Meerha."

The woman chuckled. "Of course, she did. Are you with the cause, then?"

"You mean the rebellion?"

"Hush!" the woman hissed. Her eyes shot from side to side, glancing around the square. "Never say that word in public."

Yonah inwardly berated herself for being so tactless. "I'm sorry. I'm not."

The woman looked Yonah up and down. "If you're not with the cause, then what do you want?"

"Meerha said you would be able to exchange some goods for lotions and creams."

The woman shook her head with a small smirk. "That girl knows how to get her way. I can help. What do you have to trade?"

Yonah withdrew a handful of rings from one of her coat pockets and held them out for the woman to see. The woman picked one up and held it up to her eye.

"Does your master know about this?"

"I don't believe that's any of your business," Yonah replied, trying to sound more confident than she felt.

The woman eyed Yonah carefully. "Why aren't you with the cause? I would have thought you'd be all for it what with your situation." She nodded at Yonah's collar.

With the events of the previous night still flashing through her mind, Yonah wondered briefly if she shouldn't try to make a difference. "I'm just trying to find my brother."

The woman's eyebrows rose. "Alright, come inside. But you breathe a word of this to anybody and there will be trouble."

"How will you manage that?" Yonah's curiosity got the better of her.

The woman had her hand pressed against the door to the building behind her as she said, "You might not be with the cause, but I am, and we have eyes and ears everywhere."

The woman led Yonah into the house. They were in a dark hallway. At the end of the hallway was a kitchen with a table and two chairs. A man sat at the table, reading a flyer. He looked up when the woman and Yonah entered the kitchen, covering the flyer with his hand.

"Meerha sent her," the woman explained. "She's not with the cause."

"I'll go mind the stall," the man said, tucking the flyer into his pocket as he stood up and walked out front.

"Off the rug," the woman said to Yonah. Yonah pressed herself against the wall and the woman folded the rug over, revealing a trapdoor in the floor. She grabbed the latch and pulled it open. There was a ladder leading downwards into darkness.

The woman took a lantern from a nearby hook and said, "Down you go."

Yonah peered down. She couldn't see a thing. "You're not going to lock me in there, are you?"

The woman looked at Yonah with disbelief. "Why would I do that?"

Yonah lowered herself onto the ladder and climbed down into the cellar. It was cool. As the woman followed her with the light, its golden glow slowly illuminated the room.

It was packed with shelves and trunks, some of which were open to reveal a variety of goods: jewelry, fabric, clothing, blankets, cookware, dishes, paintings, books. One corner was piled with furniture. Everywhere Yonah looked there was stuff piled on stuff tucked into more stuff.

The woman walked over to one shelf and read the labels on some bottles. She picked up a few and turned to Yonah. "I think Meerha will appreciate these. Now, what do you propose is a fair trade for this?"

Yonah eyed the bottles and held out two bracelets to the woman. The woman looked at the bracelets.

"One ring, too, I think," she said.

Yonah added a ring to the pile.

"Make it another."

Yonah hesitated. This woman seemed like a decent human being. She had already let Yonah know that she was involved with the rebellion, a secret she wouldn't want just anybody knowing. She seemed to treat Yonah as an equal. "I don't think that's fair," Yonah said.

"Alright, alright. It's a deal."

They exchanged their goods and began to head back up to the main floor.

"Can I ask why you have all of this stuff?" Yonah said.

"For occasions such as this," the woman answered. "And if I'm in a spot of trouble, I can sell something."

Yonah decided it was a solid business.

They climbed back up to the kitchen on the main floor. The woman closed the trapdoor and reset the rug over it.

"You can tell Meerha I say hello," she said. "As for you, good luck with whatever it is you're trying to do. Stay out of trouble."

"Thank you for your help." Yonah stood there awkwardly, trying to formulate her next sentence.

The woman raised her eyebrows at Yonah with an impatient look.

Yonah said, "Is Meerha with the cause?"

The woman pursed her lips. "That's something you'll have to ask Meerha about."

It seemed she had stumbled upon a well-established rebellion group. Yonah had so many questions about what they did, how they planned to change things. But she was afraid to ask.

She politely thanked the woman once more, then left.

ARMED WITH THE SKINCARE products, Yonah found her way back to The White Stallion. She sat down at a table in the back and waited patiently for Meerha to come to her.

"So, you found my contacts alright?" Meerha said, stepping up to the table.

Yonah nodded. "And I brought you some things." She subtly handed Meerha a small jar.

"Lovely. I haven't seen your brother around here." She pocketed the jar. "But I have a friend who's a musician at The Nine Tails in Basee. He's coming to visit me soon, so I'll pass along your brother's description to him."

"Thank you," Yonah said. It wasn't much, but it was something. She felt helpless at this point. All she could do was wait. But for how long? She didn't even know if Obi was still a sailor or if he had been shuffled off to some other part of the world.

With her questions still tugging at her mind, Yonah asked Meerha in a hushed tone, "Are you with the cause?"

A playful smirk crossed Meerha's lips. "Now, why should I answer that when you've already told me that you're not?"

"Because…" Yonah hesitated. Her father had been a protester of the slave trade from the very beginning. She was proud of that. It had also gotten him killed. "Because I might be changing my mind?"

Meerha said kindly, "'Might be' isn't a very compelling argument."

"I want to find my brother and sister," Yonah said. "But I'm also so angry at all the things we go through because of the slavery act. My master—" she cut herself off. She didn't know who was listening.

Meerha leaned close to Yonah and said in a quiet voice, "Does your master hurt you?"

Yonah felt ashamed as she said it. "Not yet."

"Well, maybe when he does, you'll finally know if you've changed your mind or not."

ON HER WAY BACK TO THE house, as she walked through the vineyard, Yonah caught sight of Bana working. She stopped walking, praying he wouldn't see her. After having watched Naris do what he did to the wine pourer, Yonah was certain something truly terrible would happen to Bana if she didn't stay away from him.

As stealthily as she could, Yonah eased her way under a section of the vine and crawled into the next row. Knowing she would be walking right past him, albeit with an entire bush between them, Yonah tried to make no noise as she walked towards the house.

She was at the end of the vineyard and about to make a mad dash for the door when Bana popped out from the other side of the vine and said, "Boo!"

Yonah shrieked and covered her mouth. He must have snuck alongside her the whole time. And she thought she had been so stealthy.

"What are you up to?" Bana asked, playfully.

"Nothing. I have to go." She rushed past without looking at him. She glanced up at the windows of the house, but she didn't see Naris' face.

Chapter Fifteen

Spending time in the vineyard was out of the question, as Yonah didn't want to get Bana in trouble. She didn't particularly want to run into Naris during the day, so she stayed away from his office. She wished she could get into the library, but it remained locked.

Yonah took to exploring the estate just beyond the edges of the vineyard. Those small adventures took her back to Naris' childhood treehouse and eventually to the stable.

The stable was a calm place filled with hay, the thick smell of horse feces, and the relaxed snorting of the horses themselves.

Yonah stepped gingerly inside. A man with a limp rounded the corner at the far end of the long building, carrying a bucket in each hand.

"Can I help you?" he said. He was middle-aged. Soft wrinkles lined his forehead and framed his brown eyes. He wore a slave collar.

"I'm just exploring," Yonah answered. "If that's alright."

He shrugged. "You know much about horses?"

"No."

"Just make sure you stay to the middle here, so none of them kick you."

Yonah stared up at the thickly muscled backsides of the horses, then looked at their metal-clad hooves.

"You must be the master's companion," the stable hand said. "The one they call Pet."

"It's Yonah." She tried to restrain the annoyance that was tingeing her voice.

"Well, I'm Seidon."

"It's nice to meet you," she said. She walked deeper into the building.

The stablemaster looked at Yonah. "You want to meet them?"

"The horses?"

Seidon chuckled. "I'll introduce you."

He walked Yonah through the stable, teaching her the name of each horse and explaining their individual characteristics.

"You can pet them, if you like," he said, already running his hand along one.

Yonah drew her hand upwards and gently placed it on the horse. Its skin flickered briefly at her touch. She smiled as she ran her hand slowly top to bottom.

"If you have time, come visit me and I'll teach you how to look after them."

She smiled at the thought, then asked, "Does the master come out here much?"

"Never. He always sends a slave ahead to grab his horse. Or I take it directly to him."

"Good." The word blurted out of Yonah's mouth without her really thinking about it.

Seidon gave Yonah a sideways glance. "You trying to avoid the master?"

Keeping her eyes on the horse as she ran her hand across its flank, Yonah answered, "We got into an argument. So, I guess so. But I have to spend each evening with him anyway." And if he found out she was spending time with the stable master he might forbid her from going there, too.

All her expectations of who Naris was had been turned upside down. He had been a gentleman to her, kind and encouraging. But that night, he had revealed himself to be something not so benevolent as he tried to make himself out to be.

Seidon didn't pry when Yonah gave no further explanation as to why she was hiding in the stable. Instead he said, "Well, it's just fine if you come out here when you need to."

Yonah gave him a smile. "Thank you."

AS YONAH WAS WALKING back into the palace, she saw Naris walking along the floating balcony at a fast pace. She froze in the doorway and stayed silent as he walked above her, hoping he would bypass her altogether. Naris turned his head and saw Yonah standing on the ground floor of the entrance hall.

"Yonah, I've been looking for you."

Her heart sank at his noticing her. "How can I help?"

As he came down the stairs, Naris said, "I couldn't work. I couldn't focus. I was thinking about you." He came to a stop right in front of her. "I know you're still upset with me and I want to make things right between us again. How can I do that? What would you like?"

"You mean, besides letting me visit with Bana again," Yonah said in a cool tone.

She could see Naris fought with himself to keep his facial expression pleasant. "Yes. Besides that."

Yonah's eyes shifted to the end of the floating balcony where the doors to the library lay.

"You can let me into the library," she said.

Naris furrowed his brows. "That would make things right between us?"

She couldn't be sure of that, but it was what she most wanted from Naris at this moment. "Yes."

They walked side by side up the stairs and along the balcony to the library doors. Naris withdrew a ring of only a few keys from his pocket and used one beautifully ornate one to open the library doors. He pushed them open and let Yonah step inside first.

She gasped upon her entry. Her father had described the libraries he had seen in his travels around Harasa; they were massive, with large shelves lining the walls, some with intricate carvings, some dark and impressive, others brightly lit with beautiful windows. This library, while tucked away in a private corner of the house, was luxurious. It was lit from a sky light that encompassed the whole ceiling. There was a reading area in the centre of the room outfitted with sheer canopies for shade. The wall across from her was covered in portraits of stern-looking men and women and families. The balcony Yonah and Naris had entered the library through wrapped around both sides of the room, stopping just short of the portrait wall. There were raised walkways for access to the free-standing shelves. Two sets of stairs led down to the main floor of the library right next to Yonah as well.

Yonah took her time to walk around the circumference of the library on the balcony – all while Naris watched her – before walking down the stairs and standing in front of the portrait wall.

They were the previous owners of Vaha – Naris' ancestors. She didn't even remember who her grandparents were, let alone their grandparents. Here, Naris' whole history was laid out before her.

"Can you guess which one is mine?" Naris asked. He had followed Yonah down the stairs and stood a few metres behind her.

Yonah scanned the wall. There were individuals and families staring stoically at her. Some were on horseback. One was surrounded by the greenery of the vineyard. Yonah finally found one painting of a man and a woman with a young boy between them. The man and woman stood with their necks long and their chins tilted upwards. The boy – probably around seven years old – seemed small between them. Yonah was sure the boy was Naris.

"This one?" she said.

"Very good," he said dryly as he stepped next to her. His eyes were on the portrait. "I remember that day. I couldn't sit still for so long. I wanted to go play. My mother scolded me all morning and finally my father hit me so hard it left a mark on my cheek. He told the artist to be sure to leave the mark out of the portrait." His eyes were hard as he looked up at the image of his family. "I have to give the artist credit; there's no visible mark. And we look like the perfect family."

"But you carry scars from that day."

Naris turned his eyes to rest on Yonah. "What do you mean?"

She boldly returned his stare. "You remember that day clearly even though it was so long ago and you were so young. It must have left quite an impression on you. Just like my worst days have left an impression on me."

They both looked back up at the portrait. Yonah thought his parents looked very stern and very proud in their portrait. Their expressions did not make Yonah want to meet the real people.

"We all carry our pasts with us, don't we?" Naris asked.

"I think so. I do, anyways."

"As do I. Maybe we can help each other with the burden."

And, somehow, through some strange magic she could not understand, Yonah found herself empathizing with Naris, wishing she could somehow aid him, wanting to be a shoulder to lean on, an ear to listen, a heart to share in love. She tried to shove the feeling aside and held her eyes on the portrait wall.

"Has your family always owned this place?"

"We know that my great-great-great grandfather owned the land." Naris pointed to a portrait closer to the ceiling that depicted a man, though not with the same skill as the more recent portraits. "His son started developing the vineyard, although it didn't start to flourish until his daughter, my great-grandmother was in charge. She's also the one who led the construction of this palace."

"A woman's touch," Yonah said jokingly. She stood in awe of the history before her. "Are all the estates so old?"

"Some are younger. And some are older."

"And have masters always been close like they are these days?"

Naris furrowed his brow. "I don't think 'close' would be the right way to describe it. I think some of the estate holders wanted to show off their wealth or prove their worth to others. Any of my family's interaction with other estates has always been for the business, except for Kejal's family. I think our great-grandfathers were friends much like we are."

"And how did your family decide to take on slaves? You would have had paid workers before the slavery act."

Naris paused as he considered his answer. "Well, my parents have always been very shrewd. The opportunity to take on slaves and ultimately save them money would have been too good to pass up in their eyes."

And in your eyes, too, Yonah thought.

"But, from what I picked up when I was younger," Naris continued slowly, "declining the use of slaves altogether wasn't really an option for the estate holders. I'm not sure if I remember correctly, but I think I recall my father telling my mother once that someone had been arrested for refusing to take on slaves and openly speaking against the slavery act. I can't be sure."

It cast a slightly different light on the whole system. If the upper class were threatened with imprisonment for not participating in the slavery system, then undoing the act would be much harder than anyone ever expected.

"It's strange how the slavery act is only ten years old," Naris muttered thoughtfully, "but its system is already so engrained in our society."

"It didn't take long for people to take advantage of it."

"You'll be free of it soon, won't you?" Naris said. He looked earnestly at Yonah.

"I turn twenty soon," she replied. Then she would be freed from her bondage and able to live her life on her own terms, able to find Sayzia and Obi.

"Maybe, once you are free," Naris said, "you'll feel differently about staying here with me."

Maybe. If she were free, if they were equals, if Naris treated her thusly, she would be tempted to stay. But she couldn't. She had plans. She and her siblings would be together again, just like the old days.

She didn't want to raise his hopes too high, but she did want to keep him happy with her for the time being, so Yonah said coyly, "I guess we'll have to see how nice you are to me in the meantime."

The side of Naris' mouth turned upward, but his eyes didn't match its uplifted expression.

"Is this all you wanted to see?" he asked. "Or were you hoping to read everything in here?"

"I'd like to read *some* things in here," Yonah said.

"What are you going to read?"

She wanted to learn about the history of estates and their owners. She wanted to learn everything she could about Sayzia and Obi's potential masters. She wanted to read up on slavery laws to see if there was a way she could free them or buy them once she was free. "Whatever I feel like," she said. "I could save you some trouble if you lent me your key to the library. Then I wouldn't have to ask you every time I wanted to come here."

"But that's no trouble," Naris said. "In fact, I would like that very much."

He stepped close to Yonah so that she could feel the warmth of his body against her. "I'll hold on to this key, so you have to come visit me during the day."

His closeness both thrilled and aggravated Yonah.

"If that's what you wish," she said, trying to keep her voice light.

"Don't you want to see me more? I did what you wanted. Now things are right between us."

"You did," Yonah replied. Whether things were 'right' between them, she couldn't say.

.

Chapter Sixteen

She asked Naris for permission to go to Kirash the following day. Once that was gained, Yonah started the long walk through the vineyard to the road at the edge of the estate.

Her eyes were taking in the greenery around her when someone touched her shoulder and said, "Yonah."

She cried out in surprise and jumped. Bana was standing next to her, smiling slightly.

"Sorry I scared you," he said. "Are you off to town again?"

Naris didn't want her talking to Bana anymore. Fearing what sort of punishment there would be for that violation, Yonah replied, "Yes," then walked at a brisk pace towards the road.

Bana started after her. "Hold on, what's your hurry?"

"I can't talk to you." Yonah didn't even look over her shoulder to say the words. She felt horrible for saying it, but it was for Bana's own good.

"Why not? Yonah."

But she ignored him, walking steadily along down the path. A hollowness spread through her chest as she walked farther and farther away from Bana.

The closer she got to Kirash, the easier it was to set the hollow feeling aside and focus on the task at hand. She let her eyes wander over the shops and the people as she went down the main street. The White Stallion came into view and Yonah picked up her pace.

She stepped into the dining hall and found an empty table. A minute later, Meerha sauntered over to Yonah and placed a cup of wine in front of her.

"Thanks, but I don't want any," Yonah said.

"Don't drink it, then, but I have to make it look like you're a customer. My contact hasn't seen your brother, but it's only been a short while. If he's still a sailor, he'll stop by Basee sometime."

Yonah's heart sank. A wasted trip to town. "You're sure your contact knows who to look for?"

"I described him exactly like you told me," Meerha said. "Yonah. Don't worry. We'll keep looking."

Yonah suddenly reached for the cup of wine and took three large gulps.

"You gonna pay for that?" Meerha said.

She only had four ora left from the amount Naris had given her for the dress maker. Yonah pressed one coin onto the tabletop. Now she had three. "How long have you been enslaved?"

Meerha took the coin and placed it into her pants pocket. "A couple years. My parents tried to keep me hidden from the Guard." She held up her fingerless hand. "I was born like this. But I got a little stir-crazy one day and went out without them knowing. The Guard caught me and here I am. It's so backwards. When I was free, I was a hindrance to society, but, now that I'm enslaved, I'm not. My hand hasn't changed."

"I'm sorry," Yonah said.

"For what?" Meerha's voice was calm and steely.

Yonah didn't know what to say. Meerha leaned forward, so she could speak softer.

"You just have to wait out your sentence, don't you? Turn twenty or do your time and then things are back to the way they were. But I'm stuck like this until the day I die. Unless *everyone* helps to change things."

Yonah's skin burned with shame as she said it. "Rebels are enslaved for life, too."

"Enslaved rebels need help, too."

Even though Yonah's fingers were still around the half-full cup of wine, Meerha snatched it from her hands and walked away. Yonah accepted the dismissal and left the noisy hall.

She was so close to freedom. It would be foolish to risk that freedom by joining the rebellion. But to bide her time and carry on with her own life wasn't the moral thing to do. Meerha was right. Everybody who was enslaved deserved to live a good life, and they needed everyone to stand up for that.

The chance of the rebellion, the abolition of the slavery act, the removal of Althu from the government might not happen in the next few years or even in Yonah's lifetime. That was what made her hesitate. She could risk a lifetime of enslavement or be with Sayzia and Obi again.

She felt a tug at her pants and Yonah looked down. A young boy whose wide-eyed stare and messy hair reminded her so much of Obi was staring up at her. There was a slave collar around his tiny neck.

"Where did you come from?" Yonah asked. She glanced around the street to see if there was an adult looking for the boy.

His lip trembled. "I'm lost."

Yonah knelt in front of the boy. "Are you with a grown-up?"

He nodded. "My Da."

"I'll help you find him." Yonah noticed the red sashes of the Guard in the crowd. They didn't notice the pair of them. "Are you supposed to be here? Or are we playing hide and seek?"

"Hide and seek."

Yonah's heartbeat quickened. Her palms started to sweat. "Okay," she breathed, trying to keep herself calm. "I'm Yonah. What's your name?"

"Ibo."

"Okay, Ibo. Which way were you going?"

"We came from back there." Ibo pointed down the main street. "We were going that way."

Yonah looked in the direction he pointed and saw a Guard walking at an easy pace towards them.

Pretending she hadn't seen the Guard, Yonah stood, taking Ibo's hand, and started walking him down the street, away from the oncoming Guard.

"Ibo, is there a Guard following us?"

The child took a moment to look over his shoulder. "Yes."

It was as if the whole of her insides were shaking. If this child was a runaway, she would certainly face terrible consequences if they were caught.

She slipped into a stall and led Ibo through the maze of tables and tent covers. They went past clothing and jewelry and food and flowers. Yonah looked over her shoulder and her eyes met with the Guard's. He nodded to her in acknowledgment and picked up his pace as he walked over to her.

Yonah tried to contain her panic as the Guard stepped next to her.

"Are you two from town?" the Guard asked. He wasn't much older than Yonah.

"A little beyond town," Yonah replied, fighting hard to hold her face in a neutral position. She wasn't doing anything wrong. She had to keep telling herself that so she would believe it. "I'm running an errand for the kitchen maid and the stable master told me to take his apprentice for a change of pace." Yonah nodded towards Ibo.

The Guard bent over and looked at the boy. "You're a stable master's apprentice, eh?"

"Yes, sir," Ibo said with a nod. Triumph ballooned through Yonah at the child's intelligence to keep up with the lie.

"You like horses, then?"

Ibo nodded again.

The Guard stood upright and said to Yonah, "Have I seen you around here before?"

She shrugged, a nonchalant move that covered for her panic. "Maybe. But I'm not here very often."

He looked between Yonah and Ibo once more. "Carry on, then."

Yonah watched him walk away, her breath caught in her throat. She eventually exhaled and turned her head to look down unseeingly at a pair of shoes on a nearby table.

"He's gone," Ibo said.

"Good." Yonah looked up again. She couldn't see any red sashes. "Good."

"Ibo," said a calm and deep voice.

Both Yonah and Ibo turned around. The man who lived with the candle seller stood in front of them. His lips curled into a proud smile. "Your father will be glad to see you." His eyes flickered to Yonah. "That was well handled. I thought you were going to run for a moment."

"You were watching?"

"I noticed you at the same time that Guard did." He stepped closer to Yonah, so he could speak without being overheard. "You've just helped this boy on his journey to freedom. He and his father are going south to Modeef."

Yonah was both frozen in fear at what might have happened if the Guard had persisted with his questions and alight with intrigue at what this man had just revealed to her.

"Why are you telling me this?"

"In case you would like to help more slaves."

She wanted to help more slaves. She wanted to help herself. She wanted to help Sayzia and Obi. Joining this movement would risk her chance at a happy reunion with her brother and sister.

"Modeef is very far," Yonah said, instead of providing an answer.

"It's the only place on the continent where slavery is outlawed."

Yonah shifted her gaze to Ibo, then dropped her eyes down to her feet.

"Well," the man said, shifting his weight in preparation to leave, "you know where to find us." He turned to leave, taking Ibo's hand. "Nobody else knows about today's mission," he added. Yonah met his hard gaze. "We'll know if you tell anyone about this." Then he left. Yonah watched them go, then briskly started her return to Vaha.

"AND WHAT IS YOUR FAVOURITE room in the house?" Naris asked her that night. They were playing a game of chess in his bedroom.

Her thoughts were on Ibo and the candle seller's husband. At Naris' question, Yonah shifted her mind to the palace.

She wasn't sure she had a favourite room. Yonah was inclined to say the library was her favourite, but she didn't want to draw any more attention to her presence there than necessary. She didn't want to mention the stable, as she wanted that to remain a safe space away from Naris. If she were in the house, she honestly preferred sitting on her balcony where it was quiet and she could breathe in the fresh air, but Yonah didn't think Naris would appreciate that answer, so she said, "The great hall. I especially like the paintings on the ceilings." There was some truth to that answer.

Naris smiled as he sipped his wine. "I haven't taken a good look at those in a long time. When I was younger, I liked to lie on the floor and stare up at them, imagining stories for the pictures."

"They don't have their own stories?"

"Oh, they do," Naris said. "But sometimes it's nice to write things your own way."

Yonah moved her bishop. "Check."

Naris smiled and easily moved another piece to remove her bishop from the board. "Do you not know the stories that belong to those paintings?"

She looked at the board with disappointment. She thought she had done a good job with that move. "I don't think so."

"Why don't I tell you them, then?" Naris stood up.

Yonah looked up at him. "Right now?"

"Yes!"

"It's dark. We won't be able to see them."

"Don't worry. I have my ways," Naris said, playfully. "Come."

He led her to the great hall. Yonah could see the outlines of the swooping artwork on the floor from the candle Naris carried, but when she looked up at the ceiling, all she could see was darkness.

"Wait here," Naris said, and disappeared, taking the candle with him.

Alone in the cave-like hall, Yonah couldn't help but let her imagination wander to monsters and ghosts hiding in the shadows. She looked up at the ceiling, remembering the beasts the artwork depicted.

Suddenly, there was a loud clang and the shutters to four large windows near the top of the walls opened. Moonlight flooded through the windows and began bouncing off several large mirrors that also hung on the walls, which illuminated the upper portion of the hall, casting a white glow on the paintings above. Yonah gasped at the beauty and the ingeniousness of the lighting process. It was as if the night sky had been brought inside.

Naris returned and triumphantly said, "There."

"That was amazing," Yonah breathed.

He smirked. "It puts on a good show. Now, what story would you like to hear?"

Yonah stepped further into the hall to examine the paintings. She saw the bear and the whale, the horseback riders, the magical woman on the cliff. And she saw two women holding each other in their arms, chaos swirling around them.

"Who are those two women?"

Naris stepped next to her. "That's Alib and Bria. They were two sisters who lived happily with their family on a farm. One day, pirates came and destroyed their farm and took the sisters. They were quickly separated, but each of them swore that they would find the other. Alib became an apprentice to a sorcerer and Bria herself became a pirate. The two of them searched the world for the other. Alib heard about a pirate ship captained by a woman, and Bria heard about a sorcerer's apprentice. Eventually, they came across each other in the middle of a market and they ran away together. When the sorcerer found out Alib had run away, he used his magic to find out where she was and sent stormy weather and bad luck after the sisters. Alib tried to fight the sorcerer's magic with her own, but she wasn't as skilled or as experienced as him. She said goodbye to her sister and let the sorcerer's magic carry her back to him. Bria tried to find her sister again, but the sorcerer had cast a spell on Alib so she would always be invisible to Bria, even if she were standing right next to her. While the sisters were never truly united, Alib often tried to see Bria in person and would send signs to her that she was watching over her. Bria saw those signs, and they gave her hope, and she never gave up trying to find Alib."

The painting on the ceiling must have been the moment the two sisters had been found out by the sorcerer, saying one last goodbye to each other. Yonah wished she had had a chance to hug Sayzia and Obi before they had been taken on their three different paths.

"Is that the real story?" Yonah asked.

"Of course. Why do you ask?"

She kept her eyes on the sisters above. "It sounds like my story."

"What do you mean?"

The image of the two women embracing each other so desperately stirred something in Yonah's heart.

"When my siblings and I were separated," Yonah said, "I swore I would

184

find them, too. But I'm no sorcerer or pirate."

"Do you even know where they are?" Naris asked.

"No," she said, coldly. "I haven't seen either of them for years."

This seemed to assuage Naris for now. There was silence between them for a moment. Naris wandered the hall with his neck craned upwards.

"This one is my favourite," he finally said.

Yonah stepped next to him and looked up. They were looking at a depiction of a bear cub facing two snakes that had reared up with fangs bared.

"The bear cub was separated from his mother and as he tried to find her, he ran into two snakes. They tried to trick him into coming home with them by saying they had delicious berries and fish and all the food he could ever want. But the bear cub said no. The snakes told him he would be very happy with them because they would love him more than his mother ever could. But the bear cub said no. Finally, the snakes grew impatient and they wrapped themselves around the bear cub and carried him home with them. The bear cub fought and screamed as loudly as he could, but the snakes managed to take him home to their cave. They reared up and struck him. The bear cub continued to fight back, but he was growing weaker. Suddenly, the bear cub's mother burst into the cave and threw the snakes away from her cub. As she fought one of the snakes, the bear cub attacked the second and together they killed the snakes and the bear cub was safe."

Yonah let the story hang in the air as she stared up at the bear and the snakes. "Are you the bear cub and the snakes your parents?"

Naris stared at Yonah. "What made you think that?"

"Am I wrong?"

He looked back up at the picture. "You know, now that you say it, I think that must have been it all along."

Her curiosity was getting the better of her. "So, who is the mama bear?"

Naris paused at this question, keeping his eyes on the painting. "I think, when I was very young, it was my grandfather. And sometimes it was my friend, Kejal. He's the one that would visit me often. And now, I'm hoping it will be you." He took her hand in his. "It seems to me we're both lonely people, Yonah. Don't you think it would be nice if we could make each other less lonely?"

Her skin prickled where his hand held hers. The prickle ran up her arm and down her torso until it seemed as though her whole body was tingling. She looked up at him in wonder and fear. Without meaning to, Yonah found herself stepping closer to Naris, and he stepped closer to her. Their eyes held firmly to each other, this time not in a battle of wills, but in a tentative dance.

Yonah wasn't sure whether she reached up to Naris, or he leaned down to her, or whether it was a little bit of both, but somehow their lips met. Yonah closed her eyes. Her heart fluttered. She felt one hand run up Naris' arm and her other hand rest on his chest. Naris placed his hands on her hips.

Their bodies were pressed against each other, yet Yonah wanted to get somehow closer. Their kisses grew hungry. Yonah clutched Naris tightly. His hands ran up her sides, past her shoulders, and caught on her collar, jarring her awake.

Yonah pulled her face away from Naris' and looked at him. He drew his hands away from her and they each took a step back. Yonah suddenly wished she was very far away.

The silence was agonizing. Yonah turned her eyes away from Naris' patient face.

"Say something, Yonah," he said.

She didn't know what to say. Her mind was racing with thoughts of happy evenings spent with Naris, his terrible cruelty, her brother and sister, slaves fighting for the rebellion.

"I love you," Naris said.

She felt like she was choking. On what, she didn't know. But there were no words. Nothing she could say would make this moment any better.

"May I go?" she finally gasped.

Naris' face folded into a sad frown. "You don't need to ask that."

Yonah started to back away towards the door. "But I do."

Chapter Seventeen

When Yonah opened her eyes the following morning, she lay in her bed staring up at the ceiling. Last night her chest had felt light, and now it pinned her down to her bed with a weight that wouldn't budge.

It was wrong. It was wrong of her to want more of those kisses, even if they filled her with a strange happiness. Naris was temperamental and violent. He was a master and she was a slave.

And Yonah knew that he at least *thought* he loved her.

She wished she had someone to talk to. First, she wished for her sister, and then for her friends from Master Puru's estate, and then for Bana.

There was one person at least that she could spend some time with, even if they didn't know each other well enough to talk about last night's events.

Just as Yonah was sliding out of the large bed, the slave woman who regularly brought her food came into the room with a tray.

"I told them that you're not the enemy," the woman said. "That you're just lucky the master took a liking to you." She set the tray on the table. "And that starving you really doesn't make anything better."

"Thank you for that," Yonah said, walking over to the table. Fruit and buns. She picked up a pre-cut piece and took a juicy bite that made her roll her eyes with pleasure. "You want some?"

The woman gave Yonah a disapproving look and silently left the room.

Yonah finished eating, then quietly made her way downstairs, feeling more nervous than ever about running into Naris. She went past the library, down the stairs to the main floor, out the back doors to the patio. She kept her eyes peeled for Bana as she walked through the vineyard towards the stable.

As she emerged from the vineyard onto the hill where the stable stood, Yonah exhaled deeply and felt the weight in her chest float away.

She stepped softly into the stable, so as not to startle the horses. It was empty, except for Seidon transferring hay from a wheelbarrow to the stalls with a pitchfork.

"Good morning," she said.

Seidon looked up at her. "Oh! Good morning! Off exploring again today?"

"Actually, I came here to talk to you specifically."

Seidon's eyebrows shifted upward. "Well, why don't you grab that pitchfork there and help me?" He nodded towards the end of the room where several tools rested against the wall.

Yonah walked to the wall and took the second pitchfork in her hand. "What are we doing?"

"Just spread the hay about evenly in all the stalls."

Yonah joined in the work and settled into a rhythm of stabbing the hay and pitching it away. She reveled in the quietness for a while. There was just the sound of hay rustling and the distant whinnying from the horses.

"Do you know Master Naris very well?" she finally asked.

"Not really," Seidon answered. "I've been here for a few years, but I don't really have very much to do with him. He seems quite sad."

"You mean since his parents died?"

Seidon shook his head. "No, he was sad before the fever took them away."

Yonah let that topic hang in the air for a moment before moving on. "Do you like Master Naris?"

An oddly downward-turned smirk showed up on Seidon's face. "He's nice when he's nice. But he has a temper."

Yonah nodded knowingly. "I'm aware."

"Well, you're the one that spends the most time with him," Seidon said. "What do you think of him?"

She rested the tips of the pitchfork on the ground and placed her hands and chin on top of the handle. "I know he's dangerous – because of his temper." She took a breath. "But he's become a friend." It was too much to say the whole truth of it all, that she had feelings for him beyond their friendship.

Seidon placed his elbow on one of the walls separating the stalls. "You consider your master a friend?"

"I know it's foolish."

"And Master Naris, what does he think of you?"

She said it sheepishly. "More than that."

Yonah watched Seidon puzzle over his answer. He said, "And I'm the one you came to talk to about this?"

"There's no one else I can talk to." She started working again, trying to hide her face from the man standing across from her.

He didn't speak for a moment. Yonah was acutely aware that Seidon remained standing, watching her. She wondered if she shouldn't have come to him.

"I'm sorry for wasting your time," she said. "I know it's silly and—"

"It's not silly," Seidon interrupted. "It's actually quite serious."

Yonah paused her work and looked up at him. His fingers were fiddling with each other as he continued to think.

"So, you think of the master more as a friend," Seidon said, thoughtfully. He picked up his knees to walk through the hay and stood next to Yonah. "If these were different times, there'd be a different discussion to be had. But, as it is, you need to be careful."

He looked deeply into Yonah's eyes. "There will come a time when you have to decide whether you choose your friendship with the master, or you choose a harder, but more rewarding, path."

She gulped. "You mean the rebellion?"

"I didn't say anything," Seidon shrugged. "Could be the rebellion, could be something else." He turned and walked back to the stall.

"Are you with the cause?" Yonah blurted.

"I am not." He seemed unperturbed by the question.

"Would you ever join?"

Seidon paused. His lips pursed in thought. "I suppose if the opportunity presented itself to me, I'd have to take it. Seems like the only thing to do." He patted his leg. "They'll never set me free with this limp."

Yonah pondered over his answer. It seemed as though the opportunity to join the rebellion was calling out to her. But to take it would mean defying Naris, and potentially ruining her relative freedom with him that enabled her to search for her brother and sister. She would be twenty soon, finally of age and set free. Joining the rebellion meant risking that freedom. Rebels, if caught, were enslaved for life.

SHE WAS SITTING ON HER bedroom balcony after lunch, watching the vineyard bustle beneath her. While she loved to sit and take in the beauty around her, she wished she were in the palace basement, a comrade among fellow workers.

She was sipping the wine Naris had called Valli after her mother. Much as it pained her to know she had given her mother's name away, the wine made Yonah feel closer to her.

There was a knock at her bedroom door.

"Come in," Yonah called.

She didn't hear the door open. Yonah stood from her seat and peered into her bedroom. It was empty.

"Come in," she called again.

Whoever was outside knocked again.

Yonah walked though the bedroom and opened the door. Naris stood in the hallway with his hands behind his back, wearing a boyish grin.

"Hello," he said brightly. "How was your morning?"

Yonah answered slowly, "It was fine…"

"Good. I'm glad." Naris's chipper demeanor suddenly cooled to uncertainty. Normally he held himself with an air of confidence, even arrogance. Now he seemed flustered. "Look, about last night, I'm not sorry for what I did, and I don't think you are either." He flashed his grin. "I think you like me, too, Yonah."

She stared at him while trying to keep her face impassive.

"But I thought I'd better give you a peace offering to show you how sorry I am for how it turned out," Naris continued. "So, I give you…"

He brought his hands in front of himself to reveal a flat rectangular box made of glass. Parts of the glass were stained black and it was checked in between clear squares.

Yonah gasped when she realized what it was.

"Your own chessboard!" Naris exclaimed. He held it out towards Yonah.

"It's beautiful," she said, taking the box from him. It was really made of two pieces of glass that were attached to a set of hinges. When opened, the box would flatten out into a chess board. Yonah peeked inside the box and found the pieces were tucked into two velvet pouches.

"Do you like it?" Naris asked.

She smiled at him. "Of course, I do. That's very kind of you."

"I went to get it this morning," he said. "And then I did only the most necessary work that had to be done, so I could take you out for the rest of the day."

"Out where?"

"I thought I'd take you out to a place I used to visit as a child." His eyes glimmered. "It'll be much faster if we go by horse."

Yonah held her breath, not wanting to give the answer she knew she was going to give. "Fine."

"Lovely! The horse should be ready for us by now."

Shaking her head, Yonah followed Naris outside to where a single horse was waiting, held in place at the reins by Seidon himself. The man raised an eyebrow at Yonah as Naris mounted the horse. She sheepishly turned her eyes away from him.

"Take my hand," Naris said to her. Yonah did as she was told and she mounted the horse and sat behind Naris.

"We should be back by sunset," he told Seidon, who simply nodded.

"Are you ready?"

Yonah wrapped her arms around Naris' torso and placed the side of her face on his back. Her heart started to pound. "Ready," she said softly.

With a kick, they were off, whizzing away from the palace in a direction Yonah had never gone before. The greenery of the vineyard gave way to the open brown and green plains. The horse broke into a full gallop and Yonah clung on tighter to Naris.

"I've got you!" he shouted. Yonah could barely hear him over the wind rushing past her ears.

Eventually, they slowed. Yonah lifted her head to peek past Naris' shoulder and saw a crevice stretching across the plain into a small canyon.

"Where are we?"

"You'll see. We'll have to walk the rest of the way, though. It's better for the horse."

Naris swung his leg over the horse's head and dropped down to the ground. He turned and held his arms out to Yonah. She lifted her right leg over the horse's backside and began to slide down. She felt Naris grab her sides to help guide her.

Once her feet were on the ground, she turned around and looked nervously up at Naris. "Thank you," she said.

Naris only stared at her. His features were soft and his eyes were searching. Yonah realized she had stopped breathing. Naris nodded once, grabbed the horse reins, and led the way to the canyon.

A wide path led down to the bottom of the canyon, winding around bushes and the odd tree. Yonah and Naris went slowly down the path, trying not to slip on any loose stones.

A sound Yonah had never heard before growing steadily louder as they climbed down. It was steady, full, and powerful, almost like a strong wind.

"What is that?" Yonah asked.

"What's what?"

"That sound."

Naris blinked at Yonah a couple times, and she saw the disbelief on his face. He broke into a smile. "You'll see."

Once at the bottom, they rounded a clump of bushes. Yonah gasped.

It was a waterfall, rushing gloriously down to the canyon. Its white rapids stood in stark contrast to the reddish-brown rocks that surrounded them.

"You've never seen a waterfall before?" Naris asked.

Yonah shook her head. "My father told me about them. He told me we'd go visit one someday."

"You told me your father was going to show you the world. Now that's my job."

Her mouth gaped open at the scene around her. She had seen grand palaces, masters clothed in nothing but the finest jewels, wealth and beauty beyond compare, but none of that matched the splendour of this natural wonder.

Naris gently grabbed her hand. "Come on."

He led her closer to the waterfall, following the stream that flowed from it. As they got closer, Yonah saw there was a pool at the bottom of the waterfall.

"It's actually quite shallow here," Naris said. "Do you know how to swim?"

Yonah shook her head.

"That's fine. Like I said, it's shallow."

He released Yonah's hand and pulled his tunic and shirt over his head, revealing his bare chest. Yonah found herself staring, then turning away, then sneaking another peek.

Naris started laughing and Yonah blushed. When he started removing his pants, Yonah held her hand to her face to shield her eyes.

"I'm not shy, Yonah!" Naris said. Then he was running past her into the water. "You can look now."

She looked up. Naris had fully submerged himself in the pool. "Care for a dip?" he asked. "You can keep your clothes on if you prefer."

Yonah folded her arms across her chest, partly out of playful defiance and partly to try to quell her beating heart. "And what are you expecting out of today?"

Naris smirked at her. "Whatever you like."

Yonah watched him for a moment. Then she looked at the water. How many times had she dreamed of jumping into the pools at Master Puru's palace?

"Don't look," she said, boldly.

Naris made a show of turning around and covering his eyes with one hand.

As fast as she could, Yonah removed her shirt and pants and silently slipped into the water. It was cold at first and she almost gasped. But at the same time, it was one of the most refreshing things she had ever felt. The water came up as high as her chest when she stood. Yonah sank the remaining few inches into the water and smiled.

"Can I look?" Naris said.

"Sorry, yes."

He turned around. "It's nice, isn't it?"

She conceded a nod. "Yes, it is."

"I used to come out here quite a bit when I was younger. My grandfather showed it to me. And Kejal's the only other person I've shown it to. Except you."

"Why haven't you shown anyone else?"

Naris leaned back and popped his toes out of the water. "I didn't want to."

"So, why did you show it to me?"

"Because I thought you'd like it."

Yonah didn't know what to say to that. She just stood there, letting the sound the of the waterfall fill the silence.

Naris swam closer to her. "Do you like it?" he said knowingly.

"Yes, I do. You already know that."

He grinned. "It's nice to hear you say it out loud."

She didn't want to get lost in her emotions again, like she did in the grand hall. She had to stay focused on doing what she could to find her brother and sister.

But there was nothing she could do to find them out here alone with Naris in this beautiful place.

"Tell me about your grandfather," she said.

"You want to talk about my grandfather?" Naris asked with displeasure.

"You don't?"

He started swimming around the circumference of the pool. "I liked him. He was kind to me. I don't know how my father is his son. But he died when I was young."

"Is that why you're sad?"

"Am I sad?"

Yonah didn't want to give away the fact that it was Seidon who suggested Naris had been sad for a long time.

"Is it why you're lonely?" she said instead.

"I was lonely without my grandfather," Naris replied. He found his way back to Yonah. "I'm not lonely when I'm with you."

They looked into each other's eyes. Sometimes she hated how Naris' gaze was constantly boring into her eyes, trying to burrow into her soul.

"I'm not so lonely either," she said suddenly. Slowly, a gentle smile crossed Naris' lips.

He found her hand in the water and whispered, "Come here." He led her around the back of the waterfall. The sound of the falling water pounding into the pool was deafening, but it created a sort of privacy wall that made Yonah feel as though the entire world had suddenly disappeared.

Naris was dumbly smiling at her still.

"What?" she said. She had to call it out to be heard.

"I think you're beautiful."

She felt like she was glowing, but she said, "No, you don't. No one does."

Naris leaned in to say into her ear. "They're all wrong. I'm the only one who really sees you."

Yonah tried to gauge whether he was telling the truth or just trying to get on her good side. The way he looked at her now made her feel light and excited.

Naris whispered in her ear again. "I'd like to kiss you again."

Yonah shrugged. "So, kiss me. That's my job, right?"

He shook his head. "I don't want you to kiss me because you have to." He looked pained. "Yonah, last night was… It meant something because we both wanted it. I know you did."

She watched him. He waited for her response.

"Just a kiss?" she said.

"Whatever you like."

For a moment, she was frozen in an in-between. The water fell next to them, the sun shone brightly, the shade from the rocks above their heads kept them cool, the pool rippled with tiny waves, Naris waited for Yonah's next move with unwavering eyes.

She was a slave and he was her master.

And he loved her, and she knew she felt something for him.

She could just leave when she turned twenty.

Yonah tentatively moved closer to Naris and pressed her lips to his. She felt her chest balloon with pleasure. The kiss was gentle at first, slow but passionate. She brought her hands to his face.

Despite the cool temperature of the water, everything felt warm. Yonah's skin felt like it was burning. She fell closer to Naris and he wrapped his arms around her, holding her bare body next to his. It was perfect and terrifying all at once.

There was nothing beyond the two of them. Nothing beyond their lips reaching for each other and their hands feeling the other's skin. The fear and hurt and anger that Yonah always carried with her melted away into hunger and curiosity. She let her hands explore Naris' body, starting with his curly hair and running down his back.

It was when Naris placed a hand on her breast that Yonah started waking up again.

She pressed away from Naris, so they were no longer touching, wrapping her arms around herself. The world came rushing back to Yonah.

"We don't have to do anymore," Naris said breathlessly.

The silence between them drew longer and longer and Yonah didn't know how to help the situation. They were suspended in a moment of stillness before the chaos of crashing down. Despite the pounding of the waterfall next to her, Yonah could hear her heart beating. She tried to avoid Naris' penetrating look. His look was always trying to pull her outward, trying to take something from her.

"Let's go back. We can break in your new chessboard." He filled in the space between them. "Does that sound alright?"

"Why are you being so nice?"

The playful smirk appeared again. "Because I like you." He started to swim back to the front side of the waterfall. "Now, you don't look when I get out. It's chilly in here."

Once they were dressed, Naris led them back up the canyon. It was a quiet walk. Just before he mounted the horse, he placed a soft kiss on Yonah's cheek that sent her face burning with a mixture of shame and pleasure.

She climbed onto the horse and sat behind Naris.

As they rode back, Yonah rested her head against Naris' back, not seeing the scenery go by, but thinking only about the waterfall and what might have happened there had she not stopped it.

Chapter Eighteen

Excitement thrilled through Yonah as she used the key to open the library door. She couldn't help but smile as she took in the beautiful room once again. It was warm and welcoming, bright and awe-inspiring.

When she had gone to Naris' office to ask for the library key, he had beamed happily at her entrance, which made her heart flutter. She wished his smile didn't have that effect on her.

"What can I do for you?" he had asked.

"I wanted to borrow your key to the library."

"Of course." Naris opened a drawer in his ornate desk and removed the key. As he handed it to Yonah he said, "You'll have to let me know what you read."

Her skin burnt where it met with Naris' hand. "Can I return this to you at dinner?"

Naris nodded. "That's fine. I wish I could join you there."

Yonah gave him a puzzled look. "Join me in reading?"

"I find the reading area beneath the skylight so pleasant." Naris' words drifted off as his eyes glazed over.

Yonah found herself sitting down in the chair on the other side of the desk. "Do you read often?"

"Sometimes. Although I don't think I'm as avid a reader as you."

"I haven't read for a long time," Yonah admitted.

"Well, there are certainly a couple books I can recommend to you if you'd like," Naris said, somewhat sheepishly. "But you should do some of your own exploring first. I'm sure you'll enjoy yourself."

And now, Yonah stood on the balcony overlooking the room teeming with shelves of books, the portrait wall, and the skylit reading area in the centre that Naris loved so much. She was drawn towards the portrait of Naris with his parents. Their cold eyes filled Yonah with a sense of rising tension, as if she were prey turning at the sound of a strange noise.

She started to meander through the shelves, reading titles along the way, getting to the know the organization of the books. She found fiction novels, books on architecture, horticultural texts. In the history section, Yonah found a book called *A History of Harasan Rebellions*. She hooked her finger at the top of the book, as if to pull it out, then changed her mind.

She instead pulled a book called *The Re-Organization of Harasa: A Recent History of Estate Boundaries*. Inside were detailed maps of the country and brief histories of the families that owned the estates throughout it, including their vocations and use of slaves.

Yonah settled herself onto a plush and colourful floor cushion with her back resting against an armchair to read. The first estate she looked up was Vaha.

"The Muran family at Vaha – a moderately-sized estate east of the town of Kirash, in the western region of Harasa – have owned the land for the past 150

years when Roban Muran purchased it from the previous owners. The land was later developed into a vineyard, which still provides wine to most of the estates in the country and beyond. The current palace was built between 80 and 90 years ago. The current masters of Vaha – Thuban and Serpa – were some of the first to bring slaves onto their estate."

Yonah glared at the last sentence. Naris' parents had no qualms with slavery when it could be used to their advantage. She flipped to the front of the book to check the publishing information. The book was only five years old and already out of date.

Using a map for reference, Yonah read the descriptions of the estates surrounding Sintash, the town in which she had been sold to Master Puru. That was the last place she had seen Sayzia. She traced the road upward and read up on the estates on the road north. They all kept slaves. Sayzia could be at any of those estates. She could even be in the northern country of Jalid.

Yonah pulled out the map she had purchased in Kirash from her pocket, found a quill and ink at a nearby side table, and copied the names of the estates from the book onto her map. Then she re-folded the map and returned it to her pocket.

She wished she could find a copy of a log that tracked all the slaves in Harasa; there would have to be one to track who had served their sentences and where they were so they could be informed of their freedom. But any slave log that Naris' family happened to have wouldn't have any information on her brother and sister.

Deciding she needed proof that she was reading 'appropriate' material and not anything that would incriminate her, Yonah pulled a fiction novel from a shelf to take back to her room. With the book under her arm, she went back to look at the portrait wall. She searched for Naris' great-grandmother, the woman who had built this palace.

Based on the date on the frame, Yonah figured she found the portrait. It depicted a solitary woman standing in front of Vaha, the edges of the image framed with greenery. The portrait hung at eye level and was large enough that it felt like the woman was really standing right in front of Yonah. The same self-righteous look that Yonah saw in Naris' parents was here in this woman, too, but Yonah almost felt that this woman, standing in front of the palace she had built, deserved that pride.

A strange, small handle made of the same gold material as the picture frame sticking out awkwardly to the side. There was no handle on the opposite side. Yonah placed her hand on the handle and gently pushed it downward. It shifted, there was a click, and the wall behind the portrait shifted.

It was a doorway. Yonah tentatively swung the wall open to reveal a dark passage. The walls were made of brick and the floor was stone. Yonah couldn't see very far into the passage because of the darkness.

She searched the reading nook for a candle and matches. They were tucked into a box that sat on a side table. After lighting the candle, Yonah stepped into the passage. She closed the secret door behind her in case anyone, particularly Naris, were to come looking for her in the library, but kept it ajar so she wouldn't accidentally lock herself inside.

With the secret door nearly shut and the only light coming from the candle, the darkness of the passage was suffocating. Yonah took one tentative step forward, then another, then another until she had worked up to a normal pace.

She came upon a staircase to her right. Yonah went upwards, her footsteps making soft tapping noises against the steps. The stairs continued up to the third floor, but Yonah saw a sliver of light down the dark passage. Being mindful of keeping silent, Yonah went towards the light.

It was another doorway. Yonah pressed her eye to the sliver and tried to make out what was on the other side. After a few moments of trying to make out an image in the golden light, Yonah realized she was looking at Naris' figure sitting at his desk in his office. Yonah gasped in surprise.

Naris suddenly sat up straight and turned his head. Yonah covered her mouth and slowed her breathing so she wouldn't make any noise. Naris's chair creaked slightly as he turned around to look directly at Yonah. But he couldn't see her, she assured herself. He couldn't see through walls. He didn't know she was there. He might not even know the passage was there. Her forehead and hands were wet with perspiration.

Naris slowly returned to his position in his chair and returned to his work and Yonah let her hand slowly fall from her mouth. She inched away from the doorway, turned, and tiptoed to the stairwell back to the library. She swung the portrait of Naris' great-grandmother shut and exhaled loudly.

There were secret passages in the palace. Based on the multiple stairwells and hallways, Yonah imagined they went everywhere through the building. Yonah thought it was a clever nod to Naris' great-grandmother, the woman who had had those passages built, to have an entrance at her portrait.

As much as Yonah wanted to explore the passageways, Naris turning to look at her had her wondering if he knew about them, too. Or had his parents passed that secret on before they unexpectedly succumbed to the sickness that devasted Harasa only a few months ago?

She picked up the novel and left the library, unhappily locking the door behind her.

Naris asked her about her visit to the library at dinner that evening. Yonah told him about the novel.

"I love that one!" he exclaimed. "You'll have to tell me how you like it."

She did not tell him about her research on the estates, nor of her discovery of the secret passageways in the palace.

The next few days felt like a dance between Yonah and Naris. He sat close to Yonah in the evenings, stole kisses each night. While she enjoyed the careful attention and sometimes let herself have a moment of carefree pleasure with Naris, Yonah tried not to let their relationship go any further, tried not to let herself fall any deeper.

One evening Naris, as they were playing a game of chess in his room, said suddenly, "I'm being patient with you, Yonah. I'm wooing you like a proper lady. You're more difficult than some of them."

Yonah tried not to reveal her disgust at the insinuation that she wasn't a 'proper lady.' It would do her no good to get into an argument with Naris. She wanted him always on her side.

She sat up tall and looked into his eyes. "You're wooing me before you take me to bed."

His look was not as steely as Yonah's. "Yes."

"What are you waiting for?" She was honestly astonished that she had managed this long to avoid any more physical intimacy, especially as Naris' slave, especially as one meant to be his sole companion.

"For love, Yonah. You know that." Neither one of them broke their gaze. "Don't you love me, yet?"

She wasn't sure what was love and what was lust and what was loneliness and what was acting. Everything jumbled together in her chest and she was never quite sure what was leading the way.

Naris tried again. "What's holding you back?"

An easy answer. "I am your slave."

"That doesn't matter." Naris shook his head.

"Yes, it does."

"I'll prove it to you."

Yonah narrowed her eyes at Naris. "How?"

"I'm having a celebration for the harvest. Guests will start arriving tomorrow. I'll introduce you as my guest, not as a slave."

Her body tensed at the thought. It was a lovely gesture, but Yonah was not looking forward to being the recipient of sideways glares each time she was introduced as Naris' 'guest.' She had no doubt that she would still be wearing her copper slave collar.

"You'll see," Naris said. "Besides, you'll be twenty soon and we can be together then."

Yonah gave him a tight-lipped smile to hide her true feelings on that idea.

Chapter Nineteen

The following afternoon, Yonah stood with Naris on the front steps of the palace, watching a man and a woman step out of a carriage while the household slaves unloaded their luggage. Naris had told Yonah to wear the blue dress and to be sure to wear some jewelry. Yonah fiddled with the gold bracelet around her wrist. She so rarely wore any of the jewelry Naris gave her; she preferred them for their value in trading.

The man and woman walked forward. Despite having been travelling, they were dressed extravagantly.

"Master Naris," the woman said brightly. "Congratulations on another successful season."

Naris bowed his head to the woman. "Thank you both for coming. I'd like to introduce you to my companion. Yonah, this is Master Varsa and Master Bano. Varsa, Bano, this is Yonah."

The masters stared at Yonah in bewilderment. Even though she knew she would not be greeted warmly, Yonah felt herself wither in embarrassment all the same.

The woman named Varsa shifted her eyes between Naris and Yonah and she stuttered, "It's nice to make your acquaintance…Yonah." Her eyes finally fell pointedly to Yonah's collar.

"And yours, too," Yonah said, unfeelingly.

"I'll have someone show you to your room," Naris said. "And there'll be refreshments waiting for you in the back." He motioned to one of the slaves and the guests disappeared into the palace. Yonah and Naris stood awkwardly together.

"They were a bit surprised, I'll admit," Naris suddenly said. "But they'll get used to it. They all will."

Yonah didn't argue. She didn't need to. With the arrival of more guests and the continued astonishment at their introduction to her, Yonah could feel Naris growing more and more incensed.

As they finally turned to move inside for that evening's feast, Naris said to Yonah, "I'll send you to town tomorrow to buy some new dresses so you can fit in with the other women. You are more of a lady than any of them."

Naris' dark mood persisted throughout dinner, which only added to Yonah's nerves at being seated beside him at the front of the dining hall. As was the custom, their table was on a raised dais where everyone could see them. Yonah tried to ignore the half-concealed glances from the guests. Instead, she looked upwards at the pictures on the ceiling, at Alib and Bria, at the bear and the snakes. She thought of her brother's *Little Bear* song. She didn't belong here with these people, even if she were free. She belonged with her brother and sister.

When she returned her gaze back to the feasting, Yonah gasped. Bana was among the guests, setting food on the tables and clearing empty dishes. He must have been brought inside to help with the influx of guests.

Yonah looked at Naris to see if he noticed her watching Bana, but his eyes were scanning the crowd with a look of displeasure.

Curiosity got the better of Yonah and she asked, "Don't you like any of these people?"

Naris smirked at her. "Like I said to you before, most of my family's interactions with the other masters have had to do with business. That's what this is. Business. It will be more fun when Kejal arrives."

"And when does he arrive?"

"Tomorrow, hopefully. I'll introduce you at dinner."

After they had eaten, Naris led Yonah off the dais and into the crowd to mingle. The guests pointedly ignored Yonah as they spoke to Naris, even when he attempted to bring her into the conversation by asking for her opinion.

One guest, a tall man with wavy shoulder length hair, rolled his eyes as Naris and Yonah joined his conversation. "Naris, really? A slave girl? What are you trying to do?"

Naris glared up at the man. "She's my friend, Zanith, and you'll treat her as such."

"Your friend?" Zanith turned to Yonah. "Pardon me, I mistook your collar as one worn by slaves, but it must be a unique accessory." His eyes moved up and down Yonah's figure. "Come on, Naris, she isn't even one of the beautiful ones."

Naris' weight shifted and, for a moment, Yonah thought he was going to hit Zanith. The man didn't notice. "Do I have to ask you leave?" Naris hissed.

"Do I have to fraternize with your slaves in order to do business with you?"

The two men held each other in their gaze, caught in a silent tug-of-war of wills.

Naris broke away first. "Come, Yonah." He took her arm and led her away, sending one last glare Zanith's way.

Although there wasn't a conversation quite as bad as the one with Zanith, the rest of the night was far less than enjoyable for Yonah. Relief washed over her when Naris finally said she could go to bed, and she practically ran from the dining hall to her bedroom. At least tomorrow she would be able to go to Kirash. Perhaps she could spend the entire day there, so she wouldn't be forced to try to talk to the guests until the evening meal.

THE WOMAN WHO NORMALLY brought Yonah's breakfast also brought a small drawstring bag jingling with coins the following day. "From Master Naris," she explained.

Yonah thanked the woman, wolfed down her breakfast, and raced down to the front doors of the palace, hoping to leave before any more guests arrived. Her heart sank when she saw a carriage stopped just at the bottom of the front steps.

Upon taking a closer look, Yonah realized the carriage was empty, despite there being a slave sitting on the drivers' bench. The guests must have already gone inside. She started down the path through the vineyard towards the road.

"Yonah."

She spun around. Seidon was standing next to the horses, holding their reins.

"Hi," she said, walking back towards the stable master. "What is it?"

"Master Naris wants you to take the carriage today."

Yonah looked at the carriage with a frown. "Why?"

Seidon shrugged. "That's what I was told."

"Do I have to?" Whoever ended up driving the carriage would know about everywhere she went in Kirash. It would be like having a chaperone.

"Well," Seidon answered, "if you were any other slave, I would tell you without a doubt that yes, you have to."

There would be other trips to Kirash. She could ask Meerha about her brother's whereabouts another time, after the guests were gone and Naris wasn't worried about forcing them into thinking she was anything but a slave.

"Fine. I will take the carriage." She opened the door and jumped inside without the assistance of a step stool.

"Enjoy yourself," Seidon said with a chuckle, peeking through the open door.

"Believe me. It'll be much better than staying here for the day."

She was, unfortunately, back by lunchtime, the carriage burdened with four boxes that contained the outfits she purchased at the dressmaker's. When Yonah hopped out of the carriage, she saw Naris waiting for her.

"I saw you coming," he said. He noticed the boxes at the back of the carriage. "That's all you bought?"

"How many did you want me to buy?"

"More than that," he said with a sigh. "Come. Everybody should be up by now. We can sit on the patio with some of them."

"Can I just wait until dinner?" Yonah asked, anxiety clutching her chest. "Nobody really wants to spend any time with me."

"*I* want to spend time with you."

"That's very nice, but I think if you want good business, you won't make the masters talk to me."

"Yonah, please." His tone was sharp. "Just get dressed into something better than that and meet me on the patio." He strode into the palace.

HER ARRIVAL ON THE PATIO, dressed in a new skirt, shirt, and shawl, sparked looks of disapproval. Yonah spent the afternoon trying to remain invisible while she sat next to Naris and, several agonizingly long hours later, they moved into the dining hall for supper. Yonah and Naris were once again seated on the dais in plain view of the even larger number of guests. She scanned the crowd for Bana to see if he was serving again. There he was near the back.

A rugged-looking man stepped onto the dais, his arms held open wide. When Naris registered the man's presence he grinned and said, "Kejal! It's so good to see you!" They embraced, clapping each other on the back.

"It's good to see you, too," the man named Kejal said. You look well."

"I am well! Look, I want you to meet Yonah. Yonah, dear, come."

Yonah stood and stepped next to Naris with her head bowed down slightly, readying herself for yet another awkward introduction. Kejal raised an eyebrow at her. Yonah remembered that she had seen Naris talking to this man once before back when she was serving at Master Puru's celebration feast.

Naris placed his hand on the small of her back and said, "This is Yonah.

She has been my companion for the last season."

"Is she why you are looking so well, then?" Kejal asked in all sincerity.

Naris looked at Yonah. "She likes to play chess with me, she's intelligent, and she understands me."

Yonah's heart warmed at Naris' sincere look.

"Not usually the hallmarks of a good companion in your book," Kejal said, with a surprised look on his face. He turned to Yonah. "I'm glad you have brought some joy back into my friend's life, whatever your method is."

Naris insisted his friend sit and they began talking about their respective businesses and news from the past month. Yonah figured out from their conversation that this was the childhood friend to whom Naris often referred.

Sitting at the table on the dais, with so many people watching her, filled Yonah with an oozing sense of dread. Naris hardly spoke to her during the meal because of the arrival of his friend, though his hand would sometimes rest on her leg, something he had never done before. The placement of his hand was both comforting and disconcerting.

An appropriate amount of time after they had finished eating, Yonah leaned over to Naris and said softly, "I was hoping I could go to my room."

Naris looked around as if he had forgotten that he was hosting a massive feast and was surrounded by dozens of guests. His eyes landed on Yonah.

"Yes. I'm sorry I haven't paid much attention to you tonight. I'll be more attentive tomorrow."

She smiled politely at him and stood up. As she wound through the tables, she forced herself to keep her chin up and keep her eyes forward. She could feel the masters looking at her, imagined they were whispering about her.

When she had finally left the dining hall, Yonah leaned against a wall and closed her eyes. Surely Naris was starting to understand that because of her slave collar, Yonah was viewed as fundamentally different from him.

"Heading to bed already? Or perhaps you have some chores to do."

Yonah opened her eyes. The tall man with the shoulder-length hair that she had been introduced to yesterday was standing a few metres away from her. Zanith. He took a few steps closer. Yonah's chest clenched.

"Are you enjoying your stay?" Yonah asked.

"It's good enough. Are you enjoying your playtime?"

In an attempt to feel less insecure, Yonah stood up taller. "I'm doing what Master Naris asks me to do."

"So, you do obey masters' orders?"

Yonah's only reply was watching Zanith carefully. He inched even closer to her. The dread she had been feeling during dinner had returned, only now it was thicker and murkier.

"Before you became a favourite of Naris," Zanith said snidely, "did you whore around with the masters? Or maybe you still do?"

"I worked in the gardens," Yonah said quickly, hoping to distract Zanith with another topic.

"The gardens." Zanith's voice was a near whisper. He was bent over Yonah, so their faces were nearly touching.

Yonah bolstered her courage and said, "I don't think you want to do this." She could only imagine how Naris might react if he found out Zanith was this close to her.

Enraged disbelief lit up Zanith's eyes. "Oh, don't I? Do you think I care what you think? You're nothing."

Yonah remained silent, though she kept her eyes on the man in front of her. She could feel her nostrils flaring in defiance. She wanted to speak, she wanted to fight back.

"Good," Zanith said. "You still know your place." He grabbed Yonah's chin in the palm of his hand and roughly pressed his lips to hers. He smelled of the wine he had been drinking. He smelled like her mother.

Yonah's hands found his chest and she shoved Zanith with all her might. "Naris wouldn't want you touching me." Her body was trembling.

The look in Zanith's eye chilled Yonah. "Why do you think I'm doing this? Now come with me." He grabbed Yonah's arm and pulled her towards the stairs. She pulled away from Zanith, but he was far stronger than her. Her sandals slid along the polished floor as she was dragged behind him.

She tried tugging out of Zanith's grip, holding onto her shoulder, so she wouldn't hurt herself. Zanith suddenly turned around and struck Yonah across the face. She cried out in surprise. Her face stung where he hit her.

Zanith was pulling her towards the stairs again.

Yonah opened her mouth, filled her lungs with breath, and let out the loudest, shrillest scream she could find within herself.

The sound echoed in the hallway. It pierced Yonah's ears. The force hurt her throat. And the exertion made her feel powerful.

"Shut up!" Zanith hit her again, silencing her scream. "What is wrong with you?"

A few guests had milled out into the hallway. They watched Yonah and Zanith with curiosity. No one was offering to help her. For a moment, Yonah thought they would all let Zanith take her to his room. Her heart began to pound and her breath quickened.

Then Naris emerged from the growing crowd and Yonah sighed with relief. When he saw Zanith's hand on Yonah, his eyes flashed with rage and he stormed over to the pair of them.

"A misunderstanding, Naris," Zanith started to say. He let go of Yonah and held his hands in front of his chest.

In one smooth motion, Naris' fist flew through the air and crashed into Zanith's jaw with a cringe-invoking thud. The force of the blow knocked Zanith to the floor as the crowd building behind Naris gave a collective gasp.

"What's the matter with you?" Zanith sputtered as he slowly stood back up.

"Never," Naris said, panting, "touch Yonah again."

"She's just a slave, Naris. Whatever you think is going on between you two is a lie. She's just following orders. She's just pretending to like you, so she can pretend to be one of us."

"Get out," Naris snapped. "Get out! You can find an inn in Kirash tonight. Just go. I'll have your things sent after you."

Zanith smiled snidely. "Fine. It's your home. You can do what you want." As he started down the hallway to the entrance hall, he nodded to Yonah. She felt her nose wrinkle upwards and her brows furrow. "Enjoy your playtime, slave," he added.

As Zanith disappeared from view, Naris turned to the onlookers. "Who would like some more wine?" The guests started to return to the dining room, some quite happy with the promise of more wine, others irately whispering to each other. Naris turned to Yonah. "Will you find someone and tell them to pack Zanith's belongings?"

Yonah nodded and started for the kitchen when Naris suddenly took her hand in his.

"Are you alright?" he asked her.

Still silent, she nodded, withdrew her hand, and quickly walked away, wanting to hide her face from the masters who still remained. She let her lips tremble and her face twist in fear and relief as she walked away, but she would not cry. No one in this palace could know she wanted to cry. Except maybe Naris.

Chapter Twenty

None of the guests mentioned the incident the following day. At least, not to Yonah and Naris.

They were seated in the shade of the patio, sharing lemonade with a few of the guests. Lounge chairs and armchairs and pouffes and floor cushions had been brought outside for the afternoon. Two slaves were stationed there in case the pitchers needed refilling or a guest needed additional service. One of them was Bana.

Yonah scratched at her skin where her dress's neckline lay. She found the fabric coarse. Naris gently placed her hand over hers and gave her a disapproving look. As she dropped her hand away, Naris continued to hold it. He ignored the masters who noticed the physical contact.

"The protesters' numbers are growing in Kelab," Yonah heard one of the guests say. He was sitting on the edge of a chaise lounge. "And every time the Guard try to do something about it, their numbers only grow."

The woman lying down next to the first speaker shuddered. "They're like insects. There are always more hiding in the shadows. I hear that the government in Jalid is actually considering abolishing slavery."

"Why would they do that?"

The woman shook her head. "There is a highly organized group up there that has been petitioning and going directly to the government to speak to them. They ought to be executed."

Yonah took note of the information.

More than once during the afternoon, Bana tried to capture Yonah's attention by smiling tentatively at her. She pretended not to see.

"You two haven't been speaking, have you?" Naris had leaned in close to Yonah, so no one would hear him.

"No, we haven't."

Naris took a long drink from his glass. He watched Bana unblinkingly. "Do you miss your conversations with him?"

Yonah looked at Naris, his eyes still on Bana. Yes, she did miss her friendship with Bana. There were no expectations there, no careful boundaries to maneuver. But she could never let Naris know that.

"Maybe a little," she answered. "But now I have you."

Naris looked at Yonah, a serious expression on his face. His eyes drilled into hers, trying to read what she really meant. The longer he looked, the more his face softened.

"Naris," called one of the guests. "Some of us were thinking about going for a ride this afternoon. Any suggestions where we should go?"

"Yes," Naris said. "I can show you on the estate map, if you like."

Several of the guests stood up to change into riding clothes. Yonah said softly to Naris, "I'm going to go inside for a moment."

"Don't stay too long," Naris instructed.

Yonah nodded to appease him, but hoped she could hide from the guests until that night's dinner.

She was on the third floor near her bedroom when she heard Bana say, "Why have you been avoiding me?"

Yonah jumped at the sound of his voice. She glared at him. "Did you follow me all the way up here?"

"I wanted to talk to you where Master Naris wouldn't see us."

"Well, I can't talk to you."

He looked pained. "Why?"

"Naris has forbidden me from speaking to you, and you must listen or you will be the one who's punished." Before Bana could respond, Yonah turned and darted down the hall. She hoped her brief explanation was enough to convince her friend to let her be, for his sake.

"He can't see us all the time, you know," Bana called after her. "He doesn't have eyes everywhere."

Yonah remembered that heart-stopping moment when she thought Naris had looked through the wall to look right at her in the secret passage.

"You don't know that," she said, walking back towards Bana. "Besides, I can't take that risk. Don't you know what happened to the wine pourer?"

Bana shifted his weight uncomfortably. "I heard he cut her hands."

"It was terrible, Bana, I watched the whole thing. All because she was doing a poor job. And last night he kicked out one of the masters for trying to—" She couldn't say the words. "But he's jealous of you and he'll do something like that to you if he finds us talking." She tried to walk away again, but he ran around her and blocked her way.

"He's jealous of me?" A playful smile lit up his face. "Why?"

"Stop it! He just wants me to have no friends here except for him and if that's what keeps you safe, then that's what I'll do. Now, please, just forget about me." She shoved past him, but Bana grabbed her arm.

"Yonah, he can't be your friend. He's your master."

"But you can't be my friend either," she hissed, reaching for his hand and peeling it away from her arm. She continued down the hall towards her bedroom and stopped suddenly.

Naris was standing in a hidden passageway, leaning against the doorway. He must have seen the whole conversation because his eyes were dark with rage. In a panic, Yonah went to go talk to him, but as soon as he registered that she was making her way toward him, he disappeared into the passageway, closing the secret door behind him.

BANA DID NOT SERVE AT dinner that night. Yonah spent all that evening scanning the crowd, hoping that he was simply eluding her gaze as he meandered among the guests. But he was not there.

Unable to wait any longer for an explanation, Yonah said to Naris, "What happened to Bana?"

Naris was quiet for a moment, a cold resentment emanating off him.

"Your friend has been punished." He didn't volunteer anymore information, so Yonah asked, "Is he alive?"

Naris' eyes fell to the floor. Yonah shuddered, fearing the worst. He said, "I think he will survive."

Yonah's shoulders fell from their stiff position, her breath released, the knot in her chest loosened a little.

"I told you not to speak to him."

"I didn't. I mean, I tried. I really did. I told him we couldn't be friends anymore. He wouldn't listen."

Naris didn't answer. Their food grew cold on their plates as the guests that crowded the dining hall filled the room with a light-heartedness that contradicted Yonah's current mood.

"You care for him," Naris said suddenly. "You were trying to protect him."

Yonah had no answer for that. Yes, she was trying to protect Bana because she cared for him. That fact wouldn't make Naris feel any better.

"Do you think he's right?" he asked.

"About what?"

"That we can't be friends. Because I'm a master and you're my slave."

The answer to that question and what Yonah wished the answer was were two different things.

"I don't think it's as simple as that."

Hope spread through Naris' features. "Because I thought that we were… This past while…" He fumbled for words. "You're the only person I've ever talked to about… anything."

She could feel her chest shaking and she tried to control her breath. She sipped her wine and looked out at the masters on the floor.

"You're the only person I've talked to about my family in a long time," she said, shocked at the truth of her own words.

"And that makes us friends, right? More than friends."

Filled with fear, not the fear of his anger or his punishment, but of something quieter and equally strong, Yonah turned her gaze back to Naris. "I don't know."

"It means something."

"Maybe," she conceded.

He reached for her hand and gave it a squeeze. "I'm sorry about your friend."

While she believed he was sorry for making her unhappy, Yonah wasn't entirely sure Naris felt any remorse for what he had done to Bana.

As soon as the feasting was over and Yonah was permitted to go to bed, she snuck down to the kitchen. Several of the slaves were still washing and drying the dishes and packing away leftover food. Yonah found the head cook sitting at a table, wiping her brow, and asked her, "Where is Bana?"

The cook looked up at Yonah with a frown. "He's not here."

"Is he alive?"

A voice from behind Yonah said, "What do you care?" The speaker was another man who normally worked in the vineyard. His red eyes revealed that he had been crying.

Yonah's heart raced. "Is he alive? What happened to him? Please!"

"He's alive," the man said with a snarl. "Barely."

"I'm so sorry," Yonah breathed. "What... Can I see him?"

The man's eyes were filled with fury as he said, "No."

She took an unwilling step back. "Will you tell me what happened?"

The man scowled at Yonah. "He cut off his hand. A reminder not to touch you again. And now he'll never be set free."

The world felt as if it was melting, or maybe she was floating. But nothing felt solid. Yonah tried to understand what the man had said. His hand. Naris cut off Bana's hand. All for talking to her.

She began to understand the violence in Naris' punishment and her fear came back. Her safety lay in the hands of a man who had no qualm with physically and violently hurting people, one who claimed to love her and grew more possessive and protective of her every day.

Chapter Twenty-One

The atmosphere at dinner the next evening was much quieter than the previous nights of feasting. While the guests enthusiastically ate as much food and drank as much wine as they could, the conversations were a little more muted, the laughter a little more gentle, and they departed for their bedrooms earlier than usual.

Naris took the early night as an opportunity to invite Yonah to spend some time in his bedroom, a practice they hadn't done since the guests arrived a few days earlier.

Wordlessly, Naris poured two glasses of wine and sat down across from Yonah, putting his feet up on a stool. She took the glass, but set it next to her with no intention of drinking it.

They sat in contented silence for a few minutes. Naris seemed to have forgotten yesterday's events with Bana, but Yonah would always remember.

Naris spoke. "It's exhausting having so many people in one's home. I know it's common for people to stay for at least a week for these things, but I just wish they didn't need to be babysat all day long."

"Do you think they'll leave soon?" Yonah asked. "They seemed tired tonight."

"I imagine they'll feel festive again tomorrow," Naris grumbled. "You've been very good through this whole thing. I'm disappointed at how you've been treated this week."

Yonah didn't want to get into another discussion on the realities of their relationship, so she stayed silent, averting her eyes.

"Why don't you go to town tomorrow?" Naris said. "You can get away from these people for a while. Here." He went to a set of drawers, pulled out a pouch, and handed it to Yonah. "Buy yourself something. Anything." With the leftover ora from her visit to the dress maker's, Yonah realized she had plenty of money to use at her leisure, money that Naris wouldn't miss because he was so wealthy.

Naris kissed the top of her head, letting his head linger next to hers as he inhaled deeply. "I'm going to bed." He went to the bed and started folding the sheets back. "You could sleep here, if you like."

The sudden invitation startled Yonah and her muscles tightened. It was likely he honestly just wanted to sleep, but she also knew that once she was there in the bed, everything else would be all too convenient.

"I think I'll sleep better in my bed," she said, hoping Naris wouldn't turn angry with her putting him off.

His face was oddly emotionless when he looked at her. "Then kiss me once before you go."

Yonah obediently walked over to Naris. Instead of leaning over to kiss her, however, Naris paused.

"Everyone else thinks we can't be together," he said.

Yonah looked at him with wide eyes, not sure what to say.

Naris kissed her. It was a deep kiss. A romantic kiss. One where he just held Yonah, didn't let his hands roam her body, just kissed her. And she kissed him back, unintentionally. Her chest ached with longing and sorrow. What might they have been if everything was different?

They locked eyes as their kiss ended.

"They don't see this part of us," Naris whispered.

She needed to go. This was one of those moments where a path had to be chosen, and Yonah didn't want to choose this path, yet.

"Goodnight, Naris," she said softly.

"Goodnight, Yonah." He dropped his arms from their embrace. "Have a good time in Kirash."

IT WAS A SUNNY WALK INTO town, but a soft breeze kept the day at a moderate temperature. The days were growing slightly cooler as winter neared. Yonah had only experienced winter in the desert region where Kelab and Master Puru's estate lay, and she was not used to the cooler temperature.

Her first order of business would require some careful exploration. Remembering her first solo excursion to Kirash and the time the Guards were chasing her, Yonah followed the street she had run down, searching for a way up. Up was where the orphans lived.

She didn't want to climb out in the open as she had done that first trip, so she took some time exploring the nearby smaller side streets for a less conspicuous path. She noticed a stack of boxes which, to the untrained eye, looked to be simply that, but actually created the perfect step ladder to an exterior stairwell that was gated at its entrance.

Checking to see that nobody was watching, Yonah easily scaled the boxes and made the small leap to the stairwell. She pulled herself over the railing and walked up, up, up. There were doors along the way, but Yonah went all the way to the rooftop. It was one of the easiest ways she had ever found up to the orphans' world.

Nobody was in sight, but that wasn't a surprise to Yonah. It was possible the children were in the town finding work. But knowing she had met them up here midday gave her hope that she would find at least one of them.

She lingered on the rooftop for a minute, then moved on to the next one. These buildings were attached and allowed for easy travel up top.

"You can't keep coming back here."

Yonah turned. It was one of the children she had met during her first solo visit to town, the oldest boy. He stood at the opposite end of the building.

"You'll draw attention to us," he added.

"I know," Yonah said. "I just wanted to give you this." She pulled out one of the two bags of money she had collected from Naris over the past few days and tossed it forward. It arced gracefully through the air and landed on the ground close to the boy with a tinkling thud. The sound gave its contents away and the boy looked at Yonah in shock.

"What for?" he asked.

"Because I know what you're going through," Yonah answered with a shrug. "Having money always makes things easier, so there you go. Use it however you need."

The boy walked slowly to the bag, keeping his eyes on Yonah, and picked it up. "Did you steal it?"

Yonah shook her head. "My master gave it to me. But you need it more."

"How come your master gave you money?"

Yonah smiled. "It's a long story."

"Well," the boy shuffled uncomfortably on the spot, "thanks."

"You're welcome. You be careful."

"Follow me. You should use this way, so you don't get caught." The boy led Yonah to a neighbouring rooftop that slanted down onto a large second storey balcony set with a few tables. The boy pointed towards a door. "The man will let you through. He knows we use this way."

Yonah thanked the boy and wished him luck before he disappeared back onto the rooftops. She went through the doorway and down a set of stairs. There was a man in a kitchen at the bottom of the stairs who gave Yonah a puzzled look, but said nothing as she walked out the front door of his shop.

Once out on the street, Yonah took a moment to figure out where in Kirash she was. She eventually wandered back to the main street and headed towards the west end of town.

When she arrived at The White Stallion, she sat at a table near the back of the pub, waiting for Meerha to find her.

The barmaid strode over with a happy smirk on her face. "It's your lucky day," she said. "My contact, Tolga, says he met your brother."

Yonah's mouth gaped open. Her chest swelled and her mouth split into a wide grin. "Really? He's sure?"

"He's positive."

"When did he come? Will he come here? Did Tolga mention me? How does he look? Did he look healthy?"

"Would you let me finish?" Meerha cut in. "Apparently, your brother doesn't quite believe you're who you say you are."

"What do you mean?"

"He wants you to prove you really are his sister by singing your special song or something."

Their *Little Bear* song. She was surprised he even remembered.

Yonah nodded. "I know the song."

"Then you're going to have to go sing it for Tolga."

"I can't sing it for you?" Yonah asked.

Meerha shook her head with a frown. "I can't sing."

So, it was with a spring in her step that Yonah set off on the long walk to Basee for the first time. She had found Obi. Now, all she needed to do was coordinate a time for them to see each other.

For the first time in a long time, Yonah felt a warmth that reminded her of home.

She smelled the sea before she reached the port city. It was tangy and pricked at her nostrils. The city itself stretched lengthwise along the coast. It was a thin strip of buildings, markets, and houses. Ships lined the city's western edge as far as the eye could see. Some of their masts stretched so high Yonah had to crane her neck backwards to see the top. Others were just small fishing boats that hung on to the coast.

There was a building near the entrance to the city with a large sign hanging over its door. The sign had a picture of a whip sprawling to the edges and yellow lettering that said, "Nine Tails." Yonah went straight inside. Meerha had told her that Tolga was a guitarist who played there. Yonah found the musician playing onstage and sat herself at the bar to wait for him to finish his set. She used one of the ora coins Naris had given her to buy a drink. Several songs later, Tolga left the stage and sat a little way down the bar from her.

Yonah stood and stepped closer to the musician. He wore no slave collar. "Are you Tolga?"

He looked up at her. "Who's asking?"

"I'm Yonah. Your friend from Kirash sent me. You found my brother?"

The man nodded in acknowledgement. "I did."

Yonah said, "Your friend says I need to teach you our song."

"That, you do." He swivelled on his stool to face her.

Yonah tentatively leaned in towards the musician and softly sang.

"Stop hiding, Little Bear.

I know you're here. I see you there.

We'll dance and play and catch some fish.

Sleep 'neath the stars, that's my one wish."

NARIS WAS QUIET AT DINNER. Normally, he would mutter the odd quip to Yonah, either to ask her opinion on a conversation or to point out a guest he didn't like. But he went the whole meal without speaking to her. In fact, he barely looked at her.

When Naris finally stood up at the end of his meal, he spoke to Yonah for the first time that evening.

"Wait for me in my room," he ordered in a dark voice. He left her without waiting for a response.

Yonah slowly stood up and did as she was told. She thought through all their recent interactions to find something that might have upset Naris. The only thing she could think of was the fact that she had gone to Basee that day. Did he have someone following her? She thought of all the places she had ever been. Basee, The White Stallion, the candle sellers' home, the map shops – it all looked suspicious for a slave.

Her hands trembled. Naris' face had been so clouded over with anger when he had instructed her to go to his room. There would be a punishment. Images of the wine pourer's hands filled her mind. She thought of poor Bana and his hand.

Perhaps she could run away. She certainly had enough money to survive a few days. But she had no where to go. The only person she knew in Kirash was the barmaid. Maybe the candle sellers would take her in and she could work for them. But if she ran, Naris would certainly send out the Guards to find her. And if he really had somebody following her, they would know to look in those places.

It seemed her only option, at the moment, was to go meet her fate. Her only consolation was that she truly did believe that Naris would be a little lenient with her punishment.

Her breath shook as she reached for the door and pushed it open.

The room was empty. Candles were already lit, illuminating the freshly made bed, the empty sitting area, their last game of chess. Naris had won the game, as usual. Yonah sat down in her usual spot, sitting tall and alert. She watched the door.

As the minutes passed by, her trembling calmed, melting away into an anxious boredom. Yonah relaxed into her chair. To pass the time, she played a game of chess against herself. Twice. She studied the wall mural. It was odd that its images brought the ocean to mind when Vaha lay in the middle of a plain.

Suddenly wanting to do something productive with her time, Yonah peered out into the hallway, but she couldn't see Naris on his way. She closed the bedroom door again and rushed over to the nightstand. Inside its drawer, she found another bag of coins. Yonah opened it and withdrew a small handful to add to her own stash. Then she rummaged around the drawer to see if there was anything else of interest.

There was a small, ornamental box made of gold and encrusted with emeralds. Yonah opened the box and found two long beaded necklaces, one white and the other black. These were typically used in marriage ceremonies.

Yonah stuffed the box back into the drawer and closed it roughly, as if its disappearance from her sight would make it disappear entirely. She didn't know how long Naris had had the box, nor what his intentions were with it, or if he had *any* intentions.

She sat back down in one of the chairs and waited, trying to put the marriage necklaces out of her mind.

Several minutes later, the bedroom door opened and Naris entered. There was a looseness in his step that Yonah recognized as drunkenness. He stopped suddenly when he saw her. His face was twisted into a sad frown.

"So, you are capable of following directions," he grumbled, walking towards the liquor cabinet. Yonah watched him carefully. "You didn't help yourself to any. Why not?"

"I wasn't thirsty."

His head rolled when he turned to look at her. He squinted his eyes, trying to get a better look. He sighed and took a seat in a chair across from her, a glass of wine in his hand.

"One o' my guests wuz in Basee t'day," he said wryly. He mumbled through his words.

She tried to convey polite interest and curiosity.

"And they saw you there."

Yonah tried to quell the trembling that was threatening to start again. She imagined her hands were as heavy as sand.

"You were at the Nine Tails." Naris took a long drink from his cup. "Did you know the Nine Tails is n'torious for being a gathering place for rad'cals and rebels?"

"I didn't know that," she answered, glad she could give an honest answer.

"Oh, you didn't know that," Naris repeated, disbelievingly. "What other business could you possibly have there when my offer was for you to visit Kirash! Not Basee!" His voice suddenly rose in anger. Yonah flinched away. "Answer me!"

Yonah would not answer. She would not reveal that she was trying to find her brother, that she had heard from him, that she was taking steps to see him in person. She would not risk his safety.

Naris stood and grabbed Yonah's wrist. His words were crisp as he spoke, his anger turning him sober. "Why were you there? Who were you talking to?"

"Nobody, I wasn't talking to anybody!"

"I should cut out your tongue to make sure you never do again!"

She was shaking as she yelled, "I'm not a rebel, I swear! I've never spoken about the rebellion with anybody!"

"You're lying!" He grabbed her other wrist and pulled her to her feet.

"And you're making me look like a fool."

She was desperate to protect herself from a terrible punishment. "I know I shouldn't have been in Basee, but I have nothing to do with the rebellion. Please, you have to believe me."

"Then what were you doing there?" he said with a snarl.

"N-nothing. I was only exploring."

Naris' eyes were glowing hot. They searched Yonah's face for the truth. "Then you must be punished for disobeying me."

Yonah's heart, already pounding, throbbed harder against her chest. "I'm sorry. Please. What are you going to do?"

Naris drew a small blade from his belt. Yonah tried to pull away from his grip. "Don't move!" he said. "You've embarrassed me enough."

He let go of her other wrist and shoved her back down into the chair. Before Yonah could stand up, he rested one of his knees next to her so that he towered over her, their bodies nearly touching. His free hand found her chin and held her face steady.

"Naris, please," Yonah whimpered. She felt tears overflowing onto her cheeks.

He didn't hear her. He leaned over her prone body, the blade held ready. Yonah was trapped under his weight.

The blade touched the centre of her bottom lip and began to saw through the skin. Yonah screamed. She felt her chin grow hot and sticky and wet. Her body writhed. She grabbed Naris' arm and tried to pull it away. He only flung her hands away and repositioned himself so her arms were pinned between his legs. His strength enraged Yonah and filled her with terror. She was at his complete mercy. Her feet scrambled on the mosaic floor, trying to find traction. The rest of her body was immobilized. The knife continued to cut through her lip. It burned.

Eventually, Naris was satisfied with his work. He pulled the knife away and stood up. Yonah curled her knees up to her chest and raised her shaking hands to her face. What was left of her lip throbbed in pain. Her jaw hung open in the least painful position she could find. Her screams and crying had turned into a round moan – it was too painful to move her lips. Tears still streamed down her face, although her heart began to slow now that the worst was over.

"Do not disobey me again," Naris said coldly. "Get out."

She stood, her legs shaking, and hobbled to the door, trying not to disturb her lip in any way.

The hallway was quiet. She had waited so long for Naris that everyone was asleep. She shuffled silently through the dark halls, not needing any light to guide her way. She had taken this path many times before in darkness. This time, the walk seemed endless. Each step made the two sides of her split bottom lip jiggle, tugging at the fresh wound.

Yonah was afraid somebody would see her like this, especially one of the other slaves. For so long, she had been untouchable and now, she was a broken, bleeding mess, just as much at Naris' mercy as the others, in just as much danger.

When she entered her own bedroom, Yonah stumbled over to her water bowl, grabbed a cloth, and dabbed at her blood-caked chin, carefully avoiding her lip. She steeled herself and looked up into the mirror that hung on her wall.

He had cut it in two, right down the middle. Her bottom lip parted at the centre, puffing at the chasm that now opened, revealing her bottom teeth.

She felt her jaw shaking and she grabbed her chin to stop the movement. Her hand on her chin brought back the memory of Naris only minutes earlier holding her chin still. Yonah gasped and closed her eyes, pressing yet more tears out through the cracks of her eyelids.

She was so alone. The one person who claimed to love her in this whole place was also the most dangerous person in her life. This was not love. This was not family.

Hot tears still running down her cheeks, Yonah laid down in her bed with her mouth hanging open, closed her eyes, and fell asleep.

Chapter Twenty-Two

When Yonah awoke, she heard soft voices.

"She finally got a taste of what we go through," a male voice muttered. "We should just leave her be. See if it'll infect."

"What a great idea," a woman said sarcastically. It was the woman who normally brought Yonah food. "Then she dies, the master grieves, and who does he take it out on? We have to get Daza, idiot."

Daza was a senior slave who had taken on the role of doctor. He was examining her cut lip when Yonah finally opened her eyes.

"How are you feeling?" he asked her, rather analytically.

"Tired," Yonah said, forgetting her lip. She flinched at its movement.

He felt her forehead. "Hmm, perhaps you've avoided infection. That's good. I'm going to stitch it up."

Yonah slowly sat up. "Now?"

"It should have been stitched hours ago." Daza searched through a large case he had brought with him. He pulled out a squat glass container, a needle, and what looked like a spool of thin thread.

He opened the glass container and scooped a dollop of balm out with his finger, which he dabbed around Yonah's lip. She pulled away.

"It hurts now, but this will make the next part better, girl."

Yonah clenched her fists tightly as he continued to dab balm on her wound. Then he threaded the needle and said, "This shouldn't hurt too badly now."

Yonah's lip had gone numb with the application of the balm. As Daza sewed her lip back together, she only felt tugging at the corners of her mouth and near the bottom of her chin. While it wasn't necessarily painful, it was uncomfortable.

A few minutes later, Daza tied the end of the thread and cut the edge. "There. That should start to feel better. It will scar, though." He looked sad. "It will be a constant reminder of your blunder."

Daza packed up his bag and stood up.

"Is your name Yonah?"

She nodded.

"The younger ones are fools to be jealous of you. You are in the most danger out of all of us. So, while your scar constantly reminds the master of whatever crime you committed, let it constantly remind you of the severity of your situation."

He was right, she realized. Naris' attachment to her wasn't an advantage. It only made him more protective, more jealous, more angry, and more violent.

YONAH DID NOT EAT IN THE dining hall in the following days despite the remaining guests, nor was she summoned to visit Naris after supper. Instead, she spent most of her time in her room, sitting on her balcony or examining her map. She thought about visiting Seidon at the stable, but she was embarrassed of her scar and what it meant. While she had feared punishment from Naris, she never thought he would do something quite so terrible to her. She had thought her relationship with Naris protected her somewhat – she was a fool.

Daza had done a fine job of stitching her lip. While it ached constantly, which was to be expected, she could see that the wound was beginning to fade from its angry red colour.

Two evenings later, the woman that normally brought food up to Yonah said, "Why don't you come downstairs?"

Yonah said cautiously, "I didn't think I was welcome there."

The slave raised her eyebrows and shrugged her shoulders. "I'm not going to beg you or anything. It's an offer. Take it or leave it."

Yonah looked up at the woman from her seat on the balcony. The woman watched her, unblinking.

Though it filled Yonah with a soft dread to do so, she said, "Alright, I'm coming."

As they walked down to the slaves' quarters, Yonah said to the woman, "I'm Yonah."

"Praha." There was no more conversation after that.

When they arrived in the kitchen in the basement, the room fell quiet. The slaves stared at Yonah with a mixture of hatred and shock.

Praha tugged at Yonah's arm and led her to a long wooden table lined with two benches. The pair of them sat and conversation slowly grew to a normal level as the rest of the household grew tired of watching Yonah.

"What do you think you're doing, Praha?" one man said, setting bowls of soup down in front of them.

"We're eating supper," Praha answered. She reached for her spoon, ignoring the frown aimed in her direction.

Yonah listened to the conversations around her as more workers sat at the table. The slaves talked of the day's work, made fun of the various masters, and teased each other. For the most part, it was a jovial occasion. There was a sense of community here and Yonah wished she could be a part of it. She merely sat and sipped her soup quietly.

"So, what is it that finally did you in?" someone asked from across the table. Yonah missed who it was, and only saw several faces watching her. The buzzing of the room had softened to silence.

"One of the masters saw me at Basee," she said softly.

"Basee?" A man chortled. "What were you doing way out there?"

"Are you part of the rebellion?"

"Do you have news from the cities?"

Questions came at her from all sides. She had no answers.

"Anybody mentions the rebellion again tonight and I'll have their knuckles rapped!" The head cook had walked into the room.

"The pet got caught in Basee," someone said to the cook.

The cook turned her eyes on Yonah. "Oh, you plan on liberating all of us? You'll get us all punished. I can see you've started with yourself."

"I'm not part of the rebellion."

"Then what were you doing all the way in Basee?" the cook asked.

Yonah only looked back into the woman's fiery gaze. She blanched when she saw a man come down the stairs behind the cook. It was Bana.

He didn't see her right away. He went to sit next to a friend. His arm was in a sling, his stump hidden.

Just as Bana sat down, he saw Yonah. He froze. Everyone around them was also staring, waiting to see what would happen. Even the air had halted.

There was fear in Bana's eyes. His eyes glanced around the room. "What are you doing here?" His gaze rested on her face. "What happened to you?"

She felt herself go red. She could feel anger and bitterness coming her way from every direction.

"I'd better go." Yonah stood up. With her eyes on the table she said to Praha, "Thank you for inviting me down here," and raced out of the hall, holding back tears as she made her way back to her bedroom.

THE GUESTS WERE FINALLY gone. Yonah still hadn't seen Naris since the incident and it had been a week. Each day, she looked into her mirror to watch how her lip healed. The two sides were beginning to join together in an attempt to make her lip whole again. The stitching thread that criss-crossed over it was doing its job.

Yonah was still embarrassed about Seidon seeing her new scar – at least she could hide the one on her arm – so she continued to avoid the stable, and she couldn't go to town without Naris' permission. Boredom started to creep into her routine.

An idea came to Yonah.

She tucked a candle into her pocket and peered out into the third-floor hallway from her bedroom. It was empty. Keeping as quiet as possible, Yonah closed the bedroom door behind her and moved to the portion of the hallway where Naris had watched her and Bana talking. She searched for anything out of place: a crack, a lever, something mismatched, anything that could potentially be a release for a secret door.

That night had confirmed Yonah's suspicion that Naris knew about the secret passageways in the palace. However, there was no reason for Yonah to believe he would be using them today. Naris was likely holed up in his office working, especially after he had spent the past week tending to the guests.

Nothing on the wall looked out of place. There was a decorative side table laden with a few pieces, but nothing happened when she moved anything. Next, she tried a wall sconce. The sconce shifted downward when Yonah tugged on it and she heard a clunk from a section of the wall.

She checked once more for anybody watching her, then shoved at the portion of wall that had shifted. Elated, Yonah withdrew the candle from her pocket, lit it with the already lit sconce, and stepped into the dark passage.

Over the next hour, Yonah meandered through the passageways, memorizing their layout. There were peepholes for just about every room, including her own, which was a disturbing discovery and reason enough for her to make sure, in the future, she looked at her map only in the tub room or her balcony. She found doorways for three bedrooms (including Naris'), the dining hall, the slaves' quarters in the basement, an exterior door at the side of the palace, and, of course, Naris' office and the library.

Although her original intention for this excursion had been to sneak into the library, Yonah wanted to head straight back to her room so she could write down a map of the passageways before she forgot. As she started back up the stairs, she heard shouting from Naris' office. There were two male voices. She inched towards the door that led to the office.

"You cannot tell me who I can and cannot speak to!" That was Naris' voice.

"You come from a long line masters who have dedicated their lives to this estate and you are risking it!"

"How is favouring someone risking this estate?"

"It is not *someone*," the other man hissed, "it is a slave girl! Instead of trying to marry one of your peers, you're presenting a slave girl as your favourite!"

Yonah wondered if Naris' friend Kejal had perhaps stayed behind after the other guests had left and was trying to convince him that his relationship with Yonah was unacceptable. But Kejal had seemed genuinely pleased at Yonah's effect on Naris. She leaned in towards the door crack to find out if she could see who was arguing with Naris.

She could only see a sliver of the room. The man in her line of vision wasn't Naris and it wasn't Kejal, either. He was a little shorter than Kejal and not so lean. His hair was streaked with grey and his face was lined with a few wrinkles.

"You're a business advisor," Naris said. "Yonah has nothing to do with my business."

"Your reputation is your business and the slave girl is affecting your reputation." The man stepped out of Yonah's line of vision, perhaps closer to Naris. "People are starting to wonder if you're sympathetic to the rebels. Others think you're just going insane. Either way, they do not want to do business with a rebel sympathizer or a lunatic."

"Then this trip to the north is perfectly timed. I'll be able to convince everyone that nothing about the business – or my sanity – has changed."

"As long as you leave the girl behind."

There was a heavy pause. "Yonah is coming with me."

"Master Naris, I must insist!"

"No, Varin, you've given me your advice and now I must ask you to leave!"

There was another pause before Yonah saw the man leave the room. Naris' figure flashed through her vision as he sat down in his chair.

Yonah started to quietly back away from the secret door and she returned to the third-floor entrance. She was surprised that Naris was still fighting for their relationship, despite the fact that they had not seen each other in days, despite the fact that he had done the thing that he swore he wouldn't do and physically hurt her.

Once back in the third-floor hallway, Yonah returned the sconce to its position, went to her bedroom, took the map and a quill outside to her balcony, and started to draw her own map of the secret passageways on the backside, all while trying to make sense of the conversation she had heard.

Naris was the only person in favour of their relationship and, with just about everyone in his life telling him of its inappropriateness, Yonah wondered how long it was before he was finally convinced of their incompatibility.

She was still on her balcony when there was a knock on her bedroom door. Yonah frantically folded up the map and tucked it into an interior pocket on her coat and hid the quill behind her back.

The slave woman – Praha – stepped out onto the balcony. "You're leaving tomorrow," she said.

"What?"

"Master Naris is going north for business and you're going with him."

Yonah remembered that Naris had told her about this trip a long time ago. "For how long?"

Praha shrugged. "Weeks? Months? You're leaving in the morning."

Yonah stood by the carriage the next morning, huddled in her travel coat. Her possessions were packed into three cases, which were already packed onto the back of the carriage. They were waiting for Naris.

After making sure the horses were ready, Seidon stepped next to Yonah and said quietly, "Everything alright?"

She nodded somberly at him.

"You look after yourself until you get back, yeah? And then come check in with me. I wish you'd have come to me after—" He didn't finish the thought.

Yonah's lower lip trembled against her will and she forced the tears back down into herself.

Naris finally emerged from the palace and strode down the steps to the carriage. Behind him, two slaves carried his luggage.

A few feet from Yonah, he stopped short, staring at her face. Although she had had her stitches removed after hearing she would be leaving Vaha, the scab was a prominent landmark upon her otherwise clear face.

Naris' impassive face twitched and Yonah caught a glimpse of shame.

Without saying a word, Naris walked past Yonah and climbed into the carriage. She followed suit, sitting next to him in silence. As the carriage rolled away, Seidon raised a hand up in farewell to Yonah. She wanted to wave back, but, so Naris wouldn't know of her attachment to the stable master, Yonah gave Seidon a simple nod as she and Naris departed on their journey north.

Chapter Twenty-Three

It was a business trip, with very little pleasure on their part. Naris and Yonah rode in silence from one estate to the next, where Naris would turn on his charm and charisma for the masters in his quest to either confirm orders, sweeten the deal, or make a new sale.

Yonah was greeted by the masters just as she expected – with an unwilling politeness at best, and downright unkindly at worst. In those worst cases, depending on Naris' mood, he would either ask her to wait by the carriage and speak alone with the master, or he would leave with her in a rage and threaten to sever ties.

Those days left Yonah unhappy, not because she wished to be welcomed into the fold by the masters, but because it meant she didn't get a chance to ask the local slaves whether they had heard of her sister.

With each estate they visited, Yonah tried to make contact with the slaves to ask if they knew anybody by the name of Sayzia. It was risky, she knew, especially with her recent altercation with Naris, but it was an opportunity she couldn't pass up. Each time she confirmed her sister wasn't at an estate, she crossed it off her map. And each time she didn't get the chance to ask, she made a note to try to come back there in the future.

The slaves always asked Yonah for word on the rebellion. It was a topic that seemed to span across the whole country, although faith and belief in the cause varied by estate. Yonah only half-heartedly let them know that she had heard Kelab was still a hot bed of rebellion activity and that organized anti-slavery groups were forming in Jalid. Her primary interest was in finding Sayzia.

In the meantime, Naris rarely looked at her, and the two of them hardly spoke. Yonah began to wonder why he had even bothered to bring her with him.

Within a week, they made it to the mountain pass that marked the boundary between Harasa and the northern country of Jalid. Here, the landscape grew different. Hills and mountains rose up, first covered in dirt and then rough browning grass. Soon, Yonah could see small drifts of snow at the mountaintops, foreshadowing the upcoming winter that would eventually close these passes for another season. Perhaps Sayzia lived among these mountains, these majestic giants that she had had no understanding of as a child.

They stopped at yet another estate, although it looked more like a pleasant farm. It was tucked in a large valley between three mountains. There was a series of wooden cottages lined up in a row, a barn, and a massive house made of dark grey brick with several chimneys billowing smoke.

Just like at every other estate they visited, Naris led the way inside with Yonah obediently following. They were greeted, to Yonah's surprise, by Naris' friend, Kejal.

"Naris, it's good to see you," Kejal said with a smile. He and Naris embraced. "How has the journey been so far?"

"We've had mixed results," Naris said darkly.

"Really. Why's that?"

"The masters have no respect."

Kejal's eyes flickered over to Yonah, then back to his friend. "For you or Yonah?"

"It's the same thing."

As Naris grumpily took off his coat, Kejal looked at Yonah again. She wished she could disappear, so she wouldn't feel his watchful gaze.

Kejal said to Naris, "Can we talk in private?"

"I don't need a lecture, Kejal," Naris snapped.

"Naris, please." Kejal said it in a friendly tone. "I'll have someone show Yonah to your room."

Naris looked sadly at Yonah, then said to his friend, "Fine."

Kejal patted his friend on the back, nodded to one of his slaves, and led Naris into another room.

"You can follow me," a woman said to Yonah, watching her uneasily. She carried a suitcase in each hand and held one out to Yonah. "Do you mind taking this?"

Yonah took the suitcase and followed the woman through the large house to a round room. It housed a short single bed.

"This is your room," said the woman, setting down the case. "Master Naris is just through that door."

"Can I ask you a question?"

"I suppose so."

"Is there a slave named Sayzia here?"

The woman blinked in surprise. "Yes, there is. Who are you?"

Yonah's mouth dropped open and her heart seemed to stop. "I'm her sister. She's here? Where can I find her?"

"She's a shepherd. She'll be somewhere in the hills."

All Yonah wanted to do was sprint outside and find Sayzia. They had already lost so much time and she couldn't bear to lose anymore. She strode over to the window and looked outside. There was no sign of a flock. She wasn't sure she could make it back in time without Naris noticing her absence.

"From what I understand, you're staying with us for a few days," the woman said suddenly. "I'm sure you'll get a chance to see her."

Yonah turned away from the window to look at the woman. "Thank you for saying that."

The woman gave Yonah a shrug and left the room.

But Yonah didn't want to wait any longer.

Naris would be with Kejal for a while. If she was still gone when he called for her, she could just say she was exploring the exterior of the house. That might still displease Naris, given their recent altercation, but she couldn't be accused of doing anything truly suspicious, unless Kejal's own home was considered a revolutionary hotspot.

Yonah left the room and walked purposefully out into the mountain air. It had more of a bite to it than the dry air on the plain, or the stickiness near the ocean.

She flagged down a nearby slave. "Do you know where the shepherds went today?"

"They've been going up that path lately." The slave motioned in one direction.

Yonah thanked the slave and started up the path. The farther she went, the more she felt a frantic pull towards her sister that made her break into a run. She was swallowed up by the mountains; they loomed high above her, cradling the path between them. The land was wet and soft. Yonah's feet slipped in the mud, and her cloth shoes were quickly wet from the grasses she trod through.

The path opened up onto a meadow. A flock of sheep speckled the green-brown ground with white spots. Yonah desperately searched for her sister. "Sayzia!"

Two faces turned towards her. She jogged to the nearest shepherd, who had sleek and straight black hair.

Yonah panted. "Is Sayzia here?"

"Who are you?" the shepherd asked. She had a slight accent.

"I'm her sister. Yonah."

The shepherd shared a meaningful look with her companion, who was walking towards them.

"Her sister," the straight-haired shepherd said to the second. They looked at her.

"They do look a bit alike." The second shepherd pointed upwards. "She's up there."

Yonah looked in the direction the shepherd pointed. She saw a small figure perched near the top of a mountain, a speck on the massive landscape.

"Sayzia!"

The figure shifted and stood.

"How do I get up there?"

The two women chuckled. "You don't go up there. They're dangerous paths. Let Sayzia come here."

While they waited, the straight-haired shepherd introduced herself as Taleea, and the other as Zahani. Yonah learned that they had been Sayzia's closest companions for nearly as long as she had been on this estate.

Zahani tilted her chin upwards to motion past Yonah's shoulder and Yonah turned around.

There was her sister, standing at the edge of the meadow. She had grown substantially over three years; her face was long and angular, and she was a little taller, although she stooped. She used a walking stick to hold some of her weight.

Yonah ran. Sayzia broke into a smile and began to jog slowly.

The sisters met and collided into a long embrace. An immediate warmth radiated through Yonah as she held her little sister.

"Sayzia, I knew I would find you! I knew it. I told you. I found you. Sayzia."

A few quiet tears were running down Sayzia's cheeks. She clung tightly to her big sister. Sayzia felt fragile and bony in Yonah's arms.

"I didn't think I would see you again," Sayzia whispered. "At least, not for a very long time." They broke their embrace and Sayzia asked, "What happened to you?" She was looking at Yonah's lip where the scab had turned into a smooth scar.

Yonah shifted as she remembered Naris' anger from that night. "It was a punishment."

"For what?"

"For overstepping my bounds." She changed the subject. "How are you?"

"Oh, I'm alright." Sayzia called out to her friends, "Do you mind if we talk for a bit?"

"Are you an idiot, Sayzia?" Zahani replied.

Taleea laughed. "Of course! We're fine."

The sisters sat together on a large rock. Sayzia moved slower than her older sister.

"So," Sayzia said as she sat with a grunt, "how did you do it? How'd you manage to find me?"

"My master sells wine. We've been travelling for a couple weeks now. I've just been asking your name at every place we stop. I knew you were north."

"How long will you stay here?"

"I don't know. It's always different. But your master is a particular friend of Naris."

Sayzia tilted her head quizzically. "You call him by his name?"

Shame burned in Yonah's chest. "It's complicated."

"I have time. My job is to stand out here."

"It's not so bad, is it?" Yonah asked. She looked out over the meadow, the sheep, the sky.

"I'm very lucky. What do you do that has you travelling with your master?"

Yonah felt a little embarrassed of her position. Even though Sayzia was lucky, she still did work. Yonah was nothing more than a decoration.

"I'm my master's personal companion."

"What does that mean?"

"It means he thinks I'm his closest friend." She neglected to mention the fact that she sometimes thought of Naris as her friend, too, though less so after her recent punishment. "But I use it to my advantage. He gives me more freedom than most slaves... usually."

"Is that why you're out here?"

"He's talking with your master," Yonah replied, shaking her head. "He doesn't know I'm out here."

"Then you should go."

Yonah shook her head. "I just found you."

"I know. And I'm glad." Sayzia stood up with much effort, pressing her weight into her walking stick. "But you have to look after yourself. I'll see you again soon."

Anxiety tugged at Yonah to go back to the house while her love for her sister tried to hold her in place. But Sayzia was usually right. Yonah stood up and hugged her sister once again.

"I'll see you soon," she whispered.

"Go find your master," Sayzia ordered.

Yonah did as she was told, jogging down the path back to the house, uplifted from seeing Sayzia after so many years of separation, scared to come crashing down if Naris knew she had gone without his knowing.

When she snuck back into the house, she had originally thought to go looking for Naris and Kejal, but realized her wet shoes and pants would give her away. She went back to the bedroom and changed clothes.

Yonah was just flopping onto the bed in exhausted relief when Naris opened the door. She stood back up.

"You've changed," Naris noted.

"I thought I'd put on something more comfortable," Yonah replied.

He gave the outfit a disapproving look. "Well, you'll have to change again for dinner in a little while."

"Yes, Master."

Naris sighed audibly. "Yonah." They stared at each other, paragraphs of unspoken words floating between them. "Never mind."

He started for the door that led to his room. Yonah said, "Do I have your permission to explore the estate when you don't need me?"

Naris paused with his hand on the door handle. "Yes." He added in a firm voice, "But only the estate."

THE FOLLOWING MORNING, Yonah ambled up the mountain path to find the three shepherds again. Yonah showed Sayzia the map she had purchased in Kirash and how she had been using it to cross off estates she knew Sayzia hadn't been sent to.

"It only was a matter of time before I figured out where you were," Yonah said.

Sayzia chuckled softly. "Then I need to ask. Have you had word from Obi?"

Yonah beamed. "I've just gotten word from him, actually. I haven't seen him yet, but soon. I managed to track him down at the port city of Basee."

Sayzia stared at her sister in wonder. "That's… amazing. How did you do it?"

"Well, like I said, my master gives me a lot more freedom than most slaves. I travelled to the nearby town and made contacts there who could look out for him."

"When will you see him?"

"I'll go to the contact as soon as I'm back at Vaha. That's Naris' estate."

Suddenly, Sayzia was coughing harshly. Yonah flinched and reached out to touch her sister. Sayzia shook her head at Yonah.

As the coughing subsided, Sayzia said, "Don't worry. I'm fine."

"You don't sound fine."

"Did you have a terrible sickness in the south a few months back? I had it for a while. The others thought I wouldn't make it. I haven't been the same since."

Yonah nodded solemnly. "We did. I lost friends to it." She recalled nursing several of her friends to their deaths. She turned to look at the other two shepherds who were off in the distance. "Are they the ones who looked after you?"

Sayzia nodded. "We've become really close. They're almost family."

Yonah's heart panged. Even her sister – solitary, cautious, quiet – had surrounded herself with people who cared for her.

"Is there much talk of the rebellion where you are?" Sayzia asked.

It was an odd question from Sayzia. Yonah thought that her sister would have thought the rebellion was a ridiculous fantasy and a waste of time.

"I haven't paid too much attention to it, although many of the slaves I spoke to on the road up here have been asking about it. And there is a presence in Kirash. I feel like I'm accused of being a part of it nearly every day."

"But you aren't?"

"No. Not yet. I'm not sure. Finding you and Obi has been my biggest concern."

"You know, it would be easier to find me and Obi if we were all free."

Yonah furrowed her brow. Sayzia was right about that. But it didn't seem as if the rebellion would be successful anytime soon. It was only in the beginning stages. It was whispers and the odd rampant household.

"Well, I'll be free in a few months," Yonah countered. "And then I can really get to work helping you and Obi."

"Hm," Sayzia said, her lips pursed.

"I hear the rebellion is getting stronger in Jalid," Yonah said.

Sayzia nodded. "I think big changes are coming. I'm ready to help if I can."

"You'll join the rebellion?"

"I feel like I have to. Won't you?"

The thought of joining the rebellion had been on Yonah's mind for a while. To join would change everything – it would be a huge betrayal of Naris' trust and it would put her safety at risk. She brought her fingertips to the scar on her lip.

"I might. I think I'm a little afraid."

"Were you afraid when your master did that to you?" Sayzia pointed at Yonah's lip. Yonah nodded.

"So, which fear are you willing to live with?"

Eventually Taleea and Zahani joined in the conversation, sharing their stories of how they came to be working as a slave for Kejal. Zahani was from a town in Harasa. Taleea was born in Jalid.

As the four of them walked back that evening with the flock, Naris was walking outside. He stopped when he saw Yonah and looked from her to Sayzia. The shepherds stood with their heads bowed, but Naris and Yonah shared a look that made the back of Yonah's jaw twinge.

Naris walked away silently and Sayzia whispered, "What was he looking at?"

Yonah watched him go, a sense of unease spreading through her body. "He knows we're sisters."

THAT NIGHT IN NARIS' BEDCHAMBER, Yonah found him sitting with a glass of wine. The fireplace was lit, casting a shadowy glow on the room. His gaze was calm and filled with curiosity. Yonah stood in the doorway, half hoping that, if she didn't enter, they wouldn't talk, and he wouldn't ask about her sister.

"So, that's your sister." It wasn't a question. He had full confidence in knowing that they had been reunited. "You two look alike."

Yonah closed the bedroom door behind her.

"You must be very happy."

She nodded gently. She was waiting for the moment when Naris told her she would be forbidden from seeing her sister again.

Naris stood and sauntered over to the liquor cabinet and poured a drink. He handed the glass to Yonah.

"You'd better get a good visit in with your sister before we head out again. It will be some time before we are back."

The corners of her lips twitched upward, but Yonah quickly hid her glee. She took the glass from Naris and nodded before taking a drink.

"I have a gift for you," he said abruptly, striding over to a table that was acting as his office. There was a pile of paper on it, pens, and a plain flat box. He retrieved the box and carried it back to Yonah. She set her glass down and took it.

"Open it," he said.

Beneath the lid lay a necklace. It was one of the most beautiful things she had ever seen. On a black leather string hung a small collection of smooth silver and sapphire beads, and in the centre of them was a large blue stone with a carving of a bird on it. She couldn't imagine wearing it herself, it was far too valuable.

Naris silently took the necklace, stepped behind Yonah, and brushed her hair to one side. Her skin trembled at his touch, which made her feel both exhilarated and terrified. Naris brought the necklace around her neck and tied it. She could feel his soft breathing on the back of her head.

"Now, let me look at you," he said, stepping back in front of her. He smiled. "Yes. Just as I imagined it."

She felt awkward with the heavy stone on her chest.

"Do you like it?" he asked.

"It's beautiful. Thank you."

"But do you like it?"

"I do. I just..." She paused. "It's too much."

He furrowed his brow, puzzled. "I disagree. It's perfect for you." He stepped closer and ran his thumb on the beads. "It's exquisite, full of life, mysterious, charming." He looked deep into her eyes. "It's you."

Yonah's heart beat harder. Her breathing stopped. She was a fly caught in a web, immobile, at the mercy of her captor. Naris leaned in and gently kissed her. Warmth spread through her body, like a soft glow. The pressure on her mouth reminded Yonah of her tender lip and she withdrew from the sensation.

She pulled away from the kiss at the same time as Naris. There was a look of amusement on his face.

"Does that mean you forgive me?" he asked. It was the first time he had mentioned that awful night.

Rage stormed through Yonah's chest at Naris thinking that she could ever forgive him for hurting her. She would not give any more thought to the warm sensation she had initially felt.

She took a step away from him, turning her eyes downward, her hand clasping the stone hanging from her neck.

"Thank you for the necklace."

They stood in an unbearable silence. Yonah kept her eyes down as she felt Naris look at her. He finally said, "You may go," and she raced out of the room.

Chapter Twenty-Four

The following morning, Yonah was walking out the bedroom door when Naris emerged from his private room. Yonah nodded politely to him, but hoped he didn't want a long conversation.

"Where's the necklace?" Naris asked.

Yonah blinked. "Pardon?"

"The necklace I gave you yesterday. I want to see you wearing it."

He had never bothered about what jewelry she wore before. "You want me to wear it now?"

"Yes, Yonah. I would like that."

He was still as he watched Yonah retrieve the necklace from one of her cases. He helped her fasten it and took a long look at her.

"There," he said with a sigh. "Are you off to visit your sister?"

Yonah's insides were twisting. Something about Naris' eyes on her and his hands on her shoulders made her feel unsafe. "Yes," she answered.

"Good. I hope you enjoy yourself."

They walked down the hall together and parted ways at the front door. Stepping out into the cool air, Yonah shook off the feeling of dread that weighed her body down and started for the meadows hidden in the mountains.

As she walked past the slaves' cottages, she heard a voice call her name. She turned and saw Zahani waving from a window. She looked upset. Yonah changed direction and went inside.

Sayzia was lying in her bed, wrapped in blankets and shivering. Her skin was wet with a cold sweat.

"What's wrong with her?" Yonah asked, kneeling next to her sister.

"It's the fever," Zahani whispered. "It's back."

"Well, how did it happen?" Anger burned inside of Yonah, wanting to find where the blame lay.

"It's always been there, Yonah. She never really got over it. It's a miracle she survived this long."

Yonah pressed the back of her hand to her little sister's forehead. It was hot.

"Yonah, I have to go to tend the sheep. Taleea's alone."

She nodded. "Go. I'll stay here."

Yonah pressed a cold washcloth to Sayzia's skin, forced her to drink water, tried to get her to eat when she was awake, but Sayzia had little interest in the outside world and the fever grew.

Yonah sang their songs to her. She told Sayzia the stories their parents used to tell them as children. She recalled the funny stories they shared. All the while, she feared that she was simply nursing her sister on her way to death, just as she had her old friends.

Late in the afternoon, Sayzia looked straight at Yonah.

"Mama?"

Yonah shook her head, tears beginning to blur her eyesight. "It's me,

Sayzia. It's Yonah. Remember? I'm here. It's been so long, but I'm here. I'm going to make sure you get better."

"When will Pa come home?"

"Sayzia, no! Please, it's me." Her tears overflowed onto her cheeks. "It's your sister, Yonah. Sayzia, please."

Her sister's eyes flickered and she fell asleep.

"HOW IS SHE?" TALEEA ASKED when she and Zahani returned from their day's work.

"The same. She slept a lot."

Taleea froze on the spot. "What are you wearing?"

"What?"

Taleea was staring at the necklace Yonah wore. "Where did you get that?"

Yonah held the stone in her hand. "My master gave it to me."

"Those carvings are precious among my people," Taleea said. "Our stories say that they were created by one of our greatest chiefs, who carved them for her greatest advisors, warriors and friends. They are rare. If that was not a gift to your master, he paid a great price for it."

Taleea was staring hard at Yonah. Her look made the hairs on Yonah's arms stand up.

"Yonah?"

It was Sayzia.

Yonah clasped her sister's hand in hers. "Sayzia. How do you feel? Are you hungry?"

Sayzia looked around groggily with squinted eyes. "I think so?" She looked at Yonah. "I saw Mama and Pa. And you and Obi were there."

Yonah shook her head. "You were just seeing things, Sayzia. You're sick."

She slowly nodded. "I know."

Yonah asked Taleea and Zahani, "Is there a healer here who could help her?"

The two shepherds shrugged. "We have one," Zahani answered, "but she wouldn't know what to do. Sayzia's the only person to have survived the sickness. There's not a lot to go on."

There was a knock and the door opened. A teenage boy peered in and said to Yonah, "Master Naris wants you."

She looked at her sister. She ached to stay.

"We'll look after her," Taleea said. "Go to your master."

Yonah and Naris played chess that night on a new set made of jade stone that Naris said he had purchased the other day. There had been a travelling salesman. Yonah wondered if it was from this salesman that Naris purchased the apparently priceless necklace.

"What are you thinking about?" he asked her as he moved a rook.

Yonah kept her eyes on the board. She thought she saw a way to win this game. She moved her bishop. "My sister is sick. With the same illness that killed so many earlier this year."

"The same illness that brought us into each other's lives. Funny thing." He spoke mostly to himself, examining the board for his next move. Yonah wasn't surprised that Naris insisted on seeing the illness as something that brought him his good fortune, but his disregard for the pain it brought others fed the angry flame inside her.

"She's too sick to work right now, and I'm not so sure she'll find proper medical attention here. I'm worried for her."

"I hope she gets better." Naris moved his knight.

A small bit of Yonah thrilled at the move, while another part of her wanted to scream in frustration at his apparent ignorance.

"I was wondering if we could bring her home with us. Then I could look after her when you don't need me. She could be my companion." She moved her queen.

Naris looked up at her, darkness in his eyes. "I thought I made it clear that she would not be going back to Vaha with us. Which was why I encouraged you to see her as much as you could on this trip."

"But she'll die here without help."

"That is not my concern. You are my sole concern."

"And my concern is my sister!"

"Your job is to be *my* companion, Yonah," he hissed, slamming a fist on the games table. "That's it. I have tried being persuasive about it. I've tried to win your favour with gifts," he motioned to the necklace she wore, "but you can't seem to understand that you are still *my* slave and you must obey me."

Tears hot with anger welled up in Yonah's eyes. Her lips pressed together, caging the angry cry that tried to escape.

"We will be leaving in two days," Naris said, coldly. "Your sister will not be coming with us." He picked up his queen and knocked Yonah's queen to the side with it, slamming his in its place. "Checkmate."

LATER THAT NIGHT, AFTER SHE could hear Naris' soft snores as she listened from her bed in the antechamber next to his room, Yonah reached under her bed for one of her cases, quietly ran her hand through it, and pulled out her map.

She used the moonlight to examine the large paper. There was Vaha, Kirash, and Basee. Northward was the mountain pass, and there was the estate belonging to Kejal.

They would need to find a centre that would have a skilled healer. After Sayzia had recovered, they would need to find another port city in order to meet up with Obi. Perhaps they could find passage back to Basee and meet him there.

There was a road leading west that passed through a town named Jakarth. That was where they would go first.

Yonah had gone out to the barn after her chess game with Naris to search for a wagon or sled. She had found a sled that was the perfect size, moved it to a corner of the barn, and gone back to her room.

Now she waited until the air grew soft with light, the sun not yet over the horizon, its rays still hidden. It was at this time before dawn that the shepherds went out with the sheep.

Yonah took a bag that was filled with her remaining money and an extra set of clothes, fetched the sled from the barn, and watched the shepherd cottage from the door. A few minutes later, Zahani and Taleea emerged and headed in the direction of the sheep shed. Yonah waited until she saw the flock disappear into the mountains before leaving the shelter of the barn.

Sayzia was asleep when Yonah entered the cottage. Yonah quietly rummaged and searched the room for anything to pack. She placed a water bottle, an extra blanket, and some boots into her sack, and placed Sayzia's walking stick on the sled. Then she nudged her sister awake.

"Mama?"

"Ssh, it's Yonah. We're going."

"Where are we going?"

"Somewhere you can get help. Can you stand up? Just for a moment?"

Sayzia had yet to open her eyes. Yonah pressed her lips together in determination and stripped the blankets off her sister. She grabbed her feet and placed them on the floor. She wrapped an arm under each of Sayzia's shoulders, lifted her off the bed, dragged her across the floor, and unceremoniously pulled her down the front steps of the cottage to the sled.

Once Sayzia was placed on the sled, Yonah wrapped her in her bed blankets, placed her sack next to her, lifted the two handles, and pulled.

Yonah hadn't done hard labour for months now, and it showed. Her hands, once calloused, were soft and stretched against the pull of the handles. Her arms felt weak; she wondered how long she would be able to keep this up.

It wasn't until they were beyond the estate grounds and on empty road that Yonah felt herself breath normally. They were safe, for now. Nobody was expecting Sayzia since she was sick, and Naris wouldn't miss Yonah until the evening meal, by which time Yonah hoped she and Sayzia would be well hidden in Jakarth.

THEY WERE FORTUNATE THERE was very little traffic on the road, and what little there was paid no attention to them. Yonah had taken care to cover up both her and Sayzia's slave collars in coats and blankets and every time someone passed by, she forced herself not to draw her hand up to her neck.

Yonah was annoyed at herself every time she paused for a break, but she didn't have the strength she once had when she worked for Puru. She released the sled handles and held her palms open. There were three big welts on them where blisters had broken open. She wished she was making better time.

"Where am I?" came Sayzia's soft voice.

"We're going to Jakarth" Yonah said, her voice hard. "I'm getting you help."

Sayzia tried to sit up in the sled. "Yonah, what have you done?" Her voice trembled.

Yonah knelt next to Sayzia. "I told you I would bring us together again."

"This isn't the way." She lied back down. "Pa, tell her." Her eyes slowly shut.

By the time they reached Jakarth, the sun had long since set and it was dark. Yonah's back, shoulders, and arms ached. She ignored the throbbing in her hands. She felt sweat droplets gliding down her back beneath her shirt and coat. As she exhaled, clouds of hot air blew from her mouth.

Yonah dragged the sled up to an inn. She wrapped her jacket tightly around her neck to hide her slave collar and stepped inside. There was a counter with a man standing behind it. She stepped up to the counter.

"I need a room for the night."

"That'll be sixty ora."

She hesitated. "I only have forty-five, but I have plenty to barter with."

"Sorry, dear, I don't take any other forms of payment."

"Please, I can make it worth your while."

The man leaned toward her, squinting his eyes. "You a slave? On the run?"

"No."

"Then open up that coat."

She didn't move, only stared pleadingly at the innkeeper.

"Look, I can't be giving shelter to runaway slaves. I'd be out of a livelihood. Might even get enslaved myself."

Yonah dropped her hands and let her coat fall open in defeat.

"Hold on. What's that?"

She looked at the man. He was pointing at her necklace.

"It's a rare stone," Yonah said. "Would this change your mind?"

"Where did you get that?"

"Will it change your mind?" she said firmly.

He glanced from the necklace to Yonah's face and back again. "You give me that necklace, and I'll let you stay in the stable."

"I need a room. I have a sick person with me."

"Two of you! Definitely the stable. Do we have a deal?"

She had no choice but to accept the offer.

The stable was significantly warmer than the outside air, but not as sheltered as Yonah would have liked for her sick sister. She settled them in a back corner of the building in a large pile of hay. A couple horses snorted softly at their new companions.

"Sayzia, sleep for tonight and we'll find you a healer in the morning," Yonah whispered to her sister, who lay curled up in a ball next to her. Yonah wrapped her arms around Sayzia and lay her head down, praying everything would turn out alright.

SHE WAS AWOKEN BY A PAIR of hands grabbing her clothing and pulling her upright. The world was black, then she saw a flame from a torch, and Naris' face in front of hers, twisted into a look of rage and relief.

"Why did you run?" he said with a snarl.

Yonah tried to pull out of his grip. She had been here before. He was far stronger than her. She couldn't give up, though.

"I'll deal with you when we get back." Naris dragged her out of the stable into the cold night air. Breath fogged in front of everyone's faces – Yonah's, Naris', Kejal's, and the guards they had brought with them. It was a cold Yonah had never experienced before. Surely, it couldn't be good for her sister's condition.

"Sayzia!" she screamed. "Sayzia!"

"Don't bother with her," Kejal said to someone else. "She's of no use to me like that."

With a newfound strength fueled by her terror, Yonah broke free of Naris. "No! Sayzia! Someone has to help her." She ran to the stable.

A hired guard stepped in her path and wrapped his arms around her when she crashed into him. She tried to clamber out of the massive man's grip. She was ensnared in a trap, panicking, whining, desperate. Tears began to stream down her face, oddly hot against the cold night.

Then she was being pulled by her hair. Naris had grabbed a large handful of hair at her scalp and was bringing her back to his horse. Yonah's desperate screams for her sister turned into screams of pain.

"Do as I say, Yonah," he said in a low tone that only the two of them could hear. "Get up."

"Naris, please, she's my sister."

"Get on the horse, now!" he yelled. "Or do I need to remind you that even you aren't safe from punishment?" He grabbed her lip as an extra reminder.

This was not the way it was supposed to happen. She had escaped. She had successfully taken her sister away. They were supposed to find Obi and live out their lives together.

Growing impatient, Naris turned Yonah roughly around and began lifting her onto the horse. She let him. He climbed on behind her and they began the journey back to the mountain estate.

They rode fast. The air bit at Yonah's face, cooling her tears. She felt trapped tucked in between Naris' body and arms, even if the cover of his body provided a little warmth. He was silent the whole ride, but his anger never faded. She felt it around them like a buzzing in the air.

When they arrived at the estate, Naris gruffly thanked Kejal, dismounted, brought Yonah down, and dragged her to his bedchamber. The fireplace was lit, but instead of giving off a soft warmth, tonight it cast an eerie glow.

"You disobeyed me," Naris said. "You made me look like a fool!" His voice was quickly rising to a shout. "I told you your sister would not be returning with us! And, still, you tried to escape! You do not get to escape! You belong to me!"

Yonah had backed away against the far wall. The room stretched long between the two of them.

"What can I do to make sure you don't forget that ever again?"

Her tears had run dry. She tried to still her trembling body.

"Don't you understand?" he said, his voice softer. He walked slowly towards her. "You are everything."

Now standing in front of her, his eyes traced her body. His gaze stopped at her neck.

"You're not wearing the necklace."

Her trembling stopped. Every nerve in Yonah's body perked to attention, waiting for the blow.

"Where is it?"

She remained silent.

"Where is it!"

"I don't have it." She let her eyes drop to the ground.

The calm fury in his voice made chills run down Yonah's neck. "What did you do with it?"

There was a heavy silence in the room for what must have been a full minute. Yonah didn't meet his eyes the entire time. She felt his stare bearing down on her, pressing against her as if he were physically holding her.

He would wait until she said it. There was nothing for her to do except admit her guilt and accept her fate.

"We needed shelter."

He still waited.

"I traded it."

There was no eruption of anger as she had expected. He quietly rested the palm of his hand on her sternum where the stone would have rested. Then he slowly drew his hand upwards until his fingers wrapped gently around her throat, the side of his hand pressing her chin up, forcing her to look at him.

Hurt. His eyes revealed pain, with an edge of anger.

"That was a gift for you."

"I'm sorry."

"You're sorry?" He squeezed and Yonah gasped. "I'm trying to tell you how much I love you and you barter away my shows of affection!"

In that moment, Yonah believed Naris would suffocate her then and there. She could still breathe now, but how many more moments before he truly gave in to his rage? She had failed. She would never see her brother and sister again.

Naris' face was twisting in and out of a scowl and a tearful frown. He was frozen in time, trying to hold back any vulnerability.

"I just—" The words burst from his mouth with a sob. "I just need you to see." Yonah was aghast to see tears running down his cheeks. "I need you to understand."

He relaxed his grip on her throat. His thumb brushed against her lips tenderly, then he moved his hand up the side of her face and to the back on her head, his fingers tangling in her hair. He stepped closer, placing his other hand on her waist and pulled her into a kiss.

Yonah stood frozen in shock as his lips pressed against hers.

But this kiss was different from before. It was rushed, desperate, and rough. Naris' hands began to run up and down her body. He pulled away from her.

"Lie down."

Her body clenched tightly as he stared hungrily down at her.

"Do as I say," he said.

She forced the words out. "You said you wanted both of us to be ready."

His face turned dark and he pulled her by the arm and pushed her onto the bed.

"Please," Yonah whined.

Naris was undressing. First his shirt, then his pants. Despite being completely naked, he was anything but vulnerable, standing over Yonah with a predatory look.

Yonah scrambled to a sitting position. "Naris, please."

He grabbed her ankle and pulled her down the bed. Lithely, he climbed over top of her.

"Naris. No. No, I don't want to!"

His hand was under her shirt, running up her belly, resting on her breast. He kissed her neck. She tried to pull away.

"The more you struggle, the more irritated I get," he said.

"Get off of me!" She pressed her hands on his hot chest and pushed hard. Taken by surprise, he slipped off the bed, landing on his feet.

His nostrils flared. He climbed back onto the bed, pinning Yonah between his knees. He placed two hands on her shirt and pulled hard, tearing through the light fabric. Yonah cried out. Then he began pulling off her bottoms. Yonah held onto the waist.

"Stop it." He struck her face and Yonah involuntarily let go at the contact. Before she could recover from the pain, Naris removed her pants.

"No!" she screamed as loud as she could. "Help me! Someone! Please, help!"

He covered her mouth and lowered his face close to hers. "You are mine. No one is coming to help."

She stared up at him in horror, stripped of her voice, her ability to move, and her own free will as the man she had once loved turned into a monster before her eyes.

SHE WAS BREAKING APART FROM the inside. Her insides felt like they had been churned and then set on fire.

Yonah curled up on the bed and wrapped her arms around her stomach. Naris fell beside her, lightly panting.

The farther away time took her from the moment, the more all her feelings dissipated into a numbness. She shook less, the sweat on her forehead cooled, the stream of tears lessened to slow single droplets, and her fear and shock bubbled away into cool nothingness. She stared straight ahead, her eyes not seeing.

The bed shifted as Naris stood up. There was a pause before he said, "Get out." She didn't hear the pain in his voice. She only heard the order.

Everything hurt as she gingerly stood up. Without looking in Naris' direction, Yonah picked up her pants, her ruined shirt, and her travel coat. She was almost at the door when Naris said, "Yonah."

She stopped, but didn't turn.

"Your sister is dead by now. When we get back to Vaha, don't go looking for your brother."

She wouldn't let herself feel anything. If she did, she was sure she truly would fall apart in front of Naris. She left the room.

One more night. And then all contact with her sister and her old life would be gone. Yonah dressed and, barefooted, walked to the shepherds' cottage.

Taleea opened the door. Her mouth dropped open as she looked at Yonah. "What happened?"

Yonah felt again. The soreness in her body. The grief for her sister. The shock of what Naris had done. The despair that she would never feel anything good again.

Yonah closed her eyes and bowed her head. She wept. Taleea pulled her inside the cottage.

Without really knowing how, Yonah found herself curled up in Sayzia's bed with a woman she didn't recognize standing over her. The woman brought a bowl to Yonah's lips and Yonah drank. The liquid inside smelled rich and tasted bitter.

"So there will be no child," the woman explained. Yonah barely heard her. She rolled over and fell asleep.

Chapter Twenty-Five

They were back in the carriage the next morning, sitting next to each other. Yonah winced the first time she tried to climb up, and Naris came to assist her. His touch made her muscles clench, brought her back to the night before, and all she wanted to do in that moment was wrench herself away from him.

At first, they didn't speak. The only sound was the wind whipping past the carriage and through the rocks that loomed overhead. Those rocks, still and imposing, watched their discomfort. Naris tried to strike up a conversation.

"It's amazing how different the landscape is here than back home. I sometimes wonder how that could have happened."

Yonah remained silent. She looked out the window at the passing mountainsides. She could see the odd goat on a cliff, defying gravity, staying upright on tiny platforms of rock. Sayzia was out there in the cold. Surely, she didn't still lie in the stable. The innkeeper must have done something with her. Had she been buried? Would the ground be too hard with winter on its way? Perhaps they burned their dead in the north.

"I think it would be nice to travel in the mountains more often. A break from the heat. What do you think?"

She was called to speak. In a dull tone, Yonah said, "It's beautiful here."

Naris continued to be attentive to her, assisting her when leaving the carriage, encouraging her to rest, double checking that she was eating enough. They played chess every night. He let her win a few times. She was unresponsive to her victories. He sometimes held her hand while they rode. It was not a comfort to her.

Her physical pain ebbed away with the passing days. She grieved for Sayzia, quietly. Naris saw the change in her disposition clearly.

When they finally arrived back at Vaha, Yonah waited patiently for everything to be unloaded and taken back into the palace. Naris noticed her still standing there.

"Would you like something?" he asked, hopeful.

"I wanted to know if you needed any more from me," she said without feeling.

Naris slumped. "No. Thank you."

Yonah turned and went straight to her room, lied down on the bed, and stared at the ceiling.

SHE DID NOT LEAVE HER ROOM for three days. Praha brought food to her, which she only picked at from time to time. She did eventually leave her bed, choosing instead to sit on the balcony outside and stare off into the distance.

Any plans she had had for finding Obi were forgotten. Any hope dissipated. Her fate was to be stuck in this beautiful prison, a doll to the cruelest man she had ever known. To add to her gloom, Yonah knew she would be punished for attempting to escape with two more years of enslavement.

"You need to get out of here."

It was Praha. She was standing in the balcony doorway holding a tray. "And you need to eat." She crouched next to Yonah, who sat leaning against the palace wall. She held out a bun. "Yonah," Praha said with force.

Yonah pulled her eyes away from the skyline, returning to reality. She looked at the bun and slowly retrieved it from Praha's outstretched hand. Praha watched as Yonah took a slow, calculated bite and chewed. She sat next to Yonah and asked, "What happened while you were away?"

Involuntarily, Yonah drew away from the question, folding her body in upon itself to grow smaller.

"You've changed. And the master."

He had only been a figment of Yonah's imagination for the past three days, only a monster in her nightmares. Praha was making him real again.

"He's not the same either," Praha reiterated.

Yonah ached to know what she meant, but didn't dare to ask.

"Whatever happened, Yonah," Praha said, "it doesn't go away by you sitting here forever."

"It doesn't go away if I see him, either." Yonah looked at the half-eaten bun in her hands. But she also didn't want the hurt to go entirely away. If it did, it meant she had forgotten Sayzia.

"Did the master bed you?"

She closed her eyes to catch the tears welling up in them.

"I thought he had done that a long time ago," Praha said casually. Yonah didn't move, couldn't speak. "It's hard at first, but it gets easier. Nothing to get so upset over."

She didn't understand.

"You should get out of here." Praha stood up, wiping dust and dirt from her clothes. She looked down at Yonah. "You're letting him win by acting like this." She turned and left Yonah by herself.

Yonah continued to slowly gnaw at the bun in her hands and watch the skyline. A gentle breeze blew her hair to the side, baring her neck to the world. Yonah wrapped her fingers around the copper collar around her neck, trying to find the strength in herself to do the next right thing.

She couldn't let him win.

The flame that had burned inside of her since the coup and grown stronger and stronger with each unfair loss she faced – her parents' murders, her capture into slavery, her separation from her siblings – had been snuffed out in the mountains. But now, there was a tiny spark, waiting for someone to fan the flame.

With anger and indignance fueling her, Yonah stood up and strode to her bedroom door. She opened it a crack and peeked outside. The hallway was empty. She quietly shut the door behind her and made her way down the hall to the sconce that opened the secret passage.

Listening hard for other footsteps in the passage, Yonah snuck down the stairs, passed by Naris' office where she saw a soft glow of light, and stepped into the library from behind his great-grandmother's portrait.

Knowing she was safe inside the library for now, Yonah heaved a sigh and closed her eyes. If Naris found out she were here, what could he possibly do to her next?

Yonah collected herself, forcing herself to stand tall on her own two feet. She began to weave in and out of the stacks, searching for something she had bypassed before.

She remembered where they were: *A History of Harasa, The Isle War, Oceanic Wars.* Yonah's eyes lit up when she saw the book called *A History of Harasan Rebellions.* She pulled the dusty tome from the shelf, sat right there on the stone floor, and began reading.

When she had finished reading for the day, Yonah snuck down to the secret side door that led to the estate grounds and made her way to the stable. The horses were in the corral, grazing. She paused for a moment to watch them from the safety of the other side of the wooden post fence, then went into the stable.

Seidon was cleaning the stalls with a shovel. He looked up at Yonah. "Was wondering when I might see you."

"I'm sorry I didn't come sooner. Do you need help?"

"I wouldn't want you to get your fancy clothes dirty. You might get in trouble. Now, are you going to tell me what happened to you?"

Yonah remembered that she hadn't really spoken to Seidon since before the night Naris punished her for going to Basee. It seemed so long ago after everything that had happened since.

"I went to Basee," she said, "and Naris didn't like that."

Seidon frowned at Yonah for a moment before returning to his work.

"He also didn't like when I tried to escape from him on our trip to the north."

This made Seidon look up at Yonah with wide eyes and an open mouth. "You tried to escape? Why?"

"My sister was there and she was sick." Yonah dropped her chin and looked down at her sandaled feet. "She's dead now."

Seidon limped next to Yonah and place a hand on her shoulder. "I'm sorry."

She nodded without looking up and placed her hand over his. Tears prickled in her eyes and dripped from her face to the floor.

"We were supposed to be together again," she muttered. With a fierceness burning inside her, Yonah looked up at Seidon. "The slavery act ruined everything. I want to help get rid of it."

Seidon's eyebrows shot up. "Do you know what you're saying?"

Yonah nodded. "Rebellions have happened in Harasa before. Some are successful by force, like the coup. Some turn into real political movements. I think that's what they're trying to do in Jalid and Kelab. They always take a lot of people."

"You got a plan or something?"

"Not yet. But you would help, if I needed it?"

Seidon stared hard at Yonah for a moment, then he slowly nodded.

THE FOLLOWING DAY, YONAH was sitting on her balcony when she heard Praha call her name from inside.

"You have a gift."

"I don't want it."

"Well, I think it needs tending to whether you want it or not."

Her curiosity peaked, Yonah stood and went inside. There was a small, covered basket resting on the table in the centre of the room. Praha stood next to it, waiting for Yonah.

Slowly, Yonah walked over to the basket and looked inside.

It was a kitten. Its black hair was soft and thick, standing up, looking like the down on a duckling. It looked up at Yonah with its large eyes and meowed softly. Entranced by the creature, Yonah reached inside and fearlessly picked it up, cradling it in her arms. It meowed at her again and stretched its claws.

"She's meant to be your companion, the master said," Praha explained.

Warmth filled Yonah's chest and she smiled down at the kitten. "She's mine." Someone that would love her, that she could talk to, that she could turn to for comfort.

"Should I tell him you like it?"

Yonah's eyes couldn't leave the kitten. However, she nodded in answer to Praha's question. "If he asks."

Praha nodded and left the room.

Yonah played with the kitten for a while before realizing it needed a name. She watched it thoughtfully, waiting for something to come to mind.

"I think I'll call you Saza. For the sister you never knew."

That same night, Naris finally summoned her to his room.

She brought Saza with her. Naris smiled at the kitten.

"She's done wonders for you," he said.

Yonah held the kitten closer. She wasn't sure how she would react when she and Naris were alone again. Right now, she felt very much as she did the first time she had been summoned to his room when she was still a slave for Puru, unsure and cautious.

"Would you like to play a game?" Naris motioned to the set-up chess board. Yonah silently sat in her usual seat, still holding Saza close. Naris poured each of them a glass of wine.

"What have you named it?" he asked, setting a cup in front of her and sitting.

Without a moment's hesitation, she answered, "Saza."

His cup paused momentarily on its way to his lips, but Naris recovered quickly. After a long drink, he set his cup down with a sigh and looked at the kitten. There was no hatred in his eyes, as Yonah thought there might be, only curiosity.

"I've reported your attempted escape," Naris said. "Your sentence has been extended two years after your twentieth birthday."

Yonah knew she would be punished for trying to run away, but that didn't stop the blow from knocking the air out of her chest. Two extra years trapped with Naris.

"White goes first," he said, turning to the board.

Their game was quiet. Yonah felt out of practice. Her attention was split between the game and noticing every movement and breath from Naris. The long-setting sun faded away and the candles became their only light.

"I'm ashamed of how I acted, Yonah," he said suddenly. "I let my temper get the better of me."

Flashes of that night came back to her. Her fear, the pain, the eventual numbness. She drank from her glass.

"I hope we can get past it," he continued. "I was hoping that... Saza would be a good first step."

Their eyes met for a long while. His pleaded and were desperately hopeful. Hers were hard, yet broken.

"Say something," he commanded.

She said it coldly. "We can get past it."

His face crumbled a little. "What do you really want to say?"

Saza meowed, drawing the attention of both Yonah and Naris to her.

"Do you think you could ever forgive me?"

She kept her eyes on the kitten. It was playing with the sleeve of her shirt. Naris slowly stood and sat next to her, keeping a small distance between them. Yonah silently pleaded that he wouldn't come any closer. He reached over her arms and softly stoked Saza and the kitten immediately nuzzled its head into his hand. A feeling of betrayal rose in Yonah's chest that Saza so easily accepted Naris' affection.

"I like her," he said, decidedly. "She has spirit, much like you."

She didn't answer. Naris inched closer, lifted his fingers to Yonah's face, and turned it towards his.

"I'm sorry."

She could not forgive him. He wasn't to be trusted. His moods were ever-changing. His words meant nothing stacked up against his actions. No matter what he claimed to feel for her, he always found a reason to treat her like all masters did – a slave with a meaningless life, except for what she could provide for him.

He kissed her forehead, then her cheek, and then her lips. Then he was tugging her clothes away from her body.

But it didn't matter if she forgave him or not. She was still a slave and he was her master. He would take whatever he wanted from her, forgiveness or not.

IT WAS LESS PAINFUL THIS TIME. She remembered the advice of one of Master Puru's slaves; think of happy things. Thinking of her family made her grieve for what was lost. Instead, she thought of the vast sky, the clouds billowing, gentle rain and how it felt on her skin, of the mountains rising up, capped with snow, how sheep looked like tufts of snow on the mountainside from afar. She thought of the fresh air on her face, how it felt running through her nose, down to fill her lungs.

When Naris fell away from her, she moved to stand, but Naris grabbed her wrist. "No, stay."

She lay back down on the bed. He curled up next to her, resting a hand on her thigh, and promptly fell asleep. She was wide awake.

This was her life now. It wasn't a surprise, but it felt worse than she had expected. She hadn't imagined that she would feel so empty, that she would feel so small and alone in a vast world of hurt and darkness. She had to remind herself that there could be more than this, that maybe she could find meaning in her empty existence.

She focused on the small, defiant flame burning within.

Chapter Twenty-Six

Yonah lied in her bed for a long time that morning. Saza the cat hopped up to paw at her stomach and lounge at her hip. Her breakfast went cold. The sun rose higher and higher.

Yonah knew what her next step was, but it meant voluntarily seeing him, seeking him out. The thought made Yonah grimace.

She finally got out of bed, dressed, and made her way to Naris' office. The door was open just a crack. When Yonah peeked inside, she saw that Naris was talking to the older man she had seen through the secret door. His business advisor.

"Then why did so many of the masters rescind their orders?" the man said accusingly.

"I know, I know," Naris groaned.

"You can use the profits from last season to help this year, but you cannot go on like this! Especially with that girl hanging around for another two years—"

Yonah knocked on the door and the conversation stopped. The business advisor opened the door and, upon seeing Yonah, narrowed his eyes at her before stepping aside so Naris could see her.

Naris' face lit up with a bright smile when he saw Yonah.

"Yonah!" he said. "To what do I owe the pleasure?"

He had always been charming, Yonah noted. She forgave herself a little for falling for it.

"I was wondering if I could go to Kirash today," she said.

While Naris' smile didn't disappear, the happy twinkle in his eye faded just a touch. He looked to his business advisor, who looked on with fury. "Yes, that would be fine. I have work to do. But you must take someone with you. To ensure you don't go wandering off."

For a brief moment, Yonah wanted to scream at this potential foil in her plans, but quickly said, "I could take the stable master. Would that be fine?"

"Yes, I think so."

Before Yonah could say anything more, Naris' business advisor promptly closed the door in her face. She stood dumb for a moment. On the other side of the door, the man spoke in hissing tones that Yonah couldn't understand. Naris answered agitatedly.

She couldn't stay and listen long, however. She had work to do as well. Yonah turned and made her way downstairs, out the back doors of the estate, and through the vineyard to the stable.

"Seidon?" she called.

"I'm here." The man peered out of one of the stalls. "What is it?"

"I'm going to Kirash, but Master Naris says I need a chaperone, so I told him I would take you."

Seidon's eyebrows shot upwards. "Did he, now?"

"I imagine he'll question you when we get back asking about where we went," Yonah added with an exasperated sigh. "I'll need you to lie for me."

"Where are you going?"

"I can't tell you that."

"That's not really fair, now, is it?"

Yonah shook her head. "No. It's not. Will you help me?"

Seidon folded his arms across his chest and watched Yonah for a moment. He finally sighed and said, "Yes, of course, I'll help you. We'll take a horse or else I'll be forever walking there."

"I can't ride."

"You can ride with me."

It was a different sensation riding with Seidon than with Naris. The older man wasn't quite as thin and Yonah opted to hook her arms beneath his shoulders, rather than around his waist. Instead of the strange heat that came from being so close to Naris, Yonah felt a calm comfort being seated behind Seidon. But the blowing wind through her hair was the same, the scenery whizzing by, the closeness with nature. She felt free out here.

Kirash was just as she remembered – loud, rushed, rich, and splendid. They rode past stalls selling clothing, candles, spices, and food, past all manner of people including vendors, slaves, and masters.

Yonah directed Seidon down the long main street to the opposite end of the town, to The White Stallion. He waited outside. It had been a several weeks since Yonah had been here, but it all felt the same with the half-filled tables and the soft murmur of the room.

Yonah sat at a table near the back and waited.

Meerha eventually came over to the table with a drink in her good hand, which she set in front of Yonah.

"It's been a while since I saw you," she said. She did a double take. "What happened to you?"

This scar would be more of an annoyance than the one she received from that bullet as a child. She would forever be explaining to people what happened to her.

"It's nothing."

Meerha leaned closer to Yonah. "Did your master do that to you?"

Yonah gave the tiniest nod.

Meerha pursed her lips and stood tall again. "I've heard from your brother. He had suggested a meeting in Basee. It was supposed to be today."

Yonah's heart split in two. She ached to see her brother. But she couldn't risk being caught going to the port city again.

"I can't go to Basee," she said, her voice shaking. She looked at up the barmaid with a pleading look. Tears welled up in her eyes. She wanted nothing more than to go see her brother, but knew it wasn't safe, that it could ruin everything.

"That's alright. That's fine," Meerha said. She awkwardly placed her hand on Yonah's back. "I can tell my contact to let your brother know."

"Can you tell him I'm sorry? And that, if he can come to Kirash, I would see him." Her words filled her with disgust. "Here." Yonah started rummaging through her coat in search of payment for Meerha.

"Keep it," Meerha said. "This one's on me."

"Thank you." Yonah stood up, leaving the drink in front of her untouched, and left the bar.

She ignored Seidon when he called her name as she trudged the rest of the way to the western edge of town and stared down the open road. Obi was out there, waiting for her. She had promised him. But this was not a battle she could fight right now.

Naris would hurt her again if, he found out. She tried to guess what her punishment might be. Re-split her lip? Cut her feet so she couldn't walk? Or maybe he would prevent her from going to Kirash ever again.

That would ruin everything.

A tear dripped down Yonah's cheek, hot with anger.

She had left her message. That was all she could do.

"You alright?" Seidon asked.

Yonah nodded stoically and turned back to Kirash. "Will you wait here while I do my next thing?"

"Yonah, are you getting yourself into trouble?" he asked in a low voice.

She gave him a hard look, but didn't answer. If she couldn't be reunited with her siblings, if the things Naris did to her would go without consequence, then everything needed to change.

She left Seidon standing at the edge of Kirash and started south. She didn't quite know the exact route, but she knew the general direction. Away from the bustle of the main street, through the quiet residential ones, until she was at the candle sellers' square.

The man was at the stall today. Yonah walked up to the stall and said to him, "What is your finest scent?"

The man gazed at Yonah, knowing in his eyes. "Have you changed your mind?"

She remembered the rules Meerha had told her. Give the reply no matter what the man says. "I prefer roses."

"Yes, yes, I know," he said with an eye roll. "What is it?"

She hesitated. "I just want to talk."

The man raised an eyebrow. "About what?"

She held her eyes firm on the man. "The cause."

He nodded knowingly at Yonah, then opened the door behind him and motioned for Yonah to go inside.

Yonah stepped around the table and entered the building. She could see the woman from her first visit sitting at the kitchen table. The woman saw Yonah and began to pack away what she was doing.

"You come to trade?" she called as Yonah walked down the hallway.

"No," Yonah answered. She stood on the rug that covered the cellar door. The kitchen was well-kept, tidy, and minimal. It didn't reflect the nature of the room that lay beneath their feet.

"Well, what is it, then?" the woman said.

Yonah inhaled. "I want to help. With the cause."

The woman cocked her head to one side. "What cause?"

This was it. No going back. "I want to help with the rebellion against the masters. I want the slaves to be free."

The woman dropped her chin and spoke in a heavy voice. "Are you willing to die for the cause?"

Yonah's nod was tentative at first, then stronger.

"Why should I trust you?"

Yonah ached for her old dream of reuniting with her brother and sister. "Because it's the only thing I have left." She added, "I've been reading about all the rebellions in Harasan history."

"She helped out during one of our recent runs." The candle seller's husband was standing in the hallway behind Yonah. "Managed to talk down a Guard when she was with a lost child."

The woman glanced at her husband, then rested her elbows on the table. "Where have you been reading these books?"

"My master has an extensive library," Yonah said. "Master Naris of Vaha."

The woman chuckled. "I know of him. That whole family. They're quite infamous in Kirash." A look of acknowledgement lit her eyes. "You must be the companion."

"I didn't realize I was so famous in town."

"Your relationship with your master is highly unusual," the woman explained. "We should use that."

Yonah awaited instructions from the woman.

"What's your name, girl?"

"Yonah."

"I'm Vitora." She motioned for Yonah to sit at the table with her. Yonah pulled out a chair and sat across from the woman. "What sort of folk does your Master Naris know?"

"He knows many of the landowners in the surrounding area. He sells to most of them."

"Does he know anybody in Kelab?"

"I don't know. In the months I've known him, he's only been as far south as Sintash."

Vitora turned her eyes down to the table and sat quietly for a moment. "How close are you to your master?"

Yonah said slowly, "He claims to be in love with me."

She saw the light behind Vitora's eyes slowly grow brighter. "Do you believe him?" the woman asked. Yonah nodded. "Then I know your job,"

Vitora said. "You are our mole and Naris is your access point.

"You are to gain Master Naris' trust, if you don't already have it, and learn everything you can about the other masters and the attitudes of the slaves on all of their estates. Find out if there are any masters who are sympathetic to the cause. See if you can't convince Naris to take you to Kelab sometimes. The closer you can get to the new president and his government, the better. Can you do that?"

A mild panic vibrated through Yonah's body, sending her stomach rippling and her heart shaking.

"How can I do all that as a slave?"

"You said the master loves you, yes?" Vitora's eyes were fiery. "Use that. Manipulate him. You have an opportunity that is extremely rare, Yonah. You just told me you were willing to risk everything to make a difference."

To make a difference. That was what she had wanted to do for Sayzia and Obi. She thought her life's purpose was to bring them back together. She had failed when she left Sayzia to die in the cold.

Perhaps she could help others like herself and her siblings have a happier ending than they did. Perhaps she could prevent the Guard from destroying more families like hers. She wanted to. She could.

"I'll do it," Yonah said forcefully.

Vitora smirked. "That's the spirit. You come to Kirash often?"

"I just need to ask Naris' permission and he lets me go."

"You just report to me here, then, alright? And," Vitora paused, "I have to say this. If you do back out or do anything to betray the cause or anyone a part of it," she paused once more, "we will have to take care of that."

Yonah felt as if the blood were draining from her face.

"Understood?"

Yonah nodded timidly before saying, "Understood."

Vitora gave her a soft smile. "But I sincerely hope it doesn't come to that, Yonah. It's all about protecting each other. We're something of a family, you know."

A family. Yonah hoped that these people would welcome her better than the household at Vaha.

With their meeting over, Vitora saw Yonah out of the house and Yonah made her way back to Kirash's main street.

Yonah's mind was reeling with the implication of what she had just done. She had given up on bringing the last bit of their broken family together. Instead, she had willingly entered a dangerous world of secrecy and betrayal.

She found Seidon and they walked back down the main street.

"Did you find success?" Seidon asked her as they walked, him leading the horse by the reins.

"I did."

"You don't look happy about it."

"It wasn't a happy task."

She had a hard job ahead of her. While she did have sway with Naris, she was still a slave, always at the mercy of his command. How would she find out whether masters were sympathetic to the cause? Masters didn't talk to slaves about such things. And how would she convince Naris to go to Kelab without it seeming suspicious? She didn't have as much power as that.

A thought struck Yonah. It was more power that she needed. More sway.

She still had the money Naris had sent with her during one of her previous visits to Kirash. He had told her to buy something for herself with it.

Yonah's eyes scanned the street, back and forth, taking in the various vendors and their wares. She finally found a stall that sold glassware.

"What are you looking for?" Seidon asked.

"Not sure," Yonah muttered in reply, her eyes on the table of wares.

There were some wine glasses that had blue and purple paint strokes along the lower half, swirling around each other like waves. Then she noticed some plain glasses with single letters intricately painted on in gold.

Yonah looked up at the seller. "Do you paint these yourself?"

He nodded.

She pointed to the blue and purple glasses. "How much would it cost to put a letter on two of these?"

"The whole thing would be thirty ora."

"I'll take it." Yonah withdrew the bag from her pocket. "An N and a Y, please."

As the vendor got to work, Seidon said to Yonah, "What's that for?"

"It's for Naris."

He rolled his eyes. "Yes, but why?"

"To please him."

"It's no wonder he wanted you chaperoned," the older man grumbled. "You're full of secrets."

Several minutes later, the glass vendor packaged the newly monogrammed wine glasses and passed them to Yonah.

"Have you finished your mysterious errands?" Seidon asked.

"Yes. Let's go back."

They mounted the horse and meandered to the edge of town. As they emerged from the crowd at the road towards Vaha, Yonah saw two boys standing on the road, looking out onto the plains. They weren't dressed like Harasans, but wore the style of clothing that came from the isle nation, and both wore slave collars. They must have been sailors, but they were unusually far from port.

One of them patted his friend on the back and started trudging back into town. His friend remained in place, his gaze unwavering. The first called back to his friend.

"Come on, Obi. We've left our message. That's all we can do."

Obi. She breathed his name. Her little brother had been sold to a captain from the isle. "Obi." It couldn't be. "Obi?" she said out loud.

The one boy who was walking towards town looked over at Yonah. She ignored him and clumsily slid off the horse, landing so poorly she had to catch herself on her hands.

"Obi?" she called.

The boy turned. His face opened up into disbelief. It was him. Her little brother.

"Yonah!"

"Obi!" She broke into a run. He ran to her, too. When they met, they fell into each other's arms, laughing and crying.

It felt wonderful to be with family again. The grief Yonah felt for Sayzia that she had tried to push away came back, making her cry. She let all her sorrow and pain out, knowing she had friendly arms to hold her. Obi wasn't a little boy anymore. He wasn't grown up, yet, but he wasn't the baby-faced boy she had lost so long ago. He was lean and muscled. He would be a man soon.

He held her at arms length. "What happened to you? The musician said he hadn't heard from you since the last time I came. We were supposed to meet today. Where did you go?" He noticed her scar. "What happened to your lip?"

She didn't want to talk about that night. "We went away. And then…" She couldn't finish. "I couldn't come anymore."

"I'm so happy to see you again!" Obi cried out, pulling Yonah in for a hug once more. He noticed his friend standing next to them and said, "This is my friend Ayin. Ayin, this is my sister Yonah."

"It's nice to meet you," the other boy said. Yonah nodded at him.

Yonah motioned to Seidon, who had ridden the horse closer to them. "This is Seidon." She looked up at the stable master. "I didn't know he'd be here. I really didn't. You can't tell Naris about this."

"Naris?" Obi asked. "Master Naris? I've heard stories about him, Yonah. Is that your master?"

She nodded briefly to her brother, then looked pleadingly up at Seidon.

"Calm yourself, Yonah," he said, "I won't tell. But we should get you somewhere a little more private if you don't want anyone else to see you."

The strange party of four migrated to a nearby pub where Obi bought them all a cup of wine.

"I still can't believe it! You're here! You're right here." He was grinning ear to ear. "When you didn't come to our meeting, Ayin and I decided to go see your Kirash contact."

"Obi decided," Ayin cut in. "I came along to make sure he went back on time."

"And the lady at The White Stallion said she just saw you and that maybe we'd find you in town still. I can't believe I found you! But you did it, Yonah. You're the one that found me. You swore you would on that day we lost each other. Next, we'll be seeing Sayzia, too."

Yonah looked sadly at him. "Obi. I saw Sayzia." She steeled herself to say the words out loud. "She's dead."

"Oh." He deflated. Yonah watched his face contort as he tried to remain composed through his new grief. "When? How?"

Her lip quivered. "I was trying to escape with her, but she was sick, and they left her out there. She would have been dead by morning." She wiped a tear from underneath her eye. "It was a few weeks ago."

Obi was trying to hold back tears of his own. He grabbed Yonah's hand. "I miss her." Yonah nodded. They sat there silently, joined in their simultaneous sorrow and joy, clinging onto each other's company.

"What about your master?" Yonah finally asked. "Does he treat you well?"

"Captain Pirung's good to us," Obi answered. "He works us hard, but he's not mean. When we reach port, he lets us have free days like this. Even gives us spending money!" He laughed.

The sound of her little brother's laughter, so unfamiliar to her, a memory she had forgotten until now, tickled Yonah's ears and lifted her heart.

"So, you're okay?" she asked.

Obi nodded and shrugged. "I'll be free in six more years. I can handle it. But if you need help—" he cut himself off suddenly, looking at Seidon sitting next to Yonah.

"You don't need to worry about me, boy," the man said.

But Obi only gave Yonah a stern look that reminded her of Sayzia.

Yonah said, "I don't need your help, Obi. Not right now."

"Are you sure?"

She nodded solemnly. She had chosen her path. "I'm glad you're okay." She shared a look with Seidon. "We should probably get back."

The four of them left the pub and stepped out into the street. Obi stood close to Yonah.

"You'll keep in touch? So I know that you're alright?"

"Yes. We can use the same contacts."

"Good." Obi stepped towards her and wrapped her up in a strong hug. She squeezed his body between her arms. Yonah didn't want to let go.

They separated. Obi sniffed. "Well, goodbye."

"Goodbye," Yonah said.

With one last look, Obi turned around and he and his friend started walking down the road through Kirash, towards Basee. Once more, Yonah watched as someone she loved grew smaller and smaller as the distance between them grew larger and larger.

Chapter Twenty-Seven

That evening, before the usual supper time, Yonah stared at her reflection in her mirror. She had chosen to dress in her favourite blue dress. She thought it made her look refined and she knew Naris liked it, too. Her hair was tied into a thick braid that ran down the back of her head and over her shoulder. Instead of trading them away, she wore some of the jewelry Naris had given her. She had even put a little bit of colour on her lips and some makeup around her eyes. Besides her scars, she thought she looked like a lady.

Her scars told the stories of her most trying days. The pink strip on her arm reminded her that the world wasn't fair and that bad things happened to good people. The white line in the middle of her lip reminded her that she wasn't immune to the consequences of her actions. The scars on her heart – from the loss of each member of her family, from the hurt she had caused Bana, from the night Naris assaulted her – reminded her that to love was a dangerous thing.

She picked up the package she had bought that day and, with a quiet determination and a fluttering heart, went to Naris' office. He was sitting at the table examining a ledger. He looked up.

"How was your excursion?" he asked. "The stable master said you made a purchase in town."

She knew Naris would question Seidon once they returned to Vaha. Whether Naris believed Seidon's half-truths about what had happened that afternoon, she wasn't entirely sure.

"I did," she answered. "I hadn't yet spent the money you gave me before." She stepped closer to Naris' desk. "May I see what you're doing? I've never really asked you about your business before."

When she had returned from meeting her brother that afternoon, Yonah had opened her map and looked at all the estates and names she had penciled onto it. Vaha and Naris, Kejal's estate in the north, Puru, Zanith, Rya, Otto, and more. She knew many things about these masters and the places they lived. She knew which ones had suffered from minor rebellions from their workers, which ones treated their slaves cruelly, and which ones were kinder. She knew where the rebellion had a stronger following. She didn't know much about the slaves and free people involved in the rebellion.

"If you're really interested. Come see," Naris said, leaning back. Yonah walked around the table and examined the papers and books.

"This is the accounting system?" she asked.

"I keep track of sales here." He pointed to a column. "These are our profits. Here's where we spend money."

"Do you think I could help?" Yonah said. "With the business?"

He looked up at her with a half smile. "What do you mean?"

"You spend so much time on it, and I don't do much around here. Maybe if I helped you, you would have less work and we could spend more...," she placed a finger on his chest, "quality time together."

He didn't move at her touch, didn't answer right away. Yonah waited anxiously. His gaze bore deep into her eyes, searching.

"What are you doing?" he said finally.

She stepped away so she could see him better. She tried to keep her face looking as calm as possible.

After looking at her map, she had snuck down to the library through the secret entrance once more. After a long search, she found a few law books, one of which was dated one year old. She used the table of contents to look up the correct section. Her heart pounded with excitement when she found a case, a single case. Since the introduction of the slavery act, there was only one incident, and it appeared to have been difficult to achieve, but it was one case. It was possible.

"I've decided," she began, "to do what you wanted me to do all along. I'm going to be your companion. I'll be your friend. I'll be your assistant in work." She leaned into his ear and whispered, "I'll be your lover." She stood up. "No fuss."

He couldn't help but look pleased. "Why the change of heart?"

She leaned against the desk, still cradling the package. "Because it will make you happy. I know all you've wanted is someone you can count on for support and affection. That's all I've wanted, too." It was time to make something of her life. "We need each other. We need to be a family."

After shelving the law book, she had strode straight to the portrait of Naris and his parents and stared up at it with a hard look. She had imagined what it might have been like to grow up an only child under the stern gaze of parents that didn't seem to love you. She had imagined the loneliness one might feel, the desperation to feel something like love.

Naris reached out and pulled Yonah closer to him by her lower back. "That's all I wanted."

She looked down at him. "Me, too. And friends – family – look after each other. Help each other. I think we could be a real family, Naris. Just you and me. What do you think?" She was slowly running her hand along his arm and around his neck.

He only nodded.

After staring into that portrait in the library, she had gone back to her room to undergo her transformation, to look like a free woman of the upper class, confident in her own skin, regal in her stature, commanding with her gaze, deserving of respect.

"We can't be a real family if I'm a slave, though. You've seen how the other masters treat me. They think we can't be together. They don't understand." She placed her hand on his cheek. "I'm not free for another two years and I can't wait that long to be with you. But I don't know how to fix it." She knew how to fix it, but she needed Naris to think of it.

She needed more freedom if she wanted to make something her of her life. At the shallowest level, she seemed to have independence, but the past few months had made it very clear that that was an illusion, that even with a master who had fallen in love with her, she was powerless.

Naris took a long deep breath. Yonah saw the glimmer of an idea in his eyes, but he wasn't saying it out loud.

"Yonah," he said, "I don't trust you right now. You tried to escape."

"And I don't trust you right now," Yonah replied. "You hurt me, when you said you wouldn't." It was a risky move, but one she thought would pay off. He seemed to like it when she was honest. "But I want to trust you again, and you want to trust me again, so I found a peace offering." She held the package out to Naris. "Instead of buying myself something, I bought something for you."

Naris slowly took the package and unwrapped it, revealing the two monogrammed and painted wine glasses. He held them both up in front of his face to read the letters.

"For Naris and Yonah," he said softly. He looked at Yonah, his eyes light. "That's very kind of you."

"They match your room," she said.

"They do." He smiled at the glasses, then at Yonah. "No one's bought me a present in years. Thank you."

"Naris, you spoke about how we're both lonely people." She looked into his eyes, trying to remember the things she liked about him. She liked their games of chess. She liked his boyish smile. She liked his enthusiasm for showing her the things that made him happy. She liked when they compared wines. She liked when he was able to show vulnerability. He was more human then. "I don't want to be lonely anymore."

"What are you saying?"

"I want to be with you. And I don't want the other masters to make fun of you anymore, or for your business advisor to question you anymore. I want us to be together without everyone else judging us." She placed a hand on his cheek. "I want to stay with you."

Silence. Naris watched Yonah intently.

Yonah looked down. "It's alright if you don't believe me right now." She made a move to walk away, but to her delight, Naris caught her hand and pulled her back toward him. Holding her hands in his own, he stood up. His eyes glistened.

"Do you mean all that?"

She nodded.

"Yonah, I…" He stopped, his eyes looking deep into hers with warmth. "You want to help me run the business?"

Again, she nodded.

"And you swear that you don't plan on running away again?"

"I swear." This was sincere.

He rubbed his mouth and beard, his eyes never leaving her. "How can I trust you?"

She placed her hands on his cheeks and gently brought her lips to his. At first, it felt unnatural. She thought back to the times he had been kind to her, to when they shared their saddest moments with each other, to when he shared his childhood with her, to when he celebrated her successes in their chess games, to when he shared a secret joke with her in front of the guests and they laughed together. Her body relaxed and she fell deeper into the kiss. He anxiously kissed her back, wrapping his arms around her. She reminded herself that he wasn't angry, that she was safe. She gently pulled away and looked up at him.

"It might take time," she whispered, "but I'll earn it back."

He looked dazed. He smiled and rested his forehead against hers.

"I want to marry you," Naris said breathlessly.

It was just what she hoped he would say.

Epilogue

Sayzia's eyes felt heavy as they slowly opened. Her mind was foggy. She inhaled deeply. With a little effort, her lungs expanded and she felt the familiar tickle in her chest. It wasn't, however, as difficult to breathe as before.

She gasped and her eyes widened as the events of last night came back to her. Yonah had taken her from the estate. They had gone all day long. It was only a matter of time before they were caught. She didn't remember what happened after that...

Sayzia looked around and found she was in a small windowless room that she didn't recognize. It was lit with a fireplace.

She needed water. There was a table next to the bed she lay in with a cup on it. Sayzia gingerly sat up with her legs hanging off the side of the bed, grabbed the cup, and smelled its contents. It was odourless. She gulped it down.

Now she was hungry.

She felt tired as she stood up, but not particularly weak. Someone extremely skilled had worked hard to get her through her fever.

Sayzia stopped at the door, afraid of what she might find on the other side. She had no idea who had picked her up that night or what they wanted from her.

No use putting it off, she thought to herself. She pulled the latch and opened the door.

There were five people gathered in the room. From the single window at the top of the wall on one side, Sayzia could tell they were in a basement. The group turned to look at her in surprise.

One man muttered something to the other four and three of the party departed up the stairs.

"How does she look?" the man asked. He turned to the woman sitting next to him. She walked towards Sayzia, looking her up and down. She placed her hand on Sayzia's forehead, tugged her chin downward to open her mouth and look inside, rested her hand on Sayzia's heart.

"She is stronger," the woman said. Her face was lined with wrinkles, revealing her age, but she held her body like a young adult.

Sayzia's stomach growled.

The man smirked. "We have food," he said, motioning to the table the group had been gathered around.

Sayzia couldn't help but stride over to the table and devour the bread and cheese before her. She sighed with satisfaction as she gulped down large chunks of the food.

After a few minutes of eating, she slowed down her pace and asked, "How did I get here?"

"The innkeeper sent someone to let our healer know," he motioned to the woman, "that there was someone left for dead in his stable. That their master had left them behind. You were brought here. You've been asleep for three days."

Sayzia thought over the meaning behind this information. "My sister is gone?"

"You were the only person there," the man said.

"My master. He isn't looking for me?"

"You have no master, now. We removed your slave collar after the fever began to go down."

Sayzia brought her hand to her neck and started at finding only bare skin. She had worn that slave collar for years.

"Why did you help me?"

The man and the healer exchanged a look. "Do you believe in a better world?" he asked. "One where nobody is a slave."

"It sounds like a nice place," Sayzia said.

"Do you believe it's possible?" The man was giving her a heavy look.

Yonah set the food in her hands down on the table. "It seems unlikely. But possible."

"Is that a world you'd like to live in?"

"Yes."

"Is it a world you would be willing to work towards?"

The memory of conversations between her and the other shepherds came back to Sayzia. What would they each do if given the opportunity to join rebellion forces?

"Are you asking me to join the rebellion?"

"Are you in favour of the rebellion?"

Never had Sayzia ever dreamed this would be a decision she would get the chance to make. She had resigned herself to life as a sickly shepherd.

"I am," she answered.

The man nodded. "Then we might have a job for you here."

Acknowledgements

A huge thank you to everyone that helped make my dream of publishing a novel come true! Thank you to my mom and dad for encouraging my love of reading and writing. Thank you to my husband for listening to my random ramblings, reading and editing chapters while being forbidden from reading the book in its entirety, and for your general support throughout this journey. Thank you to my brother and sister and any other friends I pestered for giving me advice when I asked. Thank you to Elaine and Bobby for reading and providing feedback on early drafts, to P.S. Malcolm for being an incredible authorship coach and giving me the confidence and knowledge to move forward with this project, to whichever anonymous author read my manuscript through the Saskatchewan Writers' Guild manuscript evaluation service, to my fellow authors in the Authorpreneur Kingdom community for their support and insight, to Hollie Godwin for editing, to moninya for providing feedback as a sensitivity reader, to my mom once again for proofreading, and to Mandi Lynn for being so patient with me and formatting the book interior and creating a beautiful book cover. And thanks to you, dear reader, for being here.

About the Author

Although Heather has been an avid writer since childhood, *A Collection of Scars* is her debut novel. Her passion for reading, writing, and learning more about the human condition led to her earning a Bachelor of Arts in English with a History minor at the University of Saskatchewan. When she's not writing, Heather is working as a group fitness and music instructor, or volunteering in her local performing arts community. She resides in Saskatoon, Canada with her husband. You can learn more about Heather and her upcoming projects at heatherhataley.com.

Printed in the USA
CPSIA information can be obtained
at www.ICGtesting.com
BVHW040003150823
668484BV00001B/3